THE

GOLDEN

BOOK

THE BLADEMASTER OF GOLARA

DAVID H. MINES

To my Mom
Thanks for all the support throughout this long journey

Contents

THE
GOLDEN BOOK
The Blademaster of Golara

CHAPTER 1

TROUBLE ON THE HOMEFRONT

As the first rays of dawn pierced through the clouds over the rocky desolate landscape, two men traveled along a dusty secluded trail, each riding a horse. Leon Jacobs, known as the Blademaster, led the way atop his brown steed. He was a tall man in his late thirties with brown skin. His eyes were brown but bloodshot from sleepless nights. His hair was black, curly like wool, and unkempt. He hadn't shaved in several weeks. He wore dirty, battle-damaged leather armor. The figure next to him, whose name was Sam, road atop a white horse. Sam was a slender but towering male Orc and his skin was brick red. He possessed pointed ears and white tusk-like teeth that protruded from his bottom lip. Sam's head was clean-shaven. He wore canvas robes and a tattered cloak around his head and neck.

"I hope today brings us better fortune, we've been coming up empty so far," complained Sam.

"Today might be the day. Think positive, happy thoughts," Leon replied with a weary smile.

They came to a stop, having reached their destination. In front of them lay the enormous and sprawling Wildcliff canyons. It's the largest canyon system in the world, a maze of towering orange sandstone formations and interconnected rock bridges. They were deep in the Orcish confederation of tribes' territory. As the Blademaster, Leon's job was to protect the kingdoms and keep the peace. He was investigating a lead he discovered a few weeks earlier after raiding a bandit camp in the human kingdom territories. There, Leon had uncovered some documents and maps. The bandits were trying to send word to other bandit groups. The messages were encoded, but the maps weren't.

"I can't fathom why your bandits want to seek refuge in such perilous lands like these here canyons, dangerous creatures lurk here," said Sam.

Sam was an old friend of Leon's and his guide through the canyons as they searched the area for other bandit camps. The canyons were enormous. With their hidden caves, it was impossible to search every inch. The map he had recovered wasn't a very good one.

"Are you okay?" Sam inquired, noticing Leon in a fog.

Leon quickly shook himself out of it and smiled. "Yeah, let's find this thing, people are counting on us."

Since the canyons were so enormous, they divided it into sections and searched one each day. Sam sighed deeply as they headed down a nearby pass into the canyon, with only one last area to search. Leon hoped today would be the day they finally found something. They traveled down the stony canyon pass, along the orange rocky walls, until they reached the canyon's floor and began their search. The canyon floor was a dangerous place, filled with giant snakes, geckos, and scorpions with large carnivorous scavenger birds flying overhead. The heat was blistering, but Leon was used to it. His job sent him around the world to the most dangerous and uncomfortable places, fighting all sorts of dangerous monsters or bandits.

Leon took a cool drink from his canteen. They rode around the canyon floor for hours, searching what caves they could reach, but they were coming up empty. After a while, they stopped for a rest at the bank of the nearby river in the cool shade of a large stone mesa.

"I'm starting to believe we're on a wild goose chase," Sam remarked as he refilled his canteen from the river.

"It can't be," replied Leon, pouring over a map. "Each of those other bandit camps leads me to the next one and that last one led me out here."

Suddenly, Leon felt a tingle through his body. "Something's wrong!" he announced as he quickly mounted his brown horse and rode off.

"What!? What's happening?!" asked a confused Sam. He quickly followed Leon as they rode through the canyons. Leon came to a large opening in the canyons when he saw it: a flipped-over covered wagon surrounded with scattered debris.

"Hello! Is anybody there?!" shouted Leon.

There was silence. Leon got off his horse to investigate the flipped wagon. Beneath the wagon was an Orc woman and her small child.

"Are you okay? What happened?" asked Leon.

The woman responded in Orcish, but Leon didn't speak much Orcish. "Umm, Trouble, What Happened?" he replied in what little Orcish he knew. The Orc woman put her finger to her mouth and pointed behind him.

"Geckos!" shouted Sam as he climbed off his horse.

Out of the canyon's walls, a swarm of three-foot-long, green-scaled, yellow-eyed geckos crawled from their holes and descended upon them. Sam quickly drew his bow and began to fire. Immediately, a sword appeared in Leon's hand. It was the sword only the Blademaster wielded, The Blade of the Elementals. The sword was a dark copper, rectangle-shaped blade with a downward-curved crossguard: the Sword of Earth. He quickly turned toward the overturned wagon and horses, pointed his sword at it, and flicked his wrist. The ground shot up around it, forming a protective dome of earth to safely encase the wagon and horses. Sam rapidly fired arrows at the approaching geckos while Leon swung at them with his sword causing jagged rocks to jut from the canyon walls, striking some of the geckos.

"There's too many of them!" shouted Sam, now down to his last few arrows.

"Come in!" shouted Leon.

Leon changed the sword's shape. It was now a long

sword with a glowing orange, hot metal blade, the Sword of Fire. Sam retreated next to Leon. Leon swung his sword overhead, creating a large flaming ring around them and the dome. Leon began to spin the ring of fire around them, faster and faster. The geckos kept their distance, before fireballs he started launching at the geckos from the ring.

"It's working!" said Sam.

Leon launched more fireballs—hitting some geckos and missing others. Suddenly, there an ear-piercing screech echoed through the canyons. The geckos immediately stopped and retreated to their nearby burrows. Leon stopped spinning the ring of fire.

"That can't be good," said Leon.

The ground beneath them began to rumble before exploding to reveal a colossal creature know as a Canyon Crawler. It was a hundred-foot-long, centipede-like creature.

"Canyon crawler!" shouted Sam. Leon once again transformed his sword. This time it became a slightly curved cutlass with a solid, cupped hilt. The blade was dark blue with a slight blue aura, the Sword of Water. The canyon crawler turned and rocketed toward Leon and Sam. Leon swung his sword, deflecting the creature with a massive wall of water. He instantly changed his sword again, to the Sword of Earth. With a simple swing of the sword, the earthen dome receded into the ground.

"Get them out of here! I'll cover you!" ordered Leon.

This time the sword was a curved scimitar with a white blade. Its cross-guard curved in different directions with a leather grip and a small chain hanging off the pommel, the Sword of Wind. Leon quickly began swinging the sword around overhead, creating a strong tempest of spinning winds around them. Sam told the woman and child to climb out from the overturned wagon and help him flip it over. The canyon crawler continued to slam against the massive spinning column of wind that Leon had created. Sam managed to connect the wagon to their horses. The three of them quickly climbed aboard the wagon.

"We're ready!" shouted Sam over the loud, whipping winds. Leon nodded in acknowledgment. With a mighty swing, he directed the swirling winds into the massive canyon crawler, sending it crashing into a nearby canyon wall. Without hesitation, Sam immediately sped off back the way they came. The canyon crawler quickly shook off the attack and counterattacked. Leon quickly rolled out of the way. Leon sent a barrage of condensed air to slash the creature. The creature began to crawl along the canyon's walls, snaking its body on the rocks to dodge slashes. Some of the slashes connected. Most didn't, and when they did, they didn't seem to bother the creature's tough armored hide.

"I'm gonna need more power," Leon said to himself. He changed his sword again, back to its fire form. He began to rocket large fireballs at the creature. This time he managed to knock the creature down, along with most of the canyon wall itself. Leon stopped to observe the pile of rocks. Some of the rocks were still on fire. Suddenly the creature launched itself out of the rubble at Leon. He managed to jump out of the way in time, but the creature's row of long razor-sharp claws still slashed Leon's side. Leon put his hand on the wound. He was bleeding—badly.

"Ugh. It's time to end this," he thought.

Leon began spinning the sword by a chain on its pommel. The faster he spun it, the more the sword became engulfed in flames. Once enough fire was built up he threw the sword at the creature like a flaming buzzsaw. The creature quickly contorted itself to avoid the attack. With its opponent disarmed the creature again launched itself at Leon. However, before the canyon crawler could attack Leon, the spinning flaming sword returned, swiftly slicing the creature in half while its attention was focused solely on Leon. The flames of the sword vanished instantly as it returned to Leon's hand. The enormous canyon crawler crashed around him in two pieces. The half with the creature's head let out a high-pitched screech of pain before burrowing into the ground.

Leon put the sword away. He then went around, grabbing a few of the dead geckos before leaving the canyons. Leon walked around for an hour, whistling for Sam. Suddenly, Sam came around the corner with the wagon and horses. He saw that Leon was grabbing his side. Sam jumped out of the wagon and rushed to Leon. Leon removed his hand, showing Sam the wound.

"Let's set up camp," said Sam.

Leon removed his armor and Sam tended to Leon's wound. "Luckily you were wearing that armor or else we wouldn't be having this conversation," said Sam.

"I prefer metal armor for this reason. I only went

leather for the canyons," said Leon.

Sam immediately went to work on Leon's wound. As the sun started to set, the Orc woman started a fire.

"How do you feel?" asked Sam, having finished wrapping a cloth bandage around his side.

"I'll live, thanks to you," said Leon. "I brought dinner."

He tossed his bag to Sam. Sam opened the bag to see the geckos. He then gutted and skinned them before setting them over the campfire. Sam talked to the Orc woman and her child around the campfire. Leon sat away from them, continuing to look over the map that had brought them to the canyons. Sam walked over to Leon.

"What's their story?" asked Leon.

"She says they were traveling from Elderfalls to Eagle Gulch before they were attacked by geckos. They tried to outrun them but their horse broke away, leaving them stranded. I guess the geckos must have attracted the canyon crawler," said Sam.

"Good thing we found them when we did," said Leon.

Sam went to check on the food. When the food was finished cooking, they sat down to eat.

"That wasn't half bad, considering," joked Leon.

"Be nice, it wasn't like I had any spices to add to it," said Sam.

Leon laughed. "Sam, I want you to take the two of them to Eagle Gulch. I'm gonna keep looking for that camp."

"I don't think that's a good idea," Sam replied, sounding worried.

"I'll be fine," said Leon with a reassuring smile.

Sam smiled back. Leon was the strongest person he knew. He figured Leon would be okay. Afterward, they packed up the camp. The Orc woman, the child, and Sam climbed into the wagon. Leon unhooked his horse from the wagon, hopped on, and rode a few feet before stopping. He rode back to the wagon.

"What's the problem? You sense something?" asked Sam.

"After you take them to Eagle Gulch, meet back at yesterday's campsite," said Leon. Sam nodded. Leon reached in his saddlebag and pulled out a wrapped package, the size of a large book, with a note attached. He handed it to Sam. It was something Leon had taken from one of the bandit camps he had raided weeks ago.

"If you don't hear from me in a week, give that to my brother, Sterling, personally. He lives near the town of Hazelhill in the human kingdoms. He'll do the rest," he said.

Sam looked uneasy. "I feel like there's something more you're not telling me."

Leon smiled. "I'm probably just being paranoid but with all that's been happening lately, better safe than sorry."

Sam nodded and put the package in his saddlebag. "I'll be off. See you back at camp."

Leon nodded and Sam headed toward Eagle Gulch. Leon rode in the opposite direction through the canyons, as the sunset and night fell. The canyon floor was cold, so he put on his cloak. He decided against lighting his lantern. He didn't want to attract any unwanted attention. He let his senses guide him through the darkness. Leon felt something and rode toward it through the darkness. He came to a stop behind another sandstone mesa tower. He climbed off his horse and looked around. He heard the sound of trickling water a few feet away. Down a nearby embankment was a slow-moving river. A sudden, bad feeling washed over him, and he spotted a small wooden boat down the river.

Leon snuck down the riverbank and crouched in the nearby greenery. The small wooden boat sailed along past Leon, smoothly and quietly, with the river's current. Leon drew his sword and turned it to its water form. He gently pulled the boat toward the shore. The bandit in the boat looked around in pure confusion as his boat began to move closer and closer to the shore before beaching itself. The bandit climbed out of the boat onto the riverbank when a tentacle of water emerged from the river and struck the man in the back of the head, knocking him out. Leon put away his sword and ran over to the downed man. He searched his pockets and found nothing. Next, he checked the small wooden boat and found a map. He compared the new map with the older one he already had. The map revealed a more detailed section of the canyon with a spot marked just down the river.

Leon pushed the boat back into the river and traveled farther down the canyon. The boat traveled along the river. quietly, until he entered a cavern. Leon used the sword's water form to steer the boat to the cavern's bank. He hopped off the boat and changed his sword again, this time to its earth form. He slid the blade into the cavern's stone wall with no resistance. Leon then tapped the hilt of the sword, using the vibrations to act as sonar. He got an impression of the cavern's tunnels and walls.

People were in the caverns. Lots of them. Leon navigated the tunnels, going deeper and deeper into the cavern until he came upon a massive chamber. The chamber was filled with tents, boxes, crates, and barrels. Torches lit the chamber, showing the numerous stalactites on the chamber ceilings.

"Another bandit camp," thought Leon.

In the center of the camp, the bandits were preparing something. Leon stealthily made his way down to the camp, weaving his way between the various tents and other objects, taking extra care to avoid the bandits. Leon wanted to avoid a fight. He wanted to see what they were up to first. In the center of the camp was something that resembled a fire pit. It looked like some kind of ritual had taken place, or was about to.

"I don't like the look of this," Leon thought to himself.

"You should have thought about that sooner," said a female voice in his head.

Leon suddenly experienced a splitting headache so powerful and painful that he passed out.

Sam had arrived at their old campsite. It had been two days since he spoke with Leon. He had returned from Eagle Gulch after safely seeing the Orc woman and her son back to the city. Sam was nervous but set up camp in preparation for Leon. He waited several days for Leon's return. A week had passed from when he last spoke with Leon. Sam sighed, packed up the camp, hopped on his horse, and rode as quickly as he could. Sam made his way to a village in the north of the Orcish territory and hitched a ride on an Orcish fishing boat back to the human kingdoms. Sam rode north as much as he could before he and his horse were exhausted. Sam finally decided to stop and rest for the night. The next morning, Sam set out for Hazelhill.

Sam rode toward Hazelhill when he spotted a house tucked away in the trees. It was a large wood and brick three-story Victorian-style house with a wraparound porch. It matched the description Leon had given him.

"I hope this is the place," he said. Sam rode to the house, dismounted his horse, and walked up the front porch to knock on the door. There was no answer. Sam knocked again, louder this time.

The door opened a bit. "What?! What?! What do you want?" asked Sterling, annoyed by all the knocking.

Sterling was a tall, slim man in her early thirties with brown skin and brown eyes. His hair was black, long, and curly, with grey at the temples.

"Leon … sent me! I've come a long way … to give you this. It's of … great importance!" gasped Sam, nearly out of breath, as he pulled the package and note from his bag.

Sterling opened the door to accept the package, then looked over it. "What's so important he couldn't deliver himself? I know we aren't on the best of terms but …" Sterling trailed off.

Sam fell silent for a moment. "Leon … is missing. He said … if he didn't return, deliver this package to you," replied Sam.

Sterling stood there in stunned silence. He swallowed hard. "Well … thank you. Do you want some water or food? You've had a long journey," offered Sterling.

"I need to get back to Eagle Gulch. If your brother was right, my people need me," Sam said as he climbed back on his horse.

"Thank you again," said Sterling.

Sam nodded to Sterling again before riding off. Sterling went back inside, closing the door behind him. He stood in the hallway and opened the letter.

Dear Sterling,

If you are reading this, that means something has happened to me. I'm writing you this letter as a precaution. While raiding bandit camps, I found this book. I found a similar book when I was younger, but I don't remember what happened to it. Anyway, Sterling, I'd like you to give this book to my son. By the way, I have a son, it's a long story, and I'll have to tell you some other time. His name is Matthew Jacobs. He lives with his mother on the Terran Plane. This book must find its way into his hands. My plan depends on this. I trust you'll be able to do this as I've already taken care of the rest.

Your brother,

Leon Jacobs

Sterling placed the letter in his pocket. Sterling unwrapped the package, revealing a golden book. He looked over it. Its cover was covered in strange symbols and solid gold. Sterling took the book upstairs with him to his trophy room. Sterling's trophy room was a large room filled with glass display cases, each holding strange magical artifacts, relics, and talismans. In the corner of the room was a large metal container with four curved legs. Sterling lifted the top off the container and a large crystal ball floated out of the container.

Sterling placed his palm on the crystal ball and closed his eyes.

"Show me, Matthew Jacobs, Terran Plain," he commanded in a clear and calm voice.

Suddenly, in his head, he saw it: the planet Earth.

His view immediately focused on the United States, then zoomed in on the state of New York. Then New York City. Now he was in Brooklyn, and then a school. Riverside Academy. Next, he saw a boy opening his locker in a school uniform.

"Well, hello there," said Sterling.

CHAPTER 2

BOOK DONATION

The warm summer breeze flowed through the open classroom windows as the sunlight rested on the desks. While the school bell rang, the students quickly entered the classroom. Matthew was the last one to enter.

Matthew Jacobs was a twelve-year-old boy. He had brown skin and eyes with short, jet black curly hair. He was wearing his school uniform, which consisted of a short-sleeved white dress shirt, a blue plaid tie, and khaki pants. Matthew took his seat in the back of the classroom by the open windows. He liked sitting by the windows for the view, but the warm summer breeze made it even more pleasant.

"Good afternoon, everyone! I hope you're all ready for today's final exam," announced Mrs. Langley, standing before her large wooden desk in the front of the room.

Mrs. Langley was the sixth-grade English teacher. She was a middle-aged woman in her late thirties, with shoulder-length dark blonde hair, brown eyes, and pale skin. She was wearing the teacher's version of the school uniform: white blouse and khaki pants. There was some mild groaning from the students.

"I'm ready Mrs. Langley! I studied really hard for this test," Sydney chimed in. The other students rolled their eyes and groaned even louder. Sydney was a twelve-year-old girl with dark, short brown hair, a round face, olive skin, and brown eyes. Sydney had a reputation for being a teacher's pet and a bossy know-it-all. None of the other kids liked her, but the teachers seemed to love her. Matthew couldn't tell if the teachers either didn't see what Sydney was doing or just liked having their egos stroked.

"Thank you, Sydney. It's nice to hear some of you take this class seriously," said Mrs. Langley. Sydney replied with a smug smile.

"Before I hand out these tests, is there anything anybody wants me to quickly go over?" asked Mrs. Langley. The class was silent. "Does everyone have a number two pencil?"

A few students raised their hands. The teacher handed out pencils, then began handing out the test. "Now during the test, there is to be no talking. If you have any questions, please raise your hand and I'll come over to you. You have to the end of class to finish the test. If you finish before then just raise your hand and I'll collect your test. Does everyone understand?" said Mrs. Langley.

The class was silent.

"Okay, begin."

Everyone opened their test packets and began taking the final exam. Matthew wasn't worried about the test. English was one of his better subjects. The only test he was worried about was his math test, which he had taken earlier. Matthew, along with several other students, finished the test earlier than the rest of the students. After Mrs. Langley began to collect the tests from the students who had already completed them, Matthew pulled out his notebook and began to doodle. A few minutes later, Mrs. Langley collected the remaining completed tests.

"Now that all the tests have been collected, I just wanted to say a few words before the bell rings. I've enjoyed teaching you all over this past semester and hope you all have learned something from me," said Mrs. Langley.

The class was silent.

"I learned many things from you, Mrs. Langley," Sydney interjected.

"Thank you, Sydney. I hope to be teaching some of you again next year," smiled Mrs. Langley.

Mrs. Langley noticed Matthew ignoring her speech. He was continuing to draw in his notebook. Upon noticing this, she began to slowly make her way over to him. She was still looking directly at Matthew. He continued to ignore her and just kept doodling in his notebook. Before she made it to his desk the school bell rang. The other kids gathered their things and franticly ran from the classroom.

"Have a nice day," said Mrs. Langley. She faked a

friendly smile. Matthew returned a polite, fake smile and got up from his desk with his notebook under his arm, then walked out of the classroom. Outside of the classroom, the hallway buzzed with groups of kids in their Riverside Academy uniforms discussing their summer plans with each other and emptying their lockers.

Matthew hadn't had any luck making any friends since he moved from Sacramento to New Jersey for his mom's new job. His mom kept insisting to him that making friends just takes time. She said that at the start of his sixth-grade year. Now, the school year was over and he still had no friends. Matthew didn't mind being alone. Most of the kids at his new school annoyed him anyway. The majority of them were snobby, rich kids who had already been kicked out of every other more prestigious private school in New York—or they were geniuses on academic scholarships. Matthew was just smart enough to get in, and his mom made enough money to afford the tuition.

Matthew wanted to go to a normal public school. His mother, however, insisted that going to private school was a great opportunity for him and his future. Being alone also gave him more time to read and work on his drawings, though his drawings still weren't very good. He walked down the crowded hallway to his locker. He opened it and grabbed his science notebook. One last class before he was free for summer vacation. He closed his locker and headed up to the third floor. The bell rang as he entered Mr. Tyler's science classroom.

Mr. Tyler was an older man in his late sixties, with

short grey hair and a large grey mustache, fair skin, brown eyes, and large glasses. He was also wearing the teacher's version of their uniform under a white lab coat. Matthew took his seat again in the back of the classroom.

"Good afternoon, students. I hope your day is going well. I'm sure we're all excited about summer vacation, so I'll be brief. The final will be based on the study guide I provided you earlier this week. Any topic on the study guide will be on the test. If it wasn't then you don't have to worry about it. Other than that, you know the drill. Clear your desk, number two pencils only, no talking, raise your hands for any questions, alright?"

Several of the students responded verbally while others simply nodded their heads. Mr. Tyler began to hand out the final exam. Matthew liked Mr. Tyler's science class—almost everyone did. He was one of the most well-liked teachers in the school. His projects and labs made learning fun, and his personality was easygoing. Matthew received his exam and got to work. The exam was relatively simple for him because he had completed the study guide and paid attention in class. After finishing the exam, Matthew began drawing in his notebook again until the bell rang.

"Have a fun and safe summer everyone," said Mr. Tyler as he waved goodbye to everyone leaving the classroom. Matthew waved goodbye to his teacher and headed downstairs to the second floor, where his locker was located. He opened it and pulled out his backpack, skateboard, and helmet. He stuffed his notebooks into his backpack. Next, he cleaned out his locker of everything else he didn't need and put it in one of the large trash cans in the hallway. He then closed his locker and headed down the stairs and out of the school building.

Matthew's school, Riverside Academy, consisted of three large buildings that formed a U-shape around a large grass quad area. The building he had just exited on the left was the classroom building. All the main subjects were taught there. Across the quad on the right was the extra-curricular building, which included the library, music room, and gym, among other facilities. The building in the middle, the Main Hall. was the largest of the three. It included the cafeteria, the Headmaster's office, and more classrooms. Matthew put his helmet on and hopped on his skateboard. He headed down the sidewalk in front of the classroom building until someone caught his eye.

It was the school librarian. Mrs. Grady was loading books into a white truck on the side of the extracurric-ular building, directly across from him. Mrs. Grady was a slim older woman in her late fifties. She was very short, with brown eyes, caramel skin, and short black hair that was graying. She had wire-framed glasses that she kept on a chain around her neck. She was wearing khaki pants and a white blouse. Matthew skateboarded across the sidewalk over to Mrs. Grady, who was standing in front of the white truck.

"Hey, Mrs. Grady. What's going on?" Matthew slowed his skateboard. to a stop beside her

"Hello, dear," Mrs. Grady greeted him with a smile. "The school is donating some of our older books to charity.

We've got a new shipment of books coming next week. We have to make room for them in the library."

"Oh." Matthew looked at all the boxes of books in the truck with interest.

"Would you like a book, Matthew?" Mrs. Grady suggested, smiling.

"Sure," Matthew accepted with a grin.

Matthew had become very friendly with Mrs. Grady over the school year. He had helped her out in the library dozens of times. He spent a lot of his free time in the school's library. Matthew hopped in the trailer. Mrs. Grady put the box of books she was carrying on the truck and headed back to the library. The trailer was stuffy, dusty, and filled with tons of boxes filled with books. Most of the boxes in the truck were closed. Matthew turned to the right and began looking through the first open box he saw. Nothing in it interested him. Matthew moved to the next box and began to look through it. Suddenly, there was a flash of bright light coming from deep within the trailer. Matthew stopped going through the box and investigated the source of the light.

Deeper in the trailer, on top of a cardboard box, he saw a large, golden book. The book's metallic surface was adorned with intricate markings, weaving a mysterious tapestry across its cover and spine. It exuded an air of enigma. Matthew picked up the book and ran his hands over the cover and down the spine. The book was lighter than it looked. It was cool to the touch, despite having been inside the warm truck. He started to open the book when Mrs.

Grady interrupted.

"Did you find a book?" she inquired, standing outside the truck holding a small cardboard box of books next to two men. Each man was carrying a much larger box than her.

"I'll take this one," replied Matthew.

Matthew then jumped out of the trailer. Mrs. Grady sat her box in the trailer and took the book. She put the glasses hanging around her neck and inspected the book.

"Hmmm. I don't recall ever seeing this book being in our library." Her voice tinged with curiosity.

"So can I keep it?" he inquired eagerly.

"Ummm ... sure." Mrs. Grady acquiesed, returning the book back to Matthew.

"Thanks, Mrs. Grady."

Matthew looked over the enigmatic tome one last time before putting it in his backpack.

"Have a good summer Matthew," Mrs. Grady bid him farewell with a smile.

"Thanks. You, too."

Matthew hopped back on his skateboard. He kicked off and headed down the sidewalk, weaving in and out of students. Matthew made his way to the front gates of the school when suddenly his phone began to ring, it was his mom.

"Hello?" he answered.

"Hi, Matthew. I'm glad I caught you," said his mom, Elizabeth Jacobs.

"Yeah."

"Well, I can only talk for a few minutes, I'm about to head into a meeting but I wanted to tell you that due to some unforeseen circumstances. I'm gonna be working later than usual today. So, it'll probably be nighttime when I come home."

"Alright," said Matthew.

"But I'll be sure to bring home something for dinner. So you won't have to cook something this time. Where are you now?" she asked.

"I'm leaving school. I'm about to go home."

"Okay. Remember, please be careful!" she continued.

Matthew heard some voices in the background of his mom's call. "I gotta go now, sweetie, I love you, bye," she said before hanging up.

"Bye."

Matthew slipped his phone back into his pocket. Matthew skateboarded past the front iron gates of his school and down the city sidewalk. He rode his skateboard for several blocks until he reached a subway tunnel entrance. Matthew hopped off his skateboard and descended the subway stairs. He swiped his metro card, headed through the turnstile, and down the steps to the subway platform.

The subway was hot and dirty—and it smelled awful. Its platform was well lit by a row of fluorescent lights hanging overhead, and it buzzed with the activity of commuters. People stood scattered around, talking on their phones, texting, reading, wearing headphones, leaning on the white tile wall away from the tracks. Matthew navigated the crowded-platform and found an empty place to stand by one of the metal columns. Matthew looked down at the subway tracks. The tracks were littered with trash as rats scurried about. Matthew stood waiting on the platform for several minutes until the subway train finally arrived.

The subway train was crowded and came to a full stop. The subway doors opened and dozens of people got off the train, but the train was still crowded. Matthew squeezed onto the train and grabbed a nearby pole. After a few seconds, the train doors closed and the train began to move. The train made several stops on the way to Penn Station with people coming and going at each stop, but the number of people on the train never really seemed to change. He exited the train at Penn Station and waded through the large crowds of commuters to catch the train back to New Jersey. Matthew boarded the train to Secaucus—he boarded just early enough to still get a seat.

Dozens of other commuters boarded the train several minutes before the train became ready to head off. The train was filled to the point of some people standing by the aisle. Luckily, Matthew only had to ride the train for a few minutes because he got off at the first stop. After several minutes the train pulled into the Secaucus train station. He moved hurriedly to get off the train while new passengers attempted to board and current passengers moved to fill the newly available seats. Matthew followed the crowd of people up the nearby escalator and into the main section of the station.

After swiping his ticket to get through the security turnstile he headed across the open foyer and down a pair of escalators. He walked down the hall and back outside. After descending two flights of stairs, he hopped on his skateboard and rode to their apartment complex. Near the train station was an apartment complex named Oasis Springs. Matthew skateboarded down the sidewalk and into the complex. A sudden, feeling of unease washed over him as he rode. Matthew immediately stopped and scanned his surroundings. A few people were walking around outside but there was nothing out of the ordinary. The feeling subsided and he continued skating past the several towering glass apartment buildings and into the lobby of the main building which was much larger than the others surrounding it with an attached parking garage. Matthew entered the pleasant, air-conditioned lobby.

The lobby bustled with activity with people sitting at the various wooden tables, chairs, and leather couches. They were reading newspapers, eating snacks, and watching the flat screen TVs in the lounge on the other side. The smell of fresh coffee filled his nose. In the middle of the lobby was a concession stand with fresh coffee, teas, and snacks for purchase with turnstiles on both sides leading to the elevators. On the right was the main desk where two people were sitting at a large, curved desk. On the left side of the lobby were all the mailboxes for the building's apartments. He swiped his complex ID card and walked through the turnstiles. Matthew headed over to check their mailbox before he went upstairs.

Inside, there were several envelopes, coupon mailers, and flyers from the complex. Matthew closed the mailbox and headed for the elevator. He rode the elevator to the fourth floor, headed down the hallway, and unlocked the door to their apartment. The strong smell of cinnamon filled the air as he entered. Their apartment was spacious and consisted of two bedrooms, two bathrooms, a kitchen, and a living room. The apartment was clean and well-furnished with pictures on the walls, comfortable furniture, and various knick-knacks on tables. Matthew sat the mail on the kitchen countertop and headed to his room on the left side of the apartment. His room was a modest size and consisted of a bed, a desk with a computer and chair, and a dresser. He placed his skateboard by the door, sat on his bed, and removed his backpack and helmet.

He noticed a picture frame on his dresser. It wasn't there when he left this morning. It was a picture of a young couple standing under a large tree. The man was holding a baby in his arms. He recognized the couple immediately. They were his parents, with him as a baby. He figured his mom must have given him the picture. It was the only picture they had together as a family before his dad left. Matthew got up from the bed and put the frame face down on the dresser.

He didn't like looking at the picture because it brought up too many unanswered questions. Matthew had put his father's absence behind him from an early age. It had reached a point where he rarely thought about him. He changed out of his uniform into a blueish grey shirt and jeans. He entered the kitchen to make something to eat. There was nothing he could make quickly for a lunch.

Matthew remembered there were places to eat at the train station. He grabbed his skateboard and helmet and locked the apartment behind him. He went through a nearby door that led to the parking garage. Zooming down the ramps on his skateboard, Matthew headed back to the train station.

Suddenly, the feeling unease washed over him again. Matthew felt a bit strange but he ignored it and it quickly subsided. At the train station, he bought a simple slice of pizza. He didn't want to eat too much and spoil his appetite. His mom was bring home dinner later. After he was done, Matthew left the train station and skateboarded to the local park in their apartment complex. The park was modest, featuring a colorful jungle gym with a slide and a swing set nestled in a sea of woodchips, framed by small trees and grass. He settled onto a nearby wooden bench. It was a Friday afternoon, and the sun was beginning to set but there were still young children playing on the playground with their parents watching nearby. He sat on the bench the few remaining kids and their parents gradually departed from the playground. He got up from the bench and sat on the swing set.

As he began gently rocking back and forth, he thought about the little kids with their parents. He remembered going to a park in California with his mom when he was younger. Matthew continued to slowly swing, back and forth, until the setting sun disappeared behind the nearby apartment buildings.

There was a rustling in the nearby bushes that drew his attention. The same unsettling feeling washed over him again, stronger this time, prickling his skin with unease. He immediately stopped swinging and cast a cautious gaze around the deserted playground. He was all alone. The last traces of daylight fading into dusk. Streetlamps flickered to life nearby, casting pools of light amidst the encroaching darkness—a subtle signal that it was time to make his way home. He felt uneasy, and it was getting late. Sensing the growing tension in the air, Matthew abandoned the swing and swiftly retrieved his skateboard from the park bench. With each passing moment, the knot of anxiety tightened in his chest, urging him to hasten his departure. Matthew entered the apartment complex and walked toward the main building. Instead of going through the lobby, Matthew opted to go through the parking garage.

CHAPTER 3

THE SECRET OF THE GOLDEN BOOK

The garage's incline was too steep for him to ride up on his skateboard, so he had to get off his board and began to walk. As Matthew reached the second level, the fluorescent lights overhead flickered ominously before plunging the garage into darkness. The security cameras, too, shut off. The abrupt blackout sent shivers down his spine, triggering a resurgence of his unsettling premonition. The parking garage was dark but there was enough light from the remaining dusk outside to make out the shapes of the parking garage's parked cars and concrete columns.

"Probably a blown fuse or something," he muttered to himself as he quickened his pace and entered the third level of the garage.

That uneasy feeling spiked intensely. It caused Matthew's legs to come to an abrupt stop next to a large concrete column in the parking garage. Without warning, the concrete column next to Matthew seemed to have exploded. He raised his arm to shield his eyes from the flying concrete debris. He looked back at the column again to see that half of it had been cleaved off. Matthew regained the feeling in his legs and attempted to run up the incline to the fourth level, but his instincts stopped him dead in his tracks. He noticed another concrete column in front of him had a large steel ax sticking out of it.

"That was almost me!" his mind raced.

This time the ax was momentarily lodged in the column, allowing Matthew to get a fleeting look at what was attacking him. He could make out only a vague sense of its shape. It looked like a tall man—but with horns. The creature backhanded Matthew, swiftly and with enough strength to send him across the garage where he collided with the back of a parked car. He slammed into the trunk so hard that he left a dent. Matthew pushed through the pain in his back and managed to scurry away. He crouched behind a row of parked cars. With a mighty grunt, the creature managed to free its ax from the column and began to search for him. Matthew's heart pounded in his chest. He tried to be as silent as possible as the creature began to search the side of the garage where he had knocked him aside. Matthew could hear the creature making a strange noise. It was sniffing.

As the creature made its way down the line of parked cars where Matthew was hiding, he noticed that every step the creature took made a strange *clop*, like it had hooves.

Matthew came to a realization. He didn't want to be stuck between the wall and a car if the creature found him. Matthew spotted a crumpled soda can nearby. He quietly began to reach for it as the creature continued its slow march the line of cars. He was able to grab the can—without making any noise and while still keeping an eye on the creature.

He tossed the soda can in the opposite direction as he darted out from behind the cars and booked it across the parking garage. For a split second, the noise fooled the creature. It gave him just enough of a head start to make it across the garage. Matthew sprinted between the parked cars on the other side. The creature was too large to fit through the space. Matthew used the parked cars as a barrier and ran up the incline to the fourth level. The fourth level didn't have as many parked cars, so Matthew couldn't use them as a barrier. The fourth level was also a little better lit, thanks to the light outside. Matthew attempted to make a run for the door but the creature caught up to him. It took a swipe at Matthew with its ax. Matthew attempted to block it with his skateboard, but it the ax simply cut it in half. Matthew chucked what was left of his skateboard at the creature, striking its head. He then rushed to hide behind another parked car.

"You'll pay for that," growled the creature.

Matthew silently crouched behind a parked car. The creature began to franticly search for him amongst the cars.

"I can't stay here forever," he realized.

Matthew thought about what would happen if someone else stumbled upon them. They could get hurt or killed.

Even if he made it to the door, the creature could just follow him into his apartment. The creature walked past the car where Matthew was hiding.

With the better lighting on the fourth level, Matthew was able to get a clearer look at the creature. It was a Minotaur. The creature had the large head of a white bull with large, white horns and a pink snout, and the body of a man covered in white fur. It had large hooves and a tail. Matthew was freaked out by the Minotaur and let out a small gasp.

"There you are!" the Minotaur bellowed as he swung his ax menacingly.

Matthew and the Minotaur circled the car. "I'm safe as long as I stay on the other side of this car," He thought. The Minotaur grew frustrated by Matthew and pushed off the car with its hoof. The car slammed into Matthew's chest, sending him and the car sliding back across several empty parking spaces. The Minotaur rushed toward the car, using its hoof to pushing off it again, this time much harder.

Matthew leapt out of the way as the car slammed into another, sending broken glass flying. Matthew ran and hid behind another car.

"I could really use a miracle right about now," he thought desperately. And miraculously, a steel longsword materialized in his hand.

"That'll have to do," he resolved.

He walked out from behind the cars holding the sword. The Minotaur stopped searching for Matthew and walked into the open.

"So, you do have the sword. Gideon was right. Hand

it over, kid, and maybe I'll let you live," demanded the Minotaur.

Matthew remained silent. He put both hands on the sword's hilt and stared down the Minotaur in defiance.

"That sword won't make any difference. You don't even know how to use it. I'll just take it off your body," the Minotaur sneered.

Matthew remained silent as the two of them stood in the middle of the fourth level. The Minotaur charged Matthew and swung the ax at him. Matthew quickly ducked under his swing and slashed the creature in the ribs before rolling out of the way.

"ARGH!" the Minotaur roared, clutching with his hand at the cut on his side. "Now you're going to get it."

The Minotaur charged him again, wildly swinging his ax. Matthew was running on pure adrenaline and instinct, making frantic dodges to avoid each attack. The Minotaur cleaved up the nearby cars, concrete columns, and the ground before he managed to hook Matthew's sword with his ax. The Minotaur used its monstrous strength to yank it from his hands. It skidded across the floor, stopping under a parked car. Matthew fell over as the Minotaur lifted its ax with both hands for a heavy, overhead chop just as a bright light began to beam from around the corner.

The Minotaur turned and jumped over the railing, fleeing the parking garage. The car, a silver Lexus, stopped next to Matthew. The window rolled down.

"Matthew?! What are you doing out here lying on the floor in the dark in the parking garage?! I could've run you over!" Mrs. Peterson scolded.

"Mrs. Peterson?!" Matthew, still seated on the ground, was surprised. The overhead lights in the parking garage sprang back to life.

"Get up off the ground! What are you doing walking through here?! You know it's for cars only. It's dangerous."

Mrs. Peterson was an overweight woman in her forties. She had short brown hair and green eyes, and her face was caked with makeup and bronzer. Mrs. Peterson was the president of the homeowner's association and one of Matthew's neighbors. She was stuck up, mean, and always in everyone else's business. He didn't care for her—but in this moment, he was glad to see her.

Matthew got up from the ground and brushed the dirt off himself. "I was just on my way back to my apartment," he explained.

"Walking through the parking garage is dangerous and is strictly prohibited. I'm too busy to speak with your mother about this now, but next time use the front lobby like everyone else."

"Okay. I'll be sure to remember that." Matthew replied, turning to walk away.

"Oh, one last thing," Mrs. Peterson interjected. "You wouldn't happen to know any information on what happened in the parking garage? A bunch of the columns and cars are damaged. This wouldn't be someone's idea of a prank, would it? You wouldn't know who was behind this, would you?"

"It was like that when I came up here," he lied.

Her eyes narrowed. "Alright. I'll alert management about this. They'll look through the security footage and bring whoever's responsible to justice. Besides, it needs to be repaired immediately, someone could get hurt," she annouced. She then rolled up the window and pulled into an available space.

Matthew ran through the door into the hall. In haste, he unlocked the door to find himself inside their dark apartment. He locked the door behind him and turned on almost every light in the apartment, then took a seat on the living room couch. He turned on the TV for the noise. Suddenly, there was a scratching noise at the apartment door and the door swung open.

"That Minotaur is back," he thought.

Matthew clenched his fists in fear and anger. He thought of the sword he had before. He wished he still had it, but it was still in the garage, under a car. He couldn't go get it while Mrs. Peterson was still there.

When he looked back at the door, Matthew saw his mother standing there holding a few bags. Her key was still stuck in the door lock. Matthew's mom was a tall slim woman in her late thirties with brown skin and eyes. She wore big, circular wire framed glasses and possessed a large mane of curly black hair. With a solid tug, she finally managed to free her key from the door and entered their apartment.

"Hi, Mom," Matthew greeted.

"A little help, please," she requested. He rushed over to grab some of the bags and help her put them on the kitchen counter. "I hope you're hungry, 'cause I brought burritos." she announced shaking a white paper bag.

Matthew and his mom sat down at the table and had dinner.

"So, how was your day?" she inquired.

"Fine. Took the last of my final exams."

"How did you do?"

"I dunno," he replied.

"Well, how do you *think* you did?" she pressed.

"Pretty good, I guess. Only the math test was hard, but we got to use a calculator."

"Well, that's good. Hey, did you see what happened in the parking garage? Several columns and cars were busted up when I was coming home. Like someone went through there with an ax or something."

Matthew swallowed hard and lied. "No. It was like that when I came home." He couldn't tell his mom what had happened in the parking garage. She'd probably think he was crazy—or just imagined it. Matthew could hardly believe it himself, and he was there when it happened.

"Well, you made it home safe, so that's what's important. I hope all that gets taken care of soon. It's dangerous."

"So how was your day?" Matthew wanting to change the subject.

"Busy," his mom replied. "I had three meetings today. I barely had time to eat lunch. Sorry about having to work late … again."

"It's okay … I'm used to it." They sat in awkward silence for a moment before Matthew asked a question. "Hey Mom, did you put that picture in my room?"

Liz hesitated before admitting. "Yes."

"Why?"

She fell silent again before she spoke. "Well, I found the picture amongst some of our older things, and I thought maybe you might want it since it's the only picture we have of all of us."

Matthew never really cared much about what happened to his dad. The thought of it rarely crossed his mind but having that picture in his room would serve as a reminder of things he had long put behind him.

"Thanks … but I don't really want the picture," Matthew replied.

"Why?"

Matthew was quiet for several moments before he replied. "Because you've rarely talked about him before, and now you just give me this picture. I don't even care about him, anyway!" His words spilled out in a rush of emotion.

"Matthew! Don't say that!" said Liz angrily. He fell silent. "Your dad is a good man."

"Then where is he?" Matthew challenged.

Matthew's mom grew quiet. "He had his reasons." Her voice began to shake. Matthew tended to avoid the topic of his father because every time it would come up, his mother would start to get teary-eyed. He knew that if he continued to push her she would start crying.

"So, Mom, what are we going to do tomorrow?" Matthew was desperate to change the subject.

Liz was silent for a few more moments. "I have to work tomorrow."

"Well … that's okay. How about on Sunday?" asked Matthew.

"I have to work then, too."

"Well, when do you not have to work?"

"Well … I'll have to work during the summer," answered his mom, in a solemn voice.

"Oh," said Matthew. He became quiet for a few seconds. "Is there any way you can get out of it? It's summer vacation."

"It's summer vacation for *you*. But I have to work. If I don't work, who else is going to pay for everything around here, huh?" said Liz defensive, tinged with frustration.

She then looked at Matthew, who was staring into his empty plate and not saying anything.

"That's fine. I didn't really care all that much, anyway," he lied masking his disappointment with false indifference..

"I'm sorry, I really am. Besides, I'll see if I can take some time off later. We'll still have fun together later this summer. Okay?" Her voice was soft as she stood up from the table.

"You don't have to take any time off for me. I'm fine. I don't care anymore. I spend my time all by myself. I'm used to it by now."

his words tinged with bitterness as he refused to look at his mom. His mom walked over to the sink and put her plate on the counter.

"Sometimes," Liz began, "you have to make sacrifices for the people you love. …Maybe when you're older, you'll be able to understand that."

Matthew got up from the table, put his plate in the sink, and went to sit on the couch in the living room. Liz came from the kitchen and looked at him who was trying his hardest to ignore her by concentrating on the TV. His mom, then she silently went to her room and closed her door. Matthew stayed up watching TV until product infomercials started to come on. went to his room to go to bed.

The sun streaked across the room and onto his face, waking him. Matthew awoke and began to look around the room. In green numbers, his digital clock read 10:49. After waking up at 6 am for months to catch the train to school, it felt good to sleep in. He then yawned and got out of his bed. In the kitchen, Matthew grabbed a box of cereal, a spoon, and a bowl. He then headed to the refrigerator, reached for the milk, and headed to the couch. Matthew sat there and watched TV and ate his breakfast. When he was done, he put his bowl in the sink. He noticed a note on the counter. It was from his mom.

Dear Matthew,

There should be enough food there for breakfast and lunch for you. Please clean up any messes you make and don't open the door to strangers. If you leave the apartment, please lock the apartment behind you and remember to keep your phone on you at all times. Do not leave the apartment complex! If you have any problems, call me at work or go down to the front desk. Hopefully, I'll be back before dinner.

Love,

Mom

Matthew set the note aside, feeling a mix of emotions as he sank back onto the couch. The solitude of the empty apartment stirred a sense of sadness and frustration within him. It seemed like work always took precedence for his mom, and it had uprooted their lives to New York, leaving behind his friends. Today, instead of a promising start to a summer full of adventure, it felt like a disappointing beginning to what he hoped wouldn't be a dismal summer. Determined to shake off the gloom, Matthew rose from the couch and left the apartment, making sure to lock the door behind him.

Venturing into the parking garage, Matthew found it a hive of activity, with orange cones, caution tape, and construction equipment scattered about. Amidst the repairs, he managed to locate the two halves of his skateboard among the scattered cars and machinery. Although he searched for the sword he lost the day before, it seemed to have vanished along with the car it had slid under.

Matthew hoped no one had snatched it while it lay on the ground. After a brief search, he resigned himself to the possibility and trudged back to the apartment. Returning to his room, Matthew set to work repairing his skateboard. Scouring the kitchen drawer, he unearthed some duct tape and wood glue. Carefully, he applied the glue to the fractured halves and reinforced it with layers of duct tape. With the repairs underway, he decided to pass the time with video games until the glue dried. Matthew played some of his video games until he became bored of that just like he did with everything else, and decided to have lunch.

They didn't have much in the apartment for lunch since they hadn't gone shopping in a few days. He managed to make a turkey sandwich with some potato chips. After lunch, he went back to his room, grabbed his skateboard, and headed outside. Matthew rode around on his skateboard for a few minutes.

"It feels good," thought Matthew. He continued to skate around until, suddenly, his board snapped in half again. Matthew picked up his skateboard and it folded completely in half. A deflated Matthew returned to the apartment. He entered his room, dropped his folded skateboard on the floor, flopped on the bed, and buried his face in his pillow.

Matthew turned his face to see his bookbag lying on the floor of his room. Hanging out of his bag was the corner of the golden book. Matthew raised his head off his pillow and stared at the book. He finally had time to read it. Matthew got up off the bed and went over to the book bag, unzipped it, lifted the book out of the bag, and carried it to his bed. The book seemed to glow. "Must be the sunlight in the room reflecting off the metal cover," he reasoned. Matthew sat on the edge of his bed and opened the book.

He was met with a blinding light bursting from its pages. Overwhelmed, he lost his senses one by one until darkness enveloped him completely.

The bright sunlight shone on Matthew's face as he stirred on the ground, still clutching the book tightly in his hand. Confusion clouded his senses, making everything seem blurry and disorienting. He struggled to move, to hear, to see clearly. Just as he began to regain his bearings, a wave of dizziness swept over him, causing him to black out once more.

When he came to, an old man hovered over him, rifling through his pockets with nimble fingers. He had already gone through his shoes, Matthew noticed, because his shoes had been pulled off his feet. The old man was so distracted going through Matthew's pockets that he didn't notice that he'd awakened.

"Hey!" shouted Matthew as soon as the scene came into view.

The old man was so startled he jumped back so hard he landed on his butt. He was wearing tattered clothing and had wild, grey hair. Matthew began to rise, slowly, on his rubbery legs while the old man seized the golden book and bolted into the brushes. Matthew hastily put on his shoes and pursued the thief.

Matthew followed the old man as closely as he could, and continued to follow him old man until they approached a large hedge wall.

In a flash, the old man jumped through the hedge. Matthew—without hesitating—leapt after him through the hedge.

CHAPTER 4

DOWN THE RABBIT HOLE

Once on the other side, Matthew discovered that the old man had completely vanished.

Matthew quickly scanned his surroundings, hoping to catch a glimpse of the thief, but he was nowhere to be found. Suddenly, it dawned on him that he was in a forest. Matthew tried to piece together his memories as to how he got here. He remembered sitting on his bed. He remembered that he opened that golden book—and then nothing.

As far as Matthew could discern, wherever he was, he must have gotten there because of some connection to that book. And now that book was gone, with some old man who could be anywhere by now. Matthew's situation was starting to look increasingly worse by the second. He was lost in a strange forest, in a strange place, and the only object that had some connection to how he got there was now gone.

He kept walking through the forest hoping for some sign of the old man. Soon, he burst into a frantic run, racing through the forest. He searched every bush; he looked up every tree. He continued to run through the forest, desperate for any sign of the old man—or anyone. After coming up empty-handed, Matthew became discouraged.

"I'm gonna be stuck here forever. If I don't find him, I don't know what I'm gonna do," thought Matthew.

He continued his fruitless search for the old man for what felt like hours, until he was just running around lost in the forest. The forest was hot. His increasing nervousness, coupled with the heat and all the running around he was doing, made him sweat. Despite his blind panic, he managed to stumble across a new part of the forest.

This part of the forest was mostly a grassy field, sprinkled with a few trees. In the center of this grassy field was a massive tree on a little hill. It was the largest tree in the field. Its abundant branches were lush with greenery. The tree's most unique feature was that it was slightly uprooted. It leaned back, tilted, with its gnarled roots forming a hole at the bottom of the tree.

Matthew felt a bit of relief. "The old man must be hiding in the tree. It must be some secret hideout or something," he reasoned. Matthew approached the tree and touched the rough bark. He glanced around for any other sign of life. All was quiet except for the birds chirping in the trees and the wind gently ruffling the leaves. He bent down and looked in the hole.

It was too dark—he couldn't see anything. Matthew looked again before sticking his hand in the hole. He reached but couldn't find anything. Matthew stood up and started to kick the tree.

"I know you're in here, old man! Get out here!" he demanded. There was no response. "Come out now and I won't have to hurt you!" he demanded, tried to sound tougher than he felt. Again, there was silence. He sighed.

"Look, just gimme my book back and I won't call the cops," he said.

Once again, there was only silence. "It must be some kind of secret lair. Maybe he crawled deeper inside? That's why he can't hear me," thought Matthew.

He got on his knees and carefully stuck his head inside the hole. Everything was silent inside the tree. It was also cold inside the tree, which was strange since it was hot outside.

"Hello? Is anybody in here?" he called out asked. He got no answer. Matthew backed out of the hole and grabbed a nearby rock sitting in the grass. He stuck his head back in the hole and dropped the rock. He listened intently for the sound of the rock striking the ground, but there was nothing. Matthew strained trying to listen, trying to hear even the faintest sound, until the dirt under his hands began to crumble from his weight and gave way.

He fell down the hole headfirst. The hole began to widen as he fell into the darkness.

"Ahhhhhhhhhhh!" Matthew screamed as he fell faster and faster, rocketing toward the ground. He fell for what felt like several minutes, while his eyes adjusted to the darkness. Suddenly, he saw what he could only guess was the bottom of the hole. He closed his eyes and braced for impact. When he felt no crushing impact from hitting the ground at high speed, he opened his eyes.

Matthew was floating three inches from the ground. Gently, his body was then lowered to the ground. He slowly stood up, and brushed himself off. Matthew quickly spun around trying to get a feel for his surroundings, but he was standing in a pitch-black room. He prepared himself in case the old man tried to ambush him.

Suddenly, the torches along the wall ignited with a strange blue flame. They illuminated the room. Matthew saw that he was standing in a large, circular brick room. Each of the bricks on the wall was carved with an ace, club, diamond, or heart symbol. The floor was a black, red, and white checkerboard tile that echoed each of Matthews's footsteps as he crossed the room into the only hallway exiting it. The hallway came to a dead end but was flanked with doors on both sides. Each of the numerous doors varied in size, shape, and color.

Matthew immediately tried to open every door, but they were all locked. Afterward, he stood there in the middle of the hallway, defeated.

"How am I ever gonna get out of here?" he wondered.

When he turned around he saw that there was now a

small, three-legged table in the hallway. The table was made from solid glass and on top of it was a tiny golden key.

"This key has to belong to one of these doors," he reasoned. Matthew tried using the key on every door in the hallway. The key, unfortunately, didn't open any of the doors and he returned it to the table. Matthew sighed. He then noticed another new addition to the hallway. Now there were small red curtains at the bottom of the dead-end wall in front of him. Matthew walked over to the small red curtains and opened them. Behind the curtain, there was a small wooden door. It was about twelve inches tall.

Matthew went back over to the glass table and picked up the key again. He used the key on the doorknob of the little door. The little golden key unlocked it. Matthew got on his knees, opened the little door, and looked through. The little door led to what looked like a garden with a row of tall hedges.

"Just my luck, the only door this key opens is too small for me to fit through," muttered Matthew.

Suddenly, one of the doors in the hallway creaked open, and a blonde girl stepped out. She was a slender twelve-year-old girl with fair skin and big blue eyes. She had long, thick blond hair that fell just past her shoulders. She wore a blue knee-length dress, white stockings, black-strapped shoes, and a black ribbon in her hair.

"Now then, surely I'll manage better this time," she said. She spoke with a British accent. Finally, someone else. Maybe they could help him.

"Hey! Do you know a way outta here?! Are you with

that old man?!" he blurted out eagerly. Matthew's sudden questions startled the girl, causing her to jump.

"Where did you come from?! No one was here a moment ago!" she exclaimed, looking around.

"I'm looking for an old man. He was wearing old, tattered clothing. His hair was grey and sticking up like he hadn't combed it in years. He would be carrying a book, it's big and gold. Have you seen someone like that?" Matthew inquired.

The girl shook her head no. "I'm afraid I haven't seen anyone matching that description. Sorry."

Matthew sighed, feeling deflated. "Well, can you help me get outta here? I've been stuck in this hallway forever."

The girl turned to Matthew. "Well, I'm no expert, but I think I've managed quite well. Perhaps we can assist each other," she suggested.

"Alright, I'm Matthew," he said.

"Hello, Matthew. My name is Alice. Pleasure," she replied, adding a little curtsy.

"So ... what's the plan?" he asked.

"Well, first I'm going to need the key that was on this table. Have you seen it?" She tapped the top of the glass table with her finger

"You mean this one?" He held up the key.

"Brilliant!" she exclaimed. Alice quickly walked over to Matthew and he handed her the key. "Next, take a drink from that glass on the table."

"There's no glass on the table," he replied confused. Matthew looked at the glass table again and suddenly noticed a little bottle. He walked over to the table and picked up the bottle. The bottle had a paper label tied around its neck by a little string. It had the words DRINK ME printed on it.

"Are you sure about this?" he asked, unsure.

"Yes. It'll be alright," Alice replied with a reassuring tone.

Matthew took a deep breath and drank from the bottle. The blue liquid rolled down from the bottle into Matthew's mouth. Matthew took a small sip of the strange blue liquid. Matthew put the bottle back down on the table and stood there for a moment. It tasted of blueberries. The table began to grow taller along with the walls of the room. Matthew spun around in bewilderment. He was now under the glass table. Matthew began to examine his hands but, as far as he could tell, they were normal.

"Great, now come over here," Alice said, towering over him.

Matthew ran to where Alice was standing. She kneeled and used the key to unlock the small door again, opening it for him.

"Are you going to drink some of that liquid, too?" he asked.

Alice pulled a piece of mushroom from one of her dress's pockets and began to nibble on it. As she did she slowly began to shrink to his size. Together they walked through the unlocked door.

The sunlight was blinding as Matthew put up his hands to shade his eyes. He looked up, amazed at the sky.

He had fallen into a hole—he must have been underground, but there was the sun, the clouds, and even a nice breeze.

"Curiouser and curiouser," said Alice, looking around in amazement.

"Where do we go now?" he asked.

"Well, I met a talking cat who suggests I speak with the queen. Surely she would know the way out," she reasoned.

"A … talking cat?" said Matthew.

"I know it probably sounds quite mad, but I don't know what else to do."

Matthew didn't have any other ideas and Alice had taken them this far. "It's worth a shot. Where do we go?" he said. Alice pointed to the large stone castle looming in the distance over the large gardens and hedge maze. They reluctantly entered the garden's hedge maze on their way to the large stone castle looming in the distance.

"You know, you're the first normal person I've met since I've been here," Alice said as they walked through the hedge maze.

"First normal person? You've met other people here?" he asked.

"Oh, lots. Mostly talking animals, some people, they all seemed quite mad, really."

Suddenly, he heard something. "Hey, do you hear that?" he asked.

They both listened close, and could hear faint voices in the distance. "Other people," he said, rushing off toward the voices.

"Oh dear, wait for me!" shouted Alice as she ran after him.

They came to an opening in the hedge maze. A rose tree, growing white roses, stood near the opening of the garden. At a nearby tree, three card men were painting the roses red.

"Why are they … painting roses?" he asked.

"Let's ask them," said Alice. She walked over to them. The men had long and flat torsos with playing card numbers on the front and simple checkered patterns on the back. Their long thin arms and legs sprouted out the edges of their flat torsos, with their heads on top. One of the gardeners spotted Alice as she approached.

"Hello there. Would you mind telling me … why you are painting those roses?" she asked.

Two of the gardeners said nothing but looked at the third. The third answered. "Why, you see, these should have been red rose trees, and we put in white ones by mistake. If the queen were to find out, we would have our heads cut off. So, we're doing our best to—"

The first gardener, who had been looking across the garden, suddenly yelled. "The queen! The queen!"

The three card-men quickly threw themselves flat upon their faces. Matthew ran to Alice. They heard the thundering of many footsteps and looked around to see what was happening. A long procession of marching card-men entered the garden. Some were soldiers holding weapons, some were holding banners and flags, and some were playing instruments. After the cards, came the courtiers, then followed the royal children. Each group was ornamented with a symbol, for the soldiers the club, the courtiers the diamond, and the royal children the heart. Alice recognized the White Rabbit amongst the crowd. The White Rabbit was wearing a fancy waistcoat, holding a bugle, and walking among the card-men. Following behind the White Rabbit was the Knave of Hearts, who was carrying the King's golden crown on a crimson velvet cushion.

Last in the grand procession was the King and Queen of Hearts. The King and Queen of Hearts were both humans—a detail that stood out from the strangeness of the rest of the procession. The Queen of Hearts was a woman in her thirties, with a nasty scowl on her face and a fancy red, black, and white dress. The King of Hearts was a man in his thirties with a big goofy smile on his face. He wore a long, curly, white powdered wig with fancy red, black, and white robes. Matthew and Alice stood there next to the gardeners. The sheer magnitude of the procession stunned them. Soon, the large procession came to a stop, opposite where Matthew and Alice were standing.

The queen looked at the two of them with a strange expression. She didn't recognize them or their unusual clothing.

"Who is this?" the queen asked the Knave of Hearts.

The Knave of Hearts was a young human male in a red and white checked robe with short black hair and a round red cap. The Knave of Hearts only bowed and smiled in reply.

"Idiot!" said the queen, rolling her eyes. She then

turned to Alice and asked, "What's your name, child?"

"My name is Alice, Your Majesty," spoke Alice, sounding very polite.

Then queen turned to Matthew. "And, your name, child?"

"Matthew."

The queen looked at him fiercely.

"Your Majesty," he added quickly.

"And who are *they*?" the queen asked, pointing to the three cards that were laying on the ground.

Matthew and Alice shrugged.

"Turn them over!" commanded the queen. The Knave carefully did so with one foot. The queen shouted again. "Get up!" The three gardeners jumped to their feet and bowed franticly to the king, the queen, and everyone else.

"Stop that!" screamed the queen. She then turned to the rose tree, where the gardeners stood. "What have you been doing here?" she asked.

"Well, Your Majesty—" said the first gardener.

"We were trying—" continued the second gardener.

"I see!" said the queen. She had been examining the red paint that dripped from the roses. "Off with their heads!"

The procession moved on. Three of the soldiers remained behind to follow the queen's instructions to execute the unfortunate gardeners. They all ran to Alice for protection.

"You shan't really be beheaded for something so minor?" Alice asked in disbelief.

The three card-soldiers began to close in on them until the King of Hearts returned and pardoned them. They hid behind a large flower pot. Without a word, the King of Hearts and the three soldiers marched off.

"Are their heads off?" shouted the queen.

"They're gone, Your Majesty!" the soldiers shouted in reply.

"Oh! That's right!" shouted the queen. She returned to Matthew and Alice. "Can you two play croquet?"

"Yes," answered Alice.

"Umm … sure," lied Matthew.

"Come along, then!" she roared.

Matthew and Alice reluctantly joined the procession. They walked for a little while until they arrived at a large clearing in the castle gardens.

"Get to your places!" commanded the queen. People began running about in all directions, tumbling up against each other. After a minute or two, they settled down. The White Rabbit blew his horn.

"Let the game begin!" he announced.

A card soldier brought over a croquet bag that contained multiple pairs of differently colored long, webbed feet. The other soldiers spread out in the open and bent forward to create croquet rings. The queen grabbed the red pair of webbed feet and pulled them out of the bag. Out of the bag came a solid red, living flamingo. The queen took a few wild practice swings. The White Rabbit set a red ball in front of her. She took another wild swing at the red ball in front of her, missing it completely. The red ball unfurled just enough to reveal that it was, in fact, a hedgehog. The red hedgehog hurried through the croquet rings the soldiers had formed. Some of the soldiers moved to where the ball was headed to help it move through the rings.

The queen stood there with a satisfied look on her face as the hedgehog ran through all the rings. The other soldiers who weren't forced to be croquet rings clapped and cheered at the queen who graciously waved, bowed, and blew kisses. Matthew and Alice looked at each other confused. They simply shrugged and began to clap as well.

"You're next, dear," said the queen said to Alice. Alice began to internally panic.

"I … uhh … sigh … yes, Your Majesty."

Alice grabbed a pair of yellow webbed feet and pulled out the yellow flamingo. The White Rabbit set a yellow ball for her. Alice set the flamingo's head behind the ball and she turned to look at Matthew, who was standing next to the queen. Matthew gave her a thumbs up and she turned back to the ball. The air was silent. She was having trouble managing her flamingo. Just as she got its neck straightened out to hit the hedgehog, it twisted itself around and looked up at her face. It gave her a puzzled expression. This caused some of the card-soldiers to snicker. When she finally got its head back down and was going to begin again, her hedgehog unrolled itself and began to crawl away. More of the card-soldiers snickered—this time, louder.

Alice continued to struggle with the flamingo and hedgehog until, frustrated, she grabbed the flamingo by the top of its neck. She gave the flamingo a wild swing and hit the ball. The hedgehog ran toward the card-soldier croquet rings but the soldiers moved out of the way of Alice's ball. The card-soldiers then erupted in laughter.

"Your turn, dear." The queen now looked at Matthew.

He sighed, walked over to the crotchet bag, and pulled out a blue flamingo. The White Rabbit placed a blue ball in front of Matthew. He swung his flamingo and managed to hit the ball, but the card-soldier rings just moved out of the way of his ball. The other card-soldiers began to laugh. Matthew sighed again, then walked back to the side of the garden where Alice and the queen were standing. The queen picked up her flamingo and walked over to her ball.

"This game is impossible," he complained, in a low voice, to Alice.

"It doesn't matter if we win. We just have to stay on her good side so she'll tell us how to leave," Alice replied.

Some of the card men and other inhabitants of Wonderland went next. For whatever reason, the queen shouted "Off with their head!" after some of their turns.

Alice grew more uneasy. Even though she hadn't had any dispute with the queen, she knew that the longer they stayed there the more likely a dispute was to happen.

"They're dreadfully fond of beheading people here. It's a great wonder that there's anyone left alive," Alice whispered to Matthew.

"Then we should probably leave before we do something to make her angry."

Matthew and Alice split up and looked around for a way to escape. They wondered whether they could get away without being seen. That's when Alice noticed a slight disruption in the air. At first it puzzled her, but she gave it a closer look. She thought it could've been the heat, but the temperature in the castle gardens was pleasant. After watching it for several moments, the disruption in the air became more pronounced. It began to curve and take the shape of a wide smile.

Alice recognized it immediately. "It's the Cheshire Cat," she whispered to Matthew, tugging on his shirt sleeve.

CHAPTER 5

ESCAPE FROM WONDERLAND

"It seems you've made a friend. How are you two getting on?" asked the Cheshire Cat, as soon as enough of its mouth had appeared for it to be able to speak.

A few moments later, its whole head appeared. The Cheshire Cat's head was the head of a large brown tabby cat. Its amber eyes were large with a wide mouth filled with teeth. Alice put down her flamingo. "I don't think the queen will help us," she said deflated.

Matthew walked over to Alice. He wasn't having any luck finding them a way out either. He then noticed the disembodied talking cat head laying in the grass. It's appearance completely caught him by surprise. He hesitated for a moment before speaking. "You wouldn't happen to know the way outta here?" Matthew asked the Cheshire Cat.

The king had noticed the two of them were no longer playing the game. He curiously approached them. "Who are you talking to?" he asked.

He spotted the Cheshire Cat's head laying in the grass, peering at it with great curiosity.

"It's a friend of mine … a Cheshire Cat," replied Alice.

"I don't like the look of it at all," complained the king, sounding uncomfortable. "However, it may kiss my hand if it likes."

"I'd rather not," replied the cat.

"Don't be rude. And don't look at me like that!" the King replied, getting behind Alice as he spoke.

"There's nothing wrong with a cat looking at a king," Alice interjected.

"Well, it must be removed," said the King. He then called over to the queen, who happened to be passing by at that moment.

"My dear! I wish you would have this cat removed!"

Without so much as looking around, the queen replied, "Off with his head!"

"Someone, fetch the executioner!" said the King eagerly.

Matthew and Alice thought they might as well go back and see how the game was progressing. They had already heard the queen sentence several of the other players to execution—all for having missed their turns. Matthew and Alice decided to go search for their hedgehogs. Alice's hedgehog was engaged in a fight with another hedgehog.

"This is an excellent opportunity for croqueting one of them with the other," thought Alice.

However, she didn't have her flamingo with her. Alice scanned the garden for her yellow flamingo. Her flamingo had gone to the other side of the garden, where it was trying to fly up into a tree. By the time she had managed to wrangled her flamingo and returned, the fight was over and both hedgehogs were out of sight. Alice tucked her flamingo under her arm and went to find Matthew.

Matthew's luck wasn't much better, since he also lost his hedgehog. They decided to return to the Cheshire Cat for help. In their absence a large crowd had gathered around it. The royal executioner, the king, and the queen were engaged in a dispute. All of them were talking over each other while the onlookers all remained silent, looking very uncomfortable. The moment Matthew and Alice appeared, the three forced them to settle the question.

The executioner argued that you couldn't cut off a head unless there was a body to cut it off from.

The king argued that anything that had a head could be beheaded.

The queen argued that if something wasn't done about it soon, she would order everyone beheaded.

Alice was quickly overwhelmed and confused by all three of their arguments. "The Cheshire Cat belongs to the duchess. You'd better ask *her* about it," she deflected.

"She's in prison. Bring her here!" the queen commanded to the executioner.

Before the executioner could go to retrieve the duchess, the Cheshire Cat's head had already begun to fade away like a puff of smoke. The king and the executioner ran around the garden looking for the cat. Everyone else went back to hitting their hedgehogs with their flamingos while the card-soldiers continued to dodge any and every hedgehog that wasn't the queen's.

"What do we do now?" asked Alice.

"Let's just go back to playing croquet until we find our opening to leave," Matthew replied.

"Alright," replied Alice, her voice filled with worry. Following his advise, Alice anxiously went back to the game. Suddenly, Alice spotted her yellow hedgehog sitting under a tree. She rushed over to it and struck it with her flamingo. This startled the hedgehog. It ran toward one of the card-men who was forming an arch. The card-man quickly moved out of the way, causing the hedgehog to go scurrying up the queen's dress.

The queen instantly let out a loud screech of horror. Everyone immediately stopped playing croquet and began to crowd around her in confusion. The queen howled and jumped around as she used her flamingo to batter the hedgehog as it moved through her dress. The queen then flopped and rolled around on the ground as everyone watched in horror. After several minutes, the hedgehog finally managed to escape from the queen's dress and scurried off toward some nearby bushes. The crowd noticed the bright yellow color of the hedgehog and looked around for its matching flamingo and it's welder.

Alice stood there, terrified, gripping her yellow flamingo.

The king, who looked concerned, ran over to the queen. "My dear! Are you okay?"

The queen was silent as she slowly rose from the ground. Loose strands of her black hair draped her face. Her gold crown had tumbled off her head. Her face and dress were smudged with dirt and grass stains, and she tightly clenched her fists. The queen's body was shaking in anger. Her face was turning bright red.

A suddenly deep unease overcame Matthew.

He quickly ran over to Alice. "Let's go!" he commanded, grabbing Alice's wrist and running into the hedge garden.

"OFF WITH THEIR HEADS!"

The queen's explosive command was so loud that the birds in nearby trees bolted into the sky. Her words echoed throughout the garden. "AFTER THEM!"

"Do you know where you're going?" Alice inquired nervously as Matthew pulled her around another corner of the hedge maze.

"Nope."

"Well, wait, we might run into a dead end."

They then turned a corner into a dead end. "Crap!" exclaimed Matthew.

"Over here, men!" shouted a card-soldier.

"They're trapped!" said another.

A group of card soldiers came around the corner, unsheathed their weapons, and began to close in on them.

"Get behind me," insisted Matthew, and Alice got behind him.

"Please, tell me you have a plan?" she hoped.

"Something like that," he replied.

One of the card-soldiers instructed the men to move in. "Move in men." commanded one of the card soldiers.

Matthew remembered the sword that appeared when he was attacked in the parking garage. "That would come in handy right about now," he thought desperately.

He closed his eyes tight and tried to concentrate on the sword. Alice nervously shut her eyes tight, too, while she gripped the back of Matthew's shirt.

"Take this! … Whoa!" shouted a card-soldier as he jumped back.

Matthew opened his eyes to find a sword in his hand. It was completely different from the one he remembered. This sword was a curved scimitar with a white blade. Its cross-guard was curved in different directions with a leather grip and a small chain hanging from the pommel. Matthew pointed his sword at the card soldiers to keep their distance.

Then one of them commanded, "He can't take us all. Charge!"

The soldiers charged Matthew and he swung his sword at them. An incredible, powerful gust of wind blasted the card-soldiers down the maze and into a hedge wall. Matthew looked at the sword and wondered what happened. He snapped out of it. "Let's go!" he shouted.

Matthew and Alice dashed around the downed card-soldiers, then continued to run through the hedge maze.

"Ugh, this place is impossible!" Matthew frustratedly shouted as they hit another dead end. Another card-soldier approached and swung his sword at him. Matthew was quick and managed to parry his attack. They locked swords. He managed to push the soldier back, but then more soldiers rushed in from the corner of the hedges.

With some distance between them, Matthew swung his sword once more, striking the soldiers with a gust of wind. Due to their flat torsos, they caught all the wind and flew back into the hedge walls.

"Perhaps, I should lead," Alice suggested.

"Great idea," he replied.

They ran past the downed soldiers and entered another one of the maze's pathways, coming upon a fork in the path.

"Right or Left?" Matthew anxiously asked Alice.

"Ummm," panicked Alice, who was quickly trying to make a decision.

"They couldn't have gotten far," shouted a distant soldier's voice. Matthew and Alice could hear that the soldier's voice was coming from the path on the right.

"Left it is," Alice declared.

They sprinted down the left path. As they ran, the Cheshire Cat's head made a sudden appearance on top of Alice's.

"I take it the game didn't go well," teased the cat, grinning.

"What was your first clue?" Matthew snapped.

"We'd like a way out of here if you don't mind, please!" shouted Alice, trying to be polite.

"Alright," conceded the cat. "Turn right here."

Matthew and Alice turned right. They darted down the path until a group of soldiers came from around the corner at the opposite end of the path.

"Here they are!" shouted one of the soldiers.

"Turn left," guided the cat.

They made a swift left turn before the soldiers caught up to them, hot on their tail.

"Turn right," the cat instructed.

Matthew quickly swung his sword behind him to slow down the gaining soldiers. Around the next corner was finally an exit to the maze.

"Finally!" said Matthew, a hint of relief in his voice.

"Goodbye," replied the cat, as his head began to fade from its place on top of Alice's.

"Wait!" shouted Alice. "We still don't know how to leave this place!"

"Hit the bricks," the cat replied, just as his head faded away completely.

The two of them exited the garden hedge maze, entering a large, open field.

"Over there!" Alice shouted, pointing to a large wooden door on the other side of the field.

"THIS WAY!" yelled one of the card-soldiers, now back in hot pursuit. Matthew and Alice rushed to the wooden door. It was completely smooth with no doorknob. Franticly, they banged on the door, trying as hard as they could to push the door open. Some of the card-soldiers began to exit the maze and charge across the open field. The wooden door finally gave way and they sprinted inside, pushing the large door closed behind them.

They were back in the multi-door hallway from earlier. Alice pulled the key out of one of her pockets and locked the now smaller doorknob behind them. Matthew ran to the glass table in the middle of the hallway.

"How do we grow back to normal size?" he asked Alice as she caught up to him.

"There!" she shouted, pointing to a little glass box under the giant glass table.

Suddenly, there was a loud bang from the other side of the locked door.

"I don't think that's gonna hold them for long," said Matthew.

Alice opened the little glass box. The box contained a small cake with the words *EAT ME* spelled out in berries. The cake was already had a little piece missing from it, like someone took it with their hand. Matthew hesitated while Alice, unconcerned, franticly used her hand to scoop up a small piece of cake and shoved it in her mouth. Within moments of eating it she began to grow back to normal size.

Another loud bang came from the other side of the locked door. Matthew scooped out a piece of cake and ate it, returning to normal size as Alice ran down the hallway into the large circular room.

"How do we get out of here?" he asked, just as another loud bang came from behind the door. This time, two of the door's hinges came off.

"They're almost through!" he urgently warned.

Alice franticly thought to herself for several moments. "I got it!" she shouted. "The bricks! It must have something to do with the bricks in this room."

Suddenly, the door flew off its hinges and slid into one of the glass table's legs. The small card-soldiers poured into the hallway, headed straight for the glass table.

"It must be one of the bricks!" she said as she moved her hands, desperately, all over the bricks. "Please help me!"

Matthew ran over to the wall and started waving his arms over the bricks. The card-soldiers, rushing down the hall, were starting to grow to full size.

"Hurry!" he shouted.

A card-soldier slashed at Alice's back while she was distracted felting around, touching the bricks. Matthew parried the attack and kicked back the soldier, who flew down the hallway with a gust of wind from a swing of his sword.

"I'll hold them off. Find that brick!" shouted Matthew.

Two more soldiers, now full size, charged down the hallway. They both attacked with quick slashes. Matthew barely blocked the onslaught as the soldiers continued to press him. They were too close for him to blast them away with a gust of wind. He had begun to tire from all the running and fighting, and he was barely holding on. Four more soldiers grew to full size.

"I got it!" shouted Alice. A brick with a heart symbol carved into it began to glow and protrude from the wall.

Several other bricks began to glow and protrude from the wall, forming a brick spiral staircase that ran along the walls of the circular room. "Let's go!" She shouted as she began to rush up the stairs.

Matthew mustered enough strength to push back both of the soldiers and, as quickly as he could, followed her up the stairs. Several more card-soldiers grew to full size and charged up the stairs behind them. Matthew followed Alice, while several card-soldiers were still in pursuit.

Soon, they had ascended the staircase so high that they could no longer see the bottom. Matthew began to slow down as the fatigue continued to set in. The soldiers were starting to catch up.

"We're almost there! I can see the hole!" she shouted.

Suddenly, the bricks started to slide back into the wall. "Not now!" Matthew yelled. Alice ran up a few more stairs and jumped for the hole. She landed halfway out of the hole and scrambled out into the forest. Matthew dug down deep within him and ran up a few more stairs before jumping, just as the last brick he was standing on completely slid back into the wall.

He was too far from the hole when he jumped. He managed to grab the ledge with one of his hands, but the force of the jump caused him to drop his sword. The white sword hit the wall before tumbling into the darkness below. A card-soldier caught his leg. Matthew had grown too tired, and began to lose his grip with the extra weight on his leg.

Alice quickly grabbed his hand. She began to pull him out of the hole. Matthew grabbed Alice with his other hand as she tried to pull him up. She struggled greatly. She was already tired and he was heavy. He began kicking the card-soldier in the face until the soldier relented and released his leg. Matthew watched as the card-soldier tumbled into the darkness below. Alice managed to pull Matthew halfway out of the hole before she tried out. He then pulled the rest of his body from the hole and laid flat on his back, out of breath, in the field.

"Do you mind … if I take a little break?" he asked.

Alice slowly walked over to a nearby tree. She collapsed under it and caught her breath.

"Well … if you insist," Alice replied between heavy breaths. After lying on his back in the grass for several minutes, Matthew felt recovered enough to get up. He brushed the dirt and grass off his jeans and walked over to where Alice was sitting below a tree.

"Is there a town or something around here?" Matthew inquired.

"Yes, there's a village not far from here, why?" she answered.

"Some old guy stole my book and it's really important I get it back. Can you take me there?" he pleaded.

"I suppose. I'm heading that way, anyway. But after that, I simply must be on my way, my dad is probably worried sick about me." Alice got up and started to brush the grass off her blue dress. When she was finished, they headed off for the village.

Alice led Matthew through the forest. They eventually made it to the main road.

"You're not from around here, are you?" Alice reasoned.

"No, I'm not. Why do you ask?" he replied.

"Well, it's quite obvious, really. You're asking me to take you to a village that's just down this road, and it's a bit … odd."

"You wouldn't believe me if I told you where I came from," explained Matthew. "But I have to get my book back."

"That must be some book."

While they walked, the sun started to set. "Not much farther now," Alice estimated.

"I hope so. It's almost dark and it feels like we've been walking forever," he complained.

"It's just over this hill."

"Do you feel that?" Matthew asked as they walked up a hill.

"No, feel what?" replied a confused Alice. "And what's that smell?"

They reached the top of the hill and saw the village they were looking for. It was on fire. "Crap!" shouted Matthew. He charged toward the village.

Alice ran after him. "Oh dear, wait for me!"

When they arrived at the village, it was under attack by knights in black armor. Some of the villagers were running, trying to escape the attack, while others were trying to put their house fires out and fight the knights.

"The black knights, they're attacking!" Alice panicked.

"I have to find that old man or else I'll be stuck here,"

demanded Matthew.

"What?! Well, perhaps he came here to try and sell it. So he'll probably be in the merchants' area," suggested Alice.

"Let's try it," he replied. They headed off to the merchants' area, where the market was located. When they arrived they discovered that most of the merchants' stands were either empty or had been destroyed.

Across the market, they were able to spot the old man among the chaos. The old man was arguing with the owner of the merchant stand, who was packing his wares in a frenzy. The old man was still holding the golden book. Matthew ran over to the old man and used both hands to grab him by his collar.

"Hey! Gimme back my book, you thief!" he demanded.

"Fine. Take it, it's worthless anyway." The old man tossed the book to Alice.

Matthew released the old man's collar. The old man ran off, disappearing into the escaping crowds. Alice handed Matthew his book.

"Now you got your book, let's get out of here!"

Alice looked around in fear. They ran past the merchant stands and down the road toward the end of the village. A black knight suddenly turned the corner and appeared before them. When he spotted them, he charged. Matthew and Alice took off down the street with the black knight in pursuit.

"We can't outrun him, we gotta lose him," suggested

Matthew.

They ran down a side street and a few back alleys until they reached a dead end.

"We're trapped! Now would be a good time for you to use that sword of yours," Alice anxiously suggested.

"I dropped it down that hole," he coyly admitted.

"Oh, dear," she replied, her spirit deflated.

"It was an accident!" Matthew tried to close his eyes and concentrate, but there was too much noise and chaos going on around him to focus. Just as the black knight was closing in on them, there was a loud roar. A gigantic, brown grizzly bear tackled the knight and began to maul him. The knight attempted to fight the large bear but it was no use.

"Hallo?! Is anybody down there?!" someone asked, in a German accent.

"Oh yes! We're down here!" franticly shouted Alice.

A small man walked down the street toward them.

"It's a Hairn," said Alice.

Bernhart was a little over four feet tall and rotund. He looked like an older man in his early fifties with short blonde hair and small circular glasses resting on a large nose above a thick mustache and bushy mutton chops that covered most of his face. He had long, pointy ears sticking out from the sides of his head and a long skinny pink tail with a tuft of blonde hair at the tip. He was holding a long wooden crossbow almost as tall as himself.

"Children!? Well, let's get you two out of here! Sonja, let's go!" he said, surprised.

The brown bear turned around, leaving behind the

screaming black knight, and ran back over to the man. They led Matthew and Alice down the street and out of the burning village. The group walked along the forest road heading away from the village. As they moved away from the village the heat of the burning buildings behind them faded away and the cold of the dark forest began to hit Matthew. The man lit a silver lantern to light their way.

"Thank you for saving our lives back there, mister," admired Alice.

"Yeah … thanks," added Matthew. He felt a little embarrassed about losing his sword and needing saving.

"Aww. It's no problem, no problem at all. Happy to help," he said humbly.

"Excuse me sir, but we haven't been properly introduced. My name is Alice." She gestured to herself, then gestured toward Matthew. "And this is Matthew."

"Hi," Matthew added.

"My name's Bernhart. Nice to meet you two," he replied.

"So, where are we heading … if you don't mind me asking?" asked Matthew.

"To a friend of mine. She runs an inn in these here woods," annouced Bernhart.

CHAPTER 6

HOMECOMING

"Are you sure that's safe? What about the black knights?" Alice worried.

"You should be safe for the night there. The black knights appear to be heading in the other direction," Bernhart answered.

"I never would have believed that the black knights would do something quite so awful," Alice lamented.

"Oh, believe it. The way I hear it, the black knights are under new leadership and are planning on stirring up big trouble," he said.

"Who are the black knights?" Matthew asked.

Bernhart and Alice looked at him surprised. "The black knights were part of the devoted army of the last emperor of the Sun Elf's empire, Terenas. Well, they were until he was killed by the Blademaster at the battle of Highstar," she replied.

"Now the black knights are no more than common bandits, thugs who simply bully and harass travelers but I never thought they would do something like this," said Bernhart.

The group walked in silence for several minutes, through the cold dark forest, until they spotted a building in the distance.

"There it is," he annouced.

On the side of the road was a large wooden building that had four floors with some of its windows lit. The group entered the building, where they were struck by the warmth from the fireplace. The room was expansive, with a massive stone fireplace in the corner near the entrance, a bar counter in the far corner, and several tables scattered throughout. It reminded Matthew of a log cabin with wooden floors and walls. Large iron chandeliers were hanging from the ceiling, helping to light the room with some lanterns on the walls. There were a few patrons in the place, one sitting in a chair reading a newspaper in front of the fireplace, another sitting at the bar talking to the bartender, with two more sitting at a nearby table eating.

Next to the bar was the entrance to the kitchen. On the other side of the room, a large wooden staircase led to the rooms upstairs.

"Guten Abend!" Exclaimed a woman with a German accent. A Hairn woman named Gerda walked over to the group. She was an older woman in her late forties and slightly shorter than Bernhart. Her tail didn't have any hair. She was wearing a dress with a waist apron and had green eyes. Her light brown hair was tied back in a long braid.

"Oh Bernhart, you're back! What was that commotion going on in town?" she asked.

"It was an attack … by the black knights," he replied.

"Oh, dear." Gerda's voice was solemn. "And who are your friends?"

"My name is Alice, pleasure to meet you," said Alice.

"I'm Matthew," he added.

"Welcome to my inn. I'm Gerda. Would you two like something to eat? The kitchen's still open. Or perhaps a room to stay in?"

"Well…..That's awfully kind of you, Miss Gerda, but I'm afraid we don't have any money," Alice sadly admitted.

"Well … I can't just throw out two poor, hungry children now, can I?" Gerda warmly smiled. "It's on the house."

"Thank you," said Matthew and Alice grateful.

"Now, this way to your table." Gerda led them to an empty table.

"I'm going for a smoke," said Bernhart, as he and Sonja headed back outside to smoke his pipe.

"Here we are, nice and comfy," said Gerda, showing Matthew and Alice to a booth. Matthew and Alice sat on opposite sides of the table. Gerda handed the two of them menus and told them to take their time before heading over to another table to talk with two other people.

Alice opened her menu and began to read it. Matthew sat the golden book next to him and opened his menu.

Suddenly, the sword appeared on the table in front of him. It looked like the first time it had appeared, when he was attacked in the parking garage: a simple, steel longsword with a gold cross-guard, now in its intricately designed scabbard.

"Great, now it wants to show up," Matthew grumbled. His eyes went from the sword on the table to his menu.

Immediately, there was a loud sound of a glass breaking. Everyone at the inn grew quiet and looked around to see who dropped the glass. In front of Matthew and Alice's table, there was a young human woman. She was a waitress at the inn. She stood there, stunned, staring at the table.

"What's all this now?" asked Gerda, turning away from the two people with whom she'd been speaking. Gerda walked over to the waitress and saw what was on Matthew and Alice's table. "Whose sword is this?" She asked calmly.

"Uhh … it's mine," Matthew sounded unsure if he wanted to answer.

"He's returned," said the waitress under her breath.

The whole room began to mutter to themselves.

"What?" asked Matthew confused.

"I can't believe I hadn't noticed it sooner. That sword you used in Wonderland. It was so obvious," replied Alice.

"Well now, I'm really glad I was so nice to you," said Gerda. "The council has to hear about this … I'll be right back," she declared as she left in a hurry.

The other people in the inn continued to talk amongst themselves, occasionally turning to look over at Matthew as the young waitress cleaned up the broken glass.

Bernhart came back inside and sat down next to Matthew.

"I miss anything?" asked Bernhart.

"The most wonderful news, Matthew is the new Blademaster," Alice whispered softly.

"Well, congrats. It's a huge honor." Bernhart patted Matthew on his shoulder.

"Uhh … thanks." Matthew quickly removed the sword from the table.

Gerda came back over. "Can you stay here until tomorrow? I'm sure the council would be very interested in meeting you."

"Uhh … I don't know if I can stay," Matthew replied unsure.

"Oh, but you must. You just have to meet the council, it's of the utmost importance."

"Uhh … sure. I guess I can meet them," said Matthew reluctantly.

"That's great news," replied Gerda. "Once they get my message they should be here tomorrow. Anyway, sorry about all of that. What would you like to drink?"

"I'll have some tea, if you have any?" asked Alice.

"What tea would you like?" Gerda asked.

"Do you perhaps have chamomile tea?" she asked.

"Yes," Gerda answered.

"Then I'll have that, thank you," said Alice.

"And for you?" Gerda said, turning her gaze to Matthew.

"… I'll have … water," he replied, as he scanned the

menu. He barely recognized anything on it.

"Okay," replied Gerda.

As she turned to leave, Bernhart said, "I'll have another pint of mead."

Gerda turned around and pointed at Bernhart. "You've already had three pints of mead, no more for you," she snapped. Gerda was stern. The other patrons began to look in their table's direction again. Bernhart slouched down in their booth. "I'll have water, also," he said.

"Two glasses of water and a hot chamomile tea coming right up." Gerda headed back to the kitchen.

"Have you decided on what you're going to get?" asked Alice.

"No, not really," answered Matthew, still struggling with the menu.

"I'd recommend the braised mammoth sausage with potatoes, it's one of the best things I've ever eaten," suggested Bernhart.

"I'll keep that in mind," replied Matthew as he looked over the menu again. "I think I'll have the roast chicken instead."

Bernhart shrugged. Gerda walked over holding a tray with two glasses of ice water, a teacup, and a small black kettle. She set the tray down and placed the waters in front of Bernhart and Matthew. She then set the teacup in front of Alice and filled the cup from the black kettle. "Careful dear, it's hot," she warned.

"Thank you," said Alice. She stirred her tea with her spoon. "Have you made any decision on what you'd like to have?" She asked. Alice went first. "I'll have the roasted beef and vegetables, please."

"Good choice," replied Gerda. "Alright, and for you?"

"I'll have the roast chicken," Matthew ordered.

"Okay, I'll take these orders to the kitchen. Your meals shouldn't take too long." Gerda turned and headed to the kitchen.

"I best be heading off to bed now. Lots of traveling to do tomorrow," announced Bernhart as he grabbed his glass of water and got up from the table.

"Thank you again for helping us," said Alice sincerely.

"Yeah, thanks again," added Matthew.

"Oh, don't worry about it. It was an honor to help you two," he said. "You know, I knew the previous Blademaster, but that whole story is best left for another time." Bernhart turned from the table and began to head to the stairs in the corner of the inn.

"Good night," said Alice.

"Night." Bernhart headed up the stairs.

"What happened to his bear?" asked Matthew.

They began to look around the inn. The inn was now empty except for a man sitting in front of the fireplace reading a newspaper while drinking a cup of tea, and another man sitting at the bar still having a conversation with the bartender. Next to the man reading the newspaper, there was a massive, brown furry ball curled up by the fireplace.

"I think it's over by the fireplace," said Matthew.

"She," corrected Alice before shouting, "Oh dear! I

had almost forgot my dad in all this excitement."

Alice leapt from the table. "I'll be back in just a moment."

Matthew had completely forgotten about his mom in all the excitement of what had happened to him. He picked up the golden book he had set next to him on his side of the booth. He put it on the table and stared at it.

"Uhh … take me home, book," he said unsure how it even worked. He opened the book and a blinding light emerged from its pages.

Everything went black. When Matthew came to, he was sprawled out on his bed, still clutching the golden book. He was back in his bedroom. He looked around his room, which was completely dark except for his digital clock that read 10:45. He leaned over to turn on his desk lamp. The bright light hurt his eyes.

"I'm gonna need glasses after all of this," he thought. Matthew moved his hand and accidentally knocked the golden book to the floor with a heavy thud.

"Matthew!?" his mom shouted from down the hall.

Matthew slowly sat up on his bed fighting the urge to vomit. He felt slightly better than the first time the book had transported him. Immediately, Matthew's door swung open. His mother was standing there looking extremely angry in the doorway.

"Matthew! Where have you been!?" she exploded. He tried to answer her but she continued to yell at him. "How many times have I told you to tell someone where you're going and to bring your phone! I've been trying to reach you for hours! I almost called the police! Do you have any idea how much I was worried about you?! You could have been killed! Anything could've happened to you! If anything ever happened to you I'd … where did you even go to, anyway?!"

Liz stopped yelling at him long enough to allow him to answer one of her questions, but she was still fuming.

"It's not my fault. It was this book," he replied, as he reached over the side of his bed to grab the book. He then handed it to her. She looked at the book in her hands. Suddenly, the look of pure anger on her face melted away and was replaced by sadness. She then put one of her hands over her mouth as tears began to stream down her face. "Not again," she murmered softly to herself.

Matthew was confused. He got up from his bed and walked over to his mom. "Mom, what's wrong? Have you seen this book before?" he asked.

She slowly nodded. "Yeah. I've seen a book like this before. Although, it was a different color last time." She wiped the tears from her eyes.

"Last time?" he asked.

"Your father had one … before … I never saw him again," she answered.

"My dad," he muttered.

She sighed. "He said he had something really important he had to do and that he was sorry and he loved us … then I never saw him again."

Matthew stood there. This was the most information he'd ever received about his father. If his father also had a book like him, then he was probably somewhere in that other world. Matthew walked over to his dresser and started packing his clothes into a duffle bag.

"What are you doing!?" asked Liz.

"I'm packing," he replied.

"Why!?" she asked.

"I have something important I have to do," he answered, feeling slightly unsure of himself.

"You're not going anywhere! You're grounded, mister!" she shouted, growing angry again.

"Mom, I found that weird book at school, then I got attacked by some kind of monster in the parking garage, and then this weird sword just appeared. People are saying I'm some kind of ... Blademaster, and that it's really important. I can't just ignore all that. I have to find out what it all means ... it could all have something to do with Dad," he solemnly explained.

Matthew's mom stood there quietly. She was holding herself and not looking at him.

He walked back over to his mom. "Mom ... what's wrong?" he asked concerned.

"It's silly," she said softly as she fought back more tears. "In the back of my mind ... there was always this nagging fear of you being called off just like your father ... and I'd never see you again." Tears rolled down her cheeks.

Matthew smiled confidently. "Don't worry, Mom. Unlike Dad, I'll come back, I promise."

She sighed and formed a weak smile. "Fine ... but just this once," she relented .

He packed his duffle bag, hugged his mom goodbye, and opened the golden book again. When Matthew opened his eyes he was back in the inn.

"Oh, there you are," said Alice surprised. She was sitting in the booth eating her food. "The food is here."

Matthew found a seat at the table where his roast chicken sat waiting for him, and set his duffle bag beside him.

"Where did you go off to?" Alice inquired.

"I went home for a little while," he replied.

"Oh." Alice stopped to drink some of her tea.

"What were you doing while I was gone?" he asked, digging into his meal.

"I had to send a message home, my dad has probably worried himself to death by now," she replied.

"Tell me about it … how did you end up in … whatever that place was?" asked Matthew.

"Wonderland, I believe I heard it referred to as," said Alice. "Well, I had just attended a gathering at my aunt's home for tea. Quite small of course, only a few friends of hers, and I was traveling home. When the most peculiar thing caught my eye," Alice explained.

"What was it?" he asked.

"It was a little white rabbit, but he was wearing a waistcoat and he had taken out a golden watch from his waistcoat pocket. Naturally, I was quite curious about it, so I followed him. He led me to this tree and popped down the hole. I guess my burning curiosity got the better of me and caused me to go in after him and I fell in," she replied.

"Did your aunt live in that burning village?" he asked concerned.

"Thankfully, no. She lives in another village back the way we came," said Alice.

After they finished their meals, Gerda walked over. "How was everything?" she asked.

"Everything was very delicious," said Alice.

"Yeah, very good," Matthew added.

"That's good. Would you like some dessert or are you done for the evening?" asked Gerda.

"I'm done," said Matthew.

"I couldn't possibly," added Alice.

"Alright, then follow me," she said. They got up from their booth and followed her up the stairs. Gerda took Matthew and Alice up three flights of stairs to the fourth floor. The hallway was dimly lit by the few lanterns on the walls spaced between every two doors. At the second door on the right side of the hall, Gerda stopped.

"This is your room, dear," said Gerda, looking at Alice as she unlocked the door using a key from a keyring she had in her pocket. Gerda walked into the darkroom and lit the lantern on the dresser. Alice went inside and sat on the bed.

"Good night," said Alice.

"Good night, dear," said Gerda.

Matthew waved to Alice and she waved back. Gerda closed the door behind her. She then led Matthew to the last door on the left side of the hall and opened the door. They walked inside and Gerda lit the lantern on the dresser.

"Have a nice night, dear," she said as she turned to leave.

"You too," he replied. Gerda closed the door behind her.

Matthew put his duffle bag on the dresser next to the lantern and sat on the bed. He then changed his clothes and got under the covers. Despite being in a strange bed he fell asleep quite easily—he was tired.

The next morning, Matthew awoke to the sound of soft knocking on his door.

"Hello, Matthew. Are you awake?" Alice wondered in a hushed tone, from the other side of the door.

"Yeah," Matthew lied.

"Oh, well that's good. Gerda asked me to tell you that the council has responded to her letter, and they are on their way. You have to be ready to speak with them."

Matthew groaned. "Alright … give me a few minutes," he said as he dragged himself out of bed and got ready for the day. He made his bed, packed his duffle bag, and left the room. He then headed back downstairs to the main dining area.

The dining area was more crowded than it was during dinner. Matthew spotted Alice sitting at a table. She looked different from last night. She had her thick blonde hair in a high ponytail and was wearing a different outfit: a white t-shirt three sizes too big for her, and large pants rolled in cuffs.

He walked over and sat down across from Alice at the table while she ate.

"Good morning," she said, taking a sip from her tea-cup.

"Morning," he replied.

"Guten Morgen," annouced Gerda as she set a plate of pancakes, eggs, hash browns, and bacon in front of Matthew.

"Uh, I didn't order yet," he said.

"Oh, I ordered for you. I do hope you don't mind," interjected Alice.

"I like pancakes," he replied.

"See, nothing to worry about. I got word the council are here and will be ready soon, I'll get you when they are," said Gerda before heading off toward the kitchen.

Matthew nodded, as he started to dig into his breakfast.

"So … are you nervous?" Alice prodded.

Matthew put a slice of his pancakes in his mouth. "Nope."

"Oh, well I suppose it's simply because you're not from here. You're about to meet kings and queens, some of the most important people in the world. Why, if it were me, I would be a nervous wreck. Why, I wouldn't even be able to eat," she anxiously admitted.

Matthew continued to eat his meal casually. "Hey, where did you get those clothes from?" he asked.

"Oh … well, my dress was rather filthy from our long journey, and Gerda had some clothes in the lost and found."

"Oh."

"Well, not quite what I had in mind, but they are

clean," she asserted, looking over her shirt. They finished their meals and Gerda walked over to their table.

"The council is ready to see you now," said Gerda.

"Good luck," exclaimed Alice with a smile.

Matthew replied with a weak smile. He followed Gerda outside. It was early, but there was a nice summer warmth and a pleasant breeze.

"Bernhart, can you take Matthew to the council, I can't leave the inn unattended," she requested.

Bernhart was sitting in one of the wooden rocking chairs on the large wraparound porch outside, smoking his pipe with his bear lying next to him. "Alright," he replied. He got out of the chair and walked over to Matthew. "Ready to go?"

"Yeah," Matthew answered.

"Stay here, girl. I'll be back," Bernhart said to Moria. Moria stayed on the porch.

Matthew followed him through the woods. "Hey Bernhart, I thought you were leaving today?" he asked.

"I'm still going to leave. I'm not an early traveler, is all. I'm in no rush," he replied.

After walking for a bit they arrived at a large camp with several white tents in the middle of the forest. The camp was filled with several heavily armored knights. They walked up to the entrance of the largest tent. Next to the entrance of the tent, there was a knight.

"Halt! State your business here," said the knight sternly.

"The new Blademaster is here to speak with the

council," said Bernhart.

The knight looked over Matthew for a few moments. Matthew felt awkward about it.

"This is the Blademaster?" asked the knight, sounding skeptical.

Bernhart and Matthew nodded.

"Please present the sword," asked the knight.

Matthew drew the sword for the knight. The knight looked upon it in stunned silence. "One moment please," said the knight.

CHAPTER 7

THE SORCERER'S NEPHEW

The knight entered the large tent, then after a few moments exited the tent.

"They will see you now, but your friend will have to wait outside," ordered the knight.

Matthew turned to look at Bernhart.

"Good luck," said Bernhart.

Matthew nodded his head and entered the tent. Inside the tent, it was cool and shaded. There were seven large chairs arranged in a semi-circle with someone sitting in each one. Suddenly, Matthew became very nervous.

The chair in the middle was filled by a human man in the fifties named Tovan Pendragon. His skin was fair and he had shoulder-length black hair with streaks of grey and a neat black goatee. He wore a golden crown on his head and long blue robes. In the chair to the right of him sat a male Hairn named Reinhardt. He had a bald head with a big nose, pointy ears with hair on the ends, and a long, thick blonde beard. He had a scar on his left eye. He also wore a silver and bronze braided crown on his head.

The Hairn king wore bronze armor. To the right of the Hairn king sat a female goblin the same size as the Hairn, named Lizlee. She had olive green skin with large pointy ears that jutted out from the sides of her head, almost like a bat. She had a large pointy nose and a pointy chin. Her hair was dyed hot pink and in two long ponytails. She had a pair of goggles resting on her forehead. She wore a leather apron over her clothes.

To the right of her was Miranda, the empress of the Sun Elves. She had orange skin with emerald green, monochrome eyes. She had long, skinny pointed ears on the side of her head that pointed straight up. Her long, thick auburn-colored hair was tied up in a high ponytail. Miranda looked easily like the youngest there—appearing to be in her early twenties. She was wearing a crimson and gold kimono dress.

On the left side of the human king, there was a Silvani, a plantlike humanoid named Sylvestris. He looked very imposing, as he was the tallest among them, even when sitting down. His skin was a light green, grass-like color, and his hair and long beard were a darker shade of green. His eyes were also white. His ears were long and pointed, sticking out of his hair. He was holding a wooden staff in his left hand and a tunic with a toga wrapped around him. On his left was a big, muscular Orc male named Kilchii. His skin was brick red. He was only a little shorter than the Silvani. The Orc had two tusk-like teeth that protruded from his bottom lip. He was wearing leather moccasins and canvas robes with a hood. He had two long, jet-black braids from his head with feathers and beads and a long goatee.

To the Orc's left was a male Kreath named Asger. He was a large humanoid with bronze-colored skin, pointed ears, yellow eyes, and a pair of thick arms resting on the armrest of the chair with another pair of arms folded on his lap, each with two thick fingers and a thumb. He had a pair of horn-like growths protruding from his forehead with long black hair and a lengthy, braided beard. He had thick legs that lead to large hooves, and a wide, muscular tail that rested beside his legs. The Kreath wore a mixture of animal furs and metal armor. He had an enormous iron ax leaning on the right of his chair.

"Ah, now we can start this meeting. Please, will you present the sword, child?" announced Tovan.

Matthew again drew the sword. The Council members began to talk amongst themselves.

"Tovan, he is way too young. Especially for what we need to be done," complianed Lizlee.

"I agree. I won't have the blood of a child on my hands if he fails," asserted Reinhardt.

"They make good points, Tovan. The boy's age could prove to be … problematic," Sylvestris remarked.

Matthew remained quiet and still, barely breathing in front of the council.

"Perhaps you are right, Sylvestris," replied Tovan, stroking his goatee. "We'll put it to a vote, then. What have you to say, Asger?"

"If the blade finds him to be a worthy warrior, then who are we to judge?" Asger boasted.

Tovan nodded. "Kilchii, your thoughts?"

"The blade has never been wrong before, perhaps the blade's seen something in this child we cannot," replied Kilchii.

"And you, Miranda?" asked Tovan.

"The blade does allow him to weld it. I say let him keep it," smiled Miranda.

Matthew blushed—he thought Miranda was exceptionally pretty.

"Your thoughts, Tovan?" Sylvestris inquired.

Tovan was silent for a few moments. "We are in a dire situation. I'm afraid we don't have the luxury of waiting for a better alternative. Make no mistake, the child's age does make me very uneasy, however … I'm afraid we have no other options after our first option ran into … complications. I guess with my vote, that's four to three," said Tovan. "But we've forgotten the most important opinion here. What is your name, child?"

"Uhh … Matthew."

"Well, Matthew, would you like to continue welding the blade? I won't sugarcoat this, this journey on which you will embark will be dangerous … you may even lose your life," he acknowledged.

Matthew looked at the sword in his hand. He remembered a few days ago that he felt like nobody—like he didn't matter. He had felt lonely and bored with his life. This was a once-in-a-lifetime chance to change that, even if it was dangerous.

"I want to keep the sword," he answered.

The members of the council talked amongst themselves again for a few moments.

"Very well," annouced Tovan.

"The reason we have all traveled here is that we have reason to believe that someone new is leading the black knights. Last night's attack clearly showed they're getting bolder. Pretty soon we may have a full-blown war on our hands. We'd like to avoid that if at all possible. We ask that you find whoever is leading them and bring them to justice," declared Tovan.

"Where am I supposed to find this person?" asked Matthew.

"Our latest intelligence has discovered a few camps of theirs in the south but they're constantly on the move and their leader is unknown," replied Tovan.

"Oh, well, if you know where they are, why don't you just take care of them?" he asked.

The council talked amongst themselves for a few moments. "Because it's the job of the Blademaster to create and protect peace in this world, and now that job is yours," said Tovan.

"Okay. How much time do I have to stop this person?" asked Matthew.

The council talked amongst themselves. "As soon as

possible would be preferable, but I suppose before the end of the summer. This is a very important task. The longer you wait, the more lives could be at stake," Tovan replied.

"Okay, is there anything else?" asked Matthew.

The Council talked amongst themselves again. "That is all, you're free to go," annouced Tovan. He bowed, then turned and prepared to exit the tent.

"I hope you know what you're doing, Tovan," remarked Sylvestris.

"As do I, old friend," replied Tovan. He exited the tent and entered the bright sunlight of the forest.

"So, how did it go?" asked Bernhart. Alice and Gerda were standing beside him.

"Well, I got my first mission," he replied.

"Ohhh. How wonderful!" smiled Gerda, clapping excitedly.

"Yeah, the only problem is … I don't know how to use it. I'm not exactly a fighter," he admitted.

"I may be able to help you with that. A friend of mine is pretty skilled with a blade. I bet he could teach you a thing or two," suggested Bernhart.

Matthew looked up with interest. "Really? That would be great, but I couldn't ask any more of you," he replied.

"Nonsense, it's no problem at all. We'll head off in a few minutes." Bernhart left and walked back to the inn.

"Uh … Can you give us a minute, Gerda?" asked Matthew.

"Oh, of course," she replied, then turned to head back to the inn.

"Well, I guess this is goodbye," said Alice.

"Yeah … uh … why don't you come along? I could use all the help I can get. Besides, I think we make a pretty good team."

Alice fell silent. "Oh … well … it's not like I wouldn't consider coming along, but I'm afraid I really must go home. I was supposed to be home yesterday before I got … sidetracked. My dad is probably worrying himself to death and … I hope you don't think it's very rude of me but, I don't know you all that well," she admitted.

"Oh … it's just … I thought we were kinda friends." He felt slightly embarrassed now, but Alice was genuinely touched by his words.

"You … consider me your friend?" she asked.

"I guess. Yeah. You're about the closest thing I've had to a friend in months … as sad as that sounds," he begrudingly admitted.

Alice fell silent again just as Gerda returned to where they were standing in the forest.

"I hate to interrupt, but I think Bernhart is ready for you," said Gerda.

They walked back through the forest in silence. When the three of them arrived at Britta's Inn, Alice quickly headed up the front porch steps and inside the inn. Britta handed Matthew his duffle bag. Bernhart was waiting for him, sitting in a large wooden cart being pulled by a brown ram the size of a horse. Moira was in the back with their bags.

"Ready to go?" he asked.

"Yeah, let's go," Matthew replied as he climbed into

the front of the cart.

"Thanks, Gerda, for everything," said Matthew.

"It's no problem, dear. Good luck on your journey and please don't be a stranger. Auf Wiedersehen!" she smiled as she waved goodbye.

Suddenly, Alice reemerged from the inn with a scrap of paper in her hand. She then handed it to Matthew.

"Well … if you're ever in Stormhaven … and you still want me to come along … good luck," said Alice. She then turned and head back to the inn. He opened the paper to see Alice's address. Matthew put the scrap of paper in his pocket, then smiled to himself.

Bernhart and Matthew then began to head down the road. After a few minutes, Matthew spoke. "So, who is this friend of yours?"

"He's a skilled swordsman, best in all the kingdoms, his brother lives around here. I figure we can just ask him where he is since he's always traveling," he speculated.

"Oh," said Matthew.

"Don't worry. If anyone can teach you, it'd be him."

They traveled for several hours until they reached the town of Hazelhill. Hazelhill was quite a ways south and was surrounded by dozens of acres of farmland and pastures. It was bigger than the town that the black knights had attacked. As they rode through the busy streets of Hazelhill, Matthew noticed armored knights everywhere. They continued through the town and into the neighboring forest until they came to stop.

Secluded and almost hidden by the forest was a house.

From the looks of it, it would be easy to miss if you didn't already know it was there. It was a large wooden and brick three-story Victorian-style house with a large wraparound front porch.

Bernhart pulled the cart up to the front porch. "Wait here," he said, as he jumped out of the cart.

He then walked up the stairs of the front porch and knocked on the door. After a few moments, the door opened and a tall, slim man leaned in the doorway. He looked like he hadn't slept or shaved in a while. He held a wooden cane with a red jewel on top of it. Bernhart and the man talked for ten minutes before Bernhart came back to the cart.

"Sterling's agreed to train you instead."

"Instead?" asked Matthew.

"Well, he doesn't know where his brother is, but Sterling agreed to train you. Don't worry, he's good enough to train you properly," said Bernhart.

Matthew grabbed his bag out of the back and got out of the cart. He walked up the front steps to Sterling. Bernhart got in his cart.

"Good luck," he said as he waved from his cart. He turned his cart around and headed back down the road. Matthew waved back and then turned back to Sterling.

"I suppose introductions are in order. Sterling Jacobs," annouced Sterling, extending his hand to Matthew.

"Matthew … Jacobs," replied Matthew.

"Do you know Leon Jacobs?" asked Matthew.

"Know him? He's my brother."

Matthew's face lit up. "I guess that makes you my uncle, right?" he said smiling.

"Yeah. I guess."

Matthew was a step closer to meeting his father, and then he remembered what Bernhart had told him.

"Bernhart said you don't know where he is?" he asked.

"No, I don't where he is," Sterling replied coldly. "My brother has always been irresponsible. He's always going off on some crazy adventure for weeks at a time, and he's always been hard to get a hold of."

"Aren't you worried about him?" Matthew asked.

Sterling sighed. "I trust his decisions, even when I can't see the logic."

Matthew stood there in silence.

"Well, come inside, you're letting all my cold air out," he complained.

Matthew followed him inside. He led Matthew down the hall into the foyer. The foyer was massive with marble floors, large marble columns, and a tall window above the spacious wooden stairs that split in two directions. Matthew stood there in the foyer.

"Is it—" he started.

"Yes, it's much larger on the inside," interrupted Sterling. "I'll show you where you'll be staying."

Sterling led him upstairs to the second door on the third floor. "You'll be staying here."

Matthew opened the door. The room was well decorated with, oil lamps, and paintings on the walls. It had a large bed with a dresser, two nightstands, and a wide window with long curtains.

"Thanks," said Matthew.

"You'll begin your training early tomorrow and dinner will be in a few minutes." Sterling turned and left.

Matthew put his bag down and sat on the bed for a few minutes. "How could he not care what happened to his brother? He also didn't seem to be very happy to meet me. This is going to be a rough couple of weeks, but I have to get through it. People are counting on me."

He got up from the bed and went back downstairs. He stood in the foyer looking around. He then heard small clanking noises. Matthew went down the hallway on the left to a dining room and kitchen. Sterling was in the kitchen.

"Take a seat," he stated. The dining room was large, with a massive silver chandelier, framed paintings on the walls, a dining cabinet, and a long table lined with tall chairs. There were already two bowls, cups, utensils, and some rolls on the table. Matthew sat down in front of one of the bowls.

Sterling emerged from the kitchen holding an iron pot. He sat the pot on the table and sat across from Matthew. "So … do you live here alone?" asked Matthew.

"Yes, I live here alone," answered Sterling.

"Oh … your house is really nice," said Matthew.

"Thanks," replied Sterling.

Matthew ladled some of the soup into his bowl and took a roll from the table. He began to eat his dinner.

"This soup is really good," complimented Matthew.

"Thanks," replied Sterling as he filled his goblet with a dark red wine.

"What kind of soup is this?" asked Matthew.

"Potato soup." Sterling took a deep sip from his goblet.

"So … what do you do for a living?" asked Matthew.

"I'm retired," Sterling replied.

"Well, what did you do before retiring?" asked Matthew.

"I was a teacher, among other things."

"What did you teach?"

"I taught students sorcery," replied Sterling.

"Wow! Like magic. So, you're like a wizard?"

"The term is sorcerer, but yes," corrected Sterling.

"Oh."

Matthew finally gave up trying to make conversation with his uncle. The two of them dined in relatively awkward silence for the rest of the meal.

"It's late. You should get some sleep, and your training begins tomorrow," Sterling declared.

"Okay. Do you want some help?" suggested Matthew.

"No, I'll clean up here."

"Okay." Matthew got up from the table and headed back to his room. He readied himself for bed and got under the covers. He hadn't thought about everything that had happened. He thought about his mom. He wondered what she was doing now. He thought about Alice. He wondered if she made it home and if her parents were as mad at her as his mom was at him. He wondered about what Bernhart was doing and if he made it home safe.

Most of all, he wondered about his dad. He wondered where he was and what he would say to him if they met. He then rolled over on his side and tried to go to sleep. He had another big day tomorrow.

The next morning, he woke up quite easily, though he didn't get a good night's rest. He was pretty antsy about the start of his training. He had never trained for anything before. He got dressed and went downstairs for breakfast. After eating breakfast in awkward silence, Sterling took Matthew to his backyard.

Sterling's backyard was simply an open, grassy area surrounded by the forest. "All right, let's start with some running. I want you to run from here to over there."

Sterling, who was standing on the porch, pointed with his cane to the far edge of his backyard. Matthew ran over to the far edge of the yard and stopped.

"Now run back," Sterling ordered.

Matthew ran back over to him. "Keep running until I tell you to stop," said Sterling having a seat on his back porch.

Matthew ran back and forth for hours. They stopped to eat lunch and then he continued to run until the sun was starting to set.

"Stop," said Sterling. Matthew was exhausted from running. His shirt was wet with sweat. His heart was pounding in his chest. He was in worse shape than he thought.

"That's enough for today, we'll continue tomorrow," said Sterling as he sat on the back porch, drinking wine from his goblet.

For the first week, Matthew just ran around his backyard. The next week, Sterling introduced weights and various exercises into the training. One day while training, Matthew asked a question.

"When am I going to start using a sword?"

"In due time," Sterling replied, sitting on the back porch drinking from his goblet.

"But it's been two weeks. I thought there would be, ya know … more swords in my sword training."

Sterling sighed and got up from his porch chair. "Alright, let's see what you got," he annouced.

He conjured a wooden practice sword in his left hand and tossed it to Matthew. He caught the sword and took some practice swings with it. It was pretty thick and heavy, but he got used to it quickly.

"Alright," he said. Matthew gripped the sword tightly with both hands and charged him on the back porch. Matthew began to swing the wooden sword at Sterling. He effortlessly sidestepped Matthew's strikes. He tried to trap Sterling in the corner of his porch but he simply sidestepped him again and casually walked down the porch steps out into his backyard. Matthew then jumped off the porch and began to swing the sword as fast as he could. Sterling used his cane to effortlessly guide away Matthew's wild strikes away from him with his cane. Matthew began moving closer and closer to Sterling, trying to move him back with his strikes, but he didn't move an inch. After this failed, Matthew jumped back from him to collect himself.

He had spent more energy than the thought trying to beat him. Sterling began to casually twirl his cane with his fingers.

"Was that it?" he scoffed.

Matthew gritted his teeth. They began to circle each other in the backyard. Matthew launched himself at him with various quick strikes and wild swings. Sterling continued to effortlessly block and sidestep Matthew's attacks.

Eventually, Sterling's patience had reached his limit. "I've seen enough."

With a lightning-fast strike, Sterling knocked Matthew's wooden sword from his hands with ease. The sword jettisoned off into the nearby grass.

Matthew's hands tingled from the force of Sterling's strike. He was stunned by the great ease he managed to do this.

Sterling then poked Matthew in his chest with his wooden cane.

"You're dead," he smirked.

CHAPTER 8

TRAINING BEGINS

S terling stood there stroking his chin, thinking to himself for a moment.

"Okay … a couple of things … first, it's not a club. You don't have to swing it like one. Second, what was your plan to beat me?" Sterling asked.

"Uh … I didn't exactly have a plan," replied Matthew.

Sterling stroked his chin some more. "But, you know, I'm more skilled than you. Approaching a more skilled advisory than you, without a plan, is a glorified death sentence," said Sterling. He then thought to himself again for a moment. "Have you ever played chess?"

"Yeah," replied Matthew.

"Well, you can think of sword fighting like chess. In chess, it's important to think ahead of your opponent, have a plan, and control the battle. You should never engage your opponent without one. It could be the difference between life and death," said Sterling. "You're younger than me, so you tried to use your youth as an advantage against me. That can be fine, but without proper technique or a plan you'll just tire yourself out and get picked apart by someone who can weather your storm."

"Oh." Matthew muttered.

"But having said all that, you're not too terrible for a beginner. You at least have some potential. It's raw … very raw, but if it can be channeled, you'll make a fine swordsman like your father. Now, let's try this again," he replied.

Matthew picked up his wooden sword and they sparred for the rest of the afternoon.

For the next two weeks, Matthew was trained in sword fighting in addition to his conditioning. One morning after breakfast, Matthew came out to find Sterling sitting in the grass instead of his usual place on the porch.

"Today I thought we'd start today by training your senses," he announced.

"What do you mean?" asked Matthew.

"Well, there's more to being a swordsman than simply swinging a sword well. It's important to hone one's ability to properly sense the world around them," he replied.

Sterling tossed Matthew his wooden training sword. "Try and hit me."

Matthew cautiously circled him. Sterling folded his arms behind his back. Matthew attacked him from behind. Sterling casually ducked his attack. Matthew immediately followed up that attack with another and he avoided it. Matthew attempted to pressure Sterling with a variety of attacks from different angles and speeds, following up each strike with another one somewhere else. Sterling moved deliberately and smoothly, just as he needed to avoid the incoming attacks, not an inch more. Matthew stopped in his tracks.

"This isn't really fair. Your reflexes are just better than mine," Matthew complained.

"How about this?"

Sterling conjured a strip of black fabric in his hand. He tied the strip around his eyes and folded his hands behind his back. "Again," he demanded.

Matthew tried again, but the results were still the same. Matthew stopped. "How can you do that?" he asked, untying his blindfold.

"Mastering your senses, enhancing your perception, can be a great asset in most occasions, especially in combat."

"Like what?"

"Like, being able to sense the presence of others or avoid incoming attacks better or even sense nearby danger among other things," Sterling explained.

"Oh … sometimes I have weird feelings sometimes in certain situations, is that it?" Matthew asked.

"Everyone has them these senses and sometimes use them unconsciously. The sword must've awoken these senses in you, but they still need to be trained if they're gonna do you any good."

"Cool. So how do I do all of those things?" asked

Matthew.

"First, you must learn to meditate. Learn to clear your mind. Have a seat," he said, patting the grass beside him. Matthew sat next to Sterling.

"Cross your legs and close your eyes."

Matthew did what was asked of him.

"Clear your mind."

Matthew attempted to do this.

"Breath in deeply and slowly," Sterling said with his eyes closed, sitting next to Matthew.

Matthew had too much on his mind to properly clear it, but he tried his best. He sat next to Sterling for what felt like an hour until he finally decided it was time to move on. In the following days, they began every day of training by meditating, followed by light cardio for warm-ups with weights and sparring, ending with more meditation.

In the following days, Matthew graduated from his wooden training sword to his Blademaster's Sword of Wind. He began trying to gain a better handle on his sword's abilities. After the day's training was over, Sterling levitated wooden targets to aid Matthew. Matthew swung his sword at the targets, sending a large gust of wind at the targets. The targets shook in place but were unharmed. He continued for hours, swinging at the various targets in a variety of attacks, but the targets remained unharmed. Frustrated, fatigued, and angry, he sent a condensed slice of air at the target, managing to leave a cut in it. In the final days of Matthew's training, he continued to experiment with his sword. He learned to summon his sword at will as well as be able to create condensed slices of air with greater ease. He discovered the ability to create tornados and whirlwinds.

"I think I'm finally getting the hang of this thing," he boasted to himself.

Tomorrow was Matthew's final day of training. He had gotten so used to being with his uncle he almost forgot what his real job was. Matthew's journey was just beginning.

After a month of training, Matthew and Sterling stood on opposite sides of Sterling's backyard.

"Consider this your final exam!" he announced.

Sterling flipped his wooden cane upside down. The smooth wooden cane began to melt away, revealing a steel rapier sword. The rapier was of an intricate design with twisting metal and jewels curled around the handguard. Matthew threw out his hand and in it his sword appeared—the Sword of Wind.

Matthew entered his fighting stance and gripped his sword with one hand. "Let's begin!" he declared.

Sterling got into a linear fencing stance and quickly attacked with a flying lunge. Matthew countered him by quickly spinning his wrist, creating a vortex of wind that pushed Sterling back. With some distance between them, Matthew immediately sent a condensed slash of air at Sterling. He easily sliced Matthew's attack in half and charged at Matthew again. Matthew sent multiple air slices at him, trying to keep his distance, but it was useless. Sterling closed the distance between them and unleashed a flurry of quick stabs. Matthew franticly parried his attacks as he began to press him. Matthew attempted to turn the tables by delivering some counters of his own, but he simply batted them aside with deflection parries.

The two of them locked blades for a moment before he began to move Matthew's blade to the side. Matthew immediately broke off as he spun around to deliver a quick slash. Sterling managed to duck under his blade just in time to jump back. Matthew then swung his sword at Sterling, unleashing a powerful gust of wind. He braced himself for the wind and slid back a few feet, but was otherwise unharmed. Matthew took this opportunity to go on the offensive. He quickly formed a small tornado and sent it spiraling at Sterling. Sterling attempted to simply move out of the way but the small tornado followed him. While he was maneuvering away from the tornado, Matthew unleashed another flurry of air slashes at him. He turned around and slashed through the tornado behind, then ran out of the way of the incoming barrage of air slices and closed in on Matthew again. He attacked Matthew with a one-arm, overhead slash. Matthew slid to the side to dodge it and immediately countered it with a slash of his own. Sterling used his blade to safely maneuver Matthew's blade away from him and jumped back. They stood on the opposite sides of the yard.

"Check this out!" boasted Matthew.

Matthew, with his right hand, began to rapidly spin his sword by the chain on the pummel. The faster he spun the sword, the more the wind around them began to whip. The trees around Sterling's yard began to sway back and forth from the strong winds. The blades of grass moved around Matthew in waves. Sterling put his forearm up to shield his eyes from the flying grass and dirt. The whipping wind had become so strong there were sounds of branches snapping in the forest around them.

"This is pretty impressive!" shouted Sterling over the loud noise of the whipping wind.

He began to advance toward Matthew. The powerful wind was slowing him down. With a mighty two-handed swing of his sword, Matthew sent all the wind he had whipped up in a massive slash of wind rocketing toward Sterling. He tried to counter Matthew with a one-handed overhead slash, but Matthew's powerful attack caught his blade. Sterling was pushed back by the force of Matthew's attack. Matthew began to smirk as Sterling struggled with being pushed toward the forest from his attack. He calmly put his other hand on his hilt and continued his overhead slash, cutting the wind in half. The two halves of the wind continued and sliced several trees in the forest behind him in half.

Matthew's smirk quickly melted off his face as he stood there half stunned and half demoralized. That was his best shot. With the wind back to normal, Matthew attempted to start spinning his sword again, but Sterling lunged at Matthew with a quick stab. Matthew blocked his attack and they locked swords. Sterling managed to gain control of Matthew's blade and began to manipulate it out of his hand, sending his sword across the yard. Matthew quickly rolled toward his sword before Sterling could take advantage of the fact that he'd disarmed him. Matthew stuck out his hand for his sword, and he felt it appear in his hand.

Suddenly, Sterling was charging at Matthew again and Matthew swung his sword at him. He quickly cut a thick whip of water in half. Sterling stopped, looking just as surprised as Matthew. Matthew looked at the sword in his hand. He didn't recognize it. It was now a slightly curved cutlass with a solid cupped hilt. The blade was dark blue with a slight blue aura around it.

"You lose," smirked Sterling. He was pointing his sword at Matthew's chest. "I know we didn't cover this, but I hoped you would know better than to get distracted during a battle."

"I got a new sword," Matthew grinned, happily waving it around.

Sterling turned his sword back into his wooden cane. "Yes, that's the Sword of Water. The sword takes on six forms. Congratulations. What is this, number two?"

Matthew ran his fingers down the edge of his new blade "Yeah, this is number two."

It was dull like the wind sword. His fingers were slightly wet. Suddenly, Matthew remembered what they were doing. "Oh, man. I lost," remembered Matthew.

"Ahhh, so you finally remembered what we were doing," replied Sterling with a soft laugh. Matthew frowned. "Of course, you lost. There was no way you could beat me."

"Gee, thanks," Matthew sighed. He looked a little hurt.

"That came out wrong. I meant you've only had a month of training. Of course you lost. The important thing is that you've improved. You've definitely improved. I feel you'll be more than capable of handling yourself out there … unless you get distracted again. Don't get distracted in a real battle. And that's why you pass your final exam."

"Wow! Really?" asked Matthew.

"Really," replied Sterling. He extended his hand to Matthew and helped him up from the grass.

"So … how good was I? Like, how hard were you trying back there? Gimme like a percentage," asked Matthew.

"Uh … thirty percent," he replied.

"Thirty percent?!" repeated Matthew.

"Well, my thirty percent is most people's eighty percent. Relax. As long as you don't get distracted again you should be fine."

"What was our first fight?" Matthew asked.

"Uhhh … three percent," he replied.

"Well … I did improve," said Matthew.

He felt better about his process. Matthew and Sterling headed inside for dinner.

Later that night, Matthew was in Sterling's library. Sterling's library was a large three-story room covered wall to wall with bookshelves. There were large windows on one side of the second floor. There was a large stone fireplace on the first floor with two leather chairs in front of it. He was sitting in a leather chair reading the golden book. Matthew had discovered that the golden book was filled with history, stories, legends, maps, and biographies of important people. He flipped through the book for hours.

Sterling walked into the library holding a goblet and

sat in a chair next to him. "It's a bit cold in here," commented Sterling.

"I guess," replied Matthew, his eyes still on the book's pages.

Sterling pointed his index and pointer fingers at the fireplace. A stream of fire erupted from his two fingertips, igniting the wood inside. He rubbed his hands together. "That's better," he said. "Tomorrow's the big day. Any plans?"

Matthew closed the book on his lap. "I have an idea … but it's a bit of a long shot."

"Let's hear what you got," said Sterling, taking a sip from his goblet.

"Well … I came across the story of Aleron's box," said Matthew. "I think it's my best shot to beat whoever's behind all of this."

"Matthew, Aleron's box is just a legend. It has been lost for centuries. It's not a good idea to hang your hat on a story," cautioned Sterling.

"I know it's a long shot, but it's all I've got right now. The box can sap the strength of anyone. If I can find it, I could use it on this guy."

"That's a big if. Why don't you just stay here longer? We could do some more training."

"I don't have time! I gotta beat this guy by the end of summer! Even if we train all that time, there's still no guarantee I could beat this guy. The box is my best shot. I know it is. I just know it," said Matthew.

"Where do you plan to start looking for it?" asked

Sterling.

"Well, I figure the great Stormhaven cathedral in Stormhaven is a good place to start. The cathedral appears in the story."

"Well, what happens if you can't find the box?" asked Sterling.

"Then … I'll just come back and figure something else out," replied Matthew with a smile.

Sterling sat there thinking to himself. "You remind me a lot of him, you know, my brother. He also had this sense of optimism. He was always so confident that every-thing would always work out."

"You talk about him like he's dead or something. Why aren't you more worried about him?" asked Matthew.

Sterling sat there for a moment before answering. "I'm afraid … the relationship between me and your father is … complicated to say the least. When you first asked me if I was worried about Leon, I wasn't—at first. He's one of the best swordsmen in the world. He was also the Blademaster before you, you know. He's more than capable on his own. He always disappeared for long periods before showing up again. But then when you showed up, and you had the sword now—do you know how the sword passes to a new wielder?"

Matthew shook his head no.

"The sword passes to a new wielder in one of two ways. Either by the death of the last wielder, or the current wielder relinquishing it. Very few Blademasters have ever relinquished the sword. So there's a good chance … Leon's dead. I'm sorry. I should've told you this earlier," said Sterling.

Matthew sat there quietly for a few moments. "So … there's still a chance he could still be alive?"

"Maybe, look … all I'm saying is that I don't want you to get your hopes up that he's alive somewhere."

"Until I know for certain that he's not, he's alive," replied Matthew, with a hint of confidence.

Sterling stood up from his chair, smiled, and laughed to himself. "I guess … you could be right. I'm heading to bed. Goodnight," said Sterling as he grabbed his goblet and headed toward the door.

"Night," replied Matthew.

Matthew woke up early the next morning. He was a little anxious to start his quest. He packed all his things, made the bed, and went downstairs. Matthew and Sterling ate breakfast in the dining room. After breakfast, they stood in the foyer.

"Before you start on your journey, I wanted to give you this," said Sterling. He handed Matthew a simple canvas backpack.

"Thanks … I can always use another bag."

"It's more than just a bag. Try putting your duffle bag inside it," said Sterling. He attempted to put his much larger duffle bag into the smaller canvas backpack.

Surprisingly, his much larger bag fit into the smaller one from Sterling.

"How did …?" Matthew started.

"It's enchanted. I've already put some other supplies

in there for your long journey."

"Thanks."

"And you'll need this as well," Sterling added, then pulled what looked like a crystal from his pocket. He handed it to Matthew.

Matthew took the crystal in his hand. The crystal was flat and shaped like an octagon. It was a light shade of purple.

"We can keep in touch using these," said Sterling as he pulled another from his pocket. "Just speak into the crystal and I'll be able to talk with you. Finally, I have one more gift to give you, but we're going to need to go outside first," said Sterling.

Matthew followed him outside. Once outside, Sterling held out his hand, palm facing up. Matthew watched him intensely. From the bottom up appeared a dark wood and metal framed chest that barely fit square in his hand. Sterling opened the chest, and out poured a strange-looking stagecoach. The bottom half of the stagecoach was dark wood with metal wheels. The top half appeared to be a wooden shack, with a pitched wooden roof and small circular windows.

Matthew was speechless.

"It might be a long journey, so you can borrow my stagecoach. You can't walk everywhere," said Sterling as he handed Matthew the chest.

"Thanks ... thanks for everything, Sterling," said Matthew sincerly.

"You're welcome ... nephew," he smirked.

Matthew smiled and stuck his hand out for a handshake. Sterling spread his arms for a hug. Matthew hugged him.

"Where are you heading to first?" Sterling asked.

"I'm heading to Stormhaven City first," replied Matthew as he climbed into the driver's seat of the stagecoach.

"Well, good luck. Come back alive, will ya?"

"How do I work this thing?" asked Matthew.

"Just say the name of your destination in a loud and clear voice."

"Stormhaven."

The wheels on the stagecoach began to roll forward. Matthew remembered the path that Bernhart used to take him to Sterling's house. Matthew traveled down the road through the forest until he came to Hazelhill, and passed through the town. He continued travelling down the road for hours. As he rode, he suddenly spotted a large wooden building on the side of the forest road. It was Gerda's Inn. As Matthew neared, he began to think for a second. He wanted to go inside to see her, but he decided against it. He figured she'd probably be too busy with the inn to have time to chat. He didn't know what he'd even say to her, anyway. He continued down the road.

A pleasant breeze blew through the forest. It was refreshing to Matthew as he rode along. After a while, he came to another village on the other side of the forest. He recognized this village. It was the one that was attacked when Alice and Matthew passed through it a month ago.

CHAPTER 9

A FRIEND IN NEED

The stagecoach carried Matthew through the village. The village looked to be in the process of rebuilding. There were villagers all over the place, many of whom carried building supplies. Armored knights stood guard everywhere. Most of the buildings in the village were charred. The badly charred ones were either roped off or were in the process of being torn down altogether.

Elsewhere in the village, other buildings were already being patched, repaired, or in the process of a complete rebuild. Traveling through the burned village troubled him. He hoped no one else had been hurt while he spent the past month training. He left the village with a renewed focus, to stop the black knights. The stagecoach turned and exited the village, this time from a third way he hadn't taken before. It was getting late and the sun was beginning to set, so he decided to rest for a while.

"Umm … how do I get this thing to stop?"

The stagecoach immediately came to a stop.

"I guess like that," Matthew said amazed.

He hopped out of the driver's seat and entered the stagecoach. Just like Sterling's house, the stagecoach was much larger on the inside. It consisted of two floors each with several rooms. The ground level's walls and the floors were made of wood and resembled a cabin. The place was furnished, floor to ceiling, with rustic furniture and décor. He began to walk around. On the ground floor, there was the main sitting room that connected to a small kitchen, dining room, and bathroom. On the second floor, there were three rooms with simple sleeping cots in each of them, with pillows and blankets. The sitting room had several chairs, a couch, bookshelves, and a coffee table. The dining room had a large wooden table for six with more rustic décor on the walls. He set his backpack on the coffee table in the main sitting room and took a seat. He began to look through the bag Sterling gave him. Inside the bag, there was a box with four sandwiches, a canteen full of water, and a small bag with forty gold coins. He put the objects back in the bag. He then ate one of the sandwiches and got ready for bed. He picked one of the rooms and went to sleep on one of the cots.

The next morning, Matthew ate another one of the sandwiches for breakfast. He got dressed and went outside. He climbed back into the driver's seat. Matthew opened the golden book to the map. He was still heading in the right direction.

"Stormhaven," he commanded. The stagecoach continued down the road for several hours until he came to another village. Two lightly armored men were standing at the entrance of the town. The stagecoach slowed down and stopped in front of the two guards standing on the road.

"State your business here!" announced one of the guards.

"I'm just a traveler, heading to Stormhaven."

"Stormhaven … huh? Why are you going to Stormhaven?"

"That's none of your business," Matthew replied.

"None of my business? Huh … sounds like you got something to hide … maybe some black knight business, huh?" accused the guard.

"Murray, he's not a black knight. He's just a kid," said the other guard.

"Oh yeah? How do we know that for certain, Frank?" asked Murray.

Frank turned to Matthew. "Are you a black knight?"

"No," he replied.

"See, Murray?" said Frank.

"Like he would tell us if he was," countered Murray.

"I'm willing to take that risk. Please go on ahead," directed Frank.

"If this town gets attacked like that other village, it's all on your head, Frank," complianed Murray.

"Please enjoy your visit to Goldcrest," said Frank.

The two guards stepped aside and let Matthew into the town.

Goldcrest was by far the biggest place he had encountered so far. The town was full of people, all walking around and talking to each other: people at the merchant stands buying items, and people driving carts and carriages down the road. Matthew continued walking down the street until he heard a high-pitched scream from the merchant stands.

"Stop! Thieves!" cried a woman as two men, each carrying a crate, darted in front of him.

In hot pursuit behind them was a thirteen boy with a large sword on his waist. The boy had brown skin. He had black dreadlocks that went to his jaw. He was wearing a green shirt, pants, and boots. Matthew hopped off the stagecoach and opened the chest he was given. The stagecoach evaporated into the chest and he took off after the thieves. He followed the group through the town until the group turned down an alley. The alley led to a dead end. The two thieves stopped and turned around.

"Looks like it's the end of the road for you guys. So, how about you just give back what you stole and you won't have to get hurt?" the kid proudly boasted.

The alley was empty except for a hay pile, some wooden barrels, a dumpster, and a wooden cart with a blanket over it. Matthew came down the alley.

"Hurt us?" said one of the thieves. Then both thieves laughed. "Now!" the other shouted.

Suddenly, four other guys appeared. One guy jumped

out of the dumpster, another guy jumped out of the hay, and two other guys came from around the corner behind them. There were four guys in front of them and two behind them. They were surrounded.

"Six on two … hardly seems like a fair fight. Maybe I should put one of my arms behind my back," he smirked.

"Why you—" growled one of the thieves.

He then drew his blade and slashed at the kid. The kid simply-sided stepped the guy's slash and punched him in the face, knocking him out.

"Next?" he asked, looking around. The other three guys in front of them drew their swords and attacked. In a flash, he drew his steel broadsword, blocking the swords of three men. He then engaged the three bandits. He effortlessly battled the bandits, dodging some of the bandit's sword strikes while parrying others and sending immediate counterattacks. The bandits continued their battle hoping to overwhelm him but to no avail. Matthew was in awe of his incredible skill. He was leagues better than Matthew. This continued for several moments with neither side gaining an advantage until the bandits began to tire. When an opening presented itself, he struck immediately, cutting them down one by one, making sure not to kill—just wound. After defeating the three in front, the two guys behind them drew their swords and attacked.

Matthew quickly summoned his sword and began to clash with one of the men.

"Look out!" Matthew warned.

He instantly turned around and locked swords with

the man. The kid manipulated his blade down and back-handed him with his fist, causing him to drop his sword. Matthew swiftly disarmed his opponent and pointed his blade at his chest. The man turned and ran out of the alley. The kid put his sword back in the sheath on his waist.

"Wow! That was awesome," complimented Matthew.

"Thanks … I'm Ike, by the way," he replied.

"Matthew."

"Nice to meet you."

Ike walked over to the thieves and picked up one of the crates. "You mind giving me a hand with these?" asked Ike.

"Yeah … sure," agreed Matthew, grabbing a crate. Matthew and Ike took the crates back to the merchant stand.

"Here you go, Mrs. Stratford," said Ike as he and Matthew dropped off the crates.

"Thank you, boys! You've done me a great service," Mrs. Stratford rejoiced.

Suddenly, Murray and a few other guards ran over to the merchant stand, their swords drawn. "What's all this commotion?! We heard there were bandits," demanded Murray.

"Oh, nice for you to show up, Murray, *after the fighting is over!*" Ike complained.

"Why am I not surprised you two troublemakers found each other?" grumbled Murray.

"Who …? You mean Matthew? He's been here for five minutes and he's already more helpful than you," replied Ike.

"Why you—" Murray took a step toward Ike. Ike put his hand on his sword hilt.

"Murray, these two boys stopped those thieves and recovered my stolen merchandise. They're heroes," interjected Mrs. Stratford as she stepped between them.

"Yeah! Why don't you do something useful for once and go arrest the real thieves, some of them are probably still in that alley down there," Ike mocked.

"Fine, let's go boys," grumbled Murray as they headed toward the alley. "You really shouldn't antagonize him like that," warned Mrs. Stratford.

"It's too easy. Do you have those things my mom asked for?" asked Ike.

"I've already put everything on her list in your cart," Mrs. Stratford confirmed.

"Thanks. See you again next week," Ike replied.

"You're welcome," said Mrs. Stratford.

Ike began to pull his cart away, but he stopped.

"Hey Matthew, thanks for the help," said Ike.

"Uhh … no problem."

"As thanks for helping me, I would like to invite you over for dinner."

"Thanks." Matthew walked over to him and the two walked together as Ike pulled his cart. Matthew and Ike left the town. Just outside Goldcrest were dozens of acres of farmland. They walked for a while until they reached Ike's house. Ike's house was a skinny, five-story wooden and stone building. The house was sitting in the middle of a large chunk of grassland. It was surrounded by a mixture of wooden and stone fences, tall garden hedges, and trees. There was a wooden shed across from the house's front porch near the front gate, a greenhouse in the back with a small pond, and another larger, wooden shed in the back-yard.

"Here we are," Ike annouced as they entered the front gate. "Oh, don't mention what happened in town to my mom," he continued. They walked up to the large front porch.

"What happened in town?" asked the little girl who was sitting on the front porch. She had brown skin with brown eyes and curly black hair in a large ponytail. She was wearing an orange dress and combing the yarn hair on her doll.

"None of your business, Kya," snapped Ike.

"Ike, is that you!?" called a woman from inside the house.

"Yeah, Mom!" shouted Ike.

Ike's mother came out of the house and stood on the porch. She was a short, plump woman in her early forties, with long, curly black hair tied up with a bandana. She was drying her hands on her waist apron.

"Mom! Ike said something happened in town and he wouldn't tell me what happened," Kya revealed .

"Why you little—" Ike clenched his fist. Kya stuck out her tongue and ran inside.

"Ike, what happened in town?" she asked with her arms crossed.

"Uh … nothing."

She glared at Ike.

"Well … uhh … Mrs. Stratford was robbed by some bandits, we helped her and … fought some bandits," Ike reluctantly admitted.

Ike's mom closed her eyes, exhaled, and rubbed her forehead. She exhaled again and then spoke, her voice calm. "You know … that I don't like you fighting bandits … but you did a good thing helping Mrs. Stratford. I'm still telling your father about this."

Ike's mom looked at Matthew. "And hello there. I'm Mrs. Townsend," she said, turning toward him with a warm smile.

"Hi, I'm Matthew."

"I invited him over for dinner … is that okay?" Ike asked.

Ike's mom gave Matthew a kind smile. "Well, the more the merrier, I always end up cooking too much food anyways." She then turned and went inside.

"Well, that went better than I expected. You mind giving me a hand with this stuff?" Ike asked.

They emptied the cart and took everything inside. Inside, the house was very cozy and lived-in. It was a little jumbled and cluttered with an array of mis-match furniture and other trappings, but still very clean. Framed, painted portraits of Ike and his family littered the walls. The smell of a delicious home-cooked meal was in the air.

"Oh, Mom says no shoes in the house. She's crazy about that," warned Ike.

"Okay," replied Matthew. They removed their shoes and left them by the front door, then passed through the kitchen where Ike's mom was cooking. Matthew and Ike placed the supplies in the pantry.

"Dinner's almost ready, boys. Help your sister set the table," said Mrs. Townsend.

Ike picked up a stack of plates sitting on the kitchen counter and Matthew grabbed some cups. He led Matthew into the dining room, where Kya was already setting the table. Ike set out the plates on the table and Matthew complemented each one with a cup. Mrs. Townsend came out of the kitchen, carrying a wooden bowl of salad with a wooden spoon sticking out. Behind her, there was a floating bowl of mashed potatoes, a gravy boat, a basket of rolls, and a platter of meatloaf. She placed the bowl on the table and waved her hands. The things behind her floated around her and placed themselves in empty places around the table.

"How did she—" Matthew began to ask.

"She's a sorceress," Ike interjected.

"I'm not a sorceress. I just know a few spells to help me around the house. Now everyone take a seat." Everyone took a seat. "I hope your father won't be too late."

The front door opened and then closed.

"Daddy's here," Kya annouced as she jumped up out of her chair and ran to the front door.

"Hello, sweetheart," said Ike's dad as he lifted Kya. Holding Kya, he walked into the dining room. Ike's dad was a tall, slim man in his early forties, who wore glasses. He had brown skin and eyes with black and grey hair.

"Hello, hello," he annouced. He set Kya down and she went back to her seat. He walked over to Ike's mom and the two kissed.

"Hello, Evelyn," said Ike's dad.

Ike then made a noise like he was holding his vomit.

"Hello, son."

"Hi, Dad," replied Ike.

"And It seems we have a guest this evening," Ike's dad continued.
Hello there."

"Hi, I'm Matthew." Matthew stood up to shake his hand.

"He's a friend of Ike's. We invited him for dinner," Mrs. Townsend added.

"Nice to meet you," said Ike's father, shaking Matthew's hand. "I hope you all weren't waiting too long for me."

"You're just in time, dear," replied Mrs. Townsend.

"Great," said Mr. Townsend rubbing his hands together as he sat down in the chair at the head of the table.

"Well everyone, dig in before it gets cold," encouraged Mrs. Townsend.

Everyone began to help themselves to dinner.

"So, how was your day, dear?" asked Mrs. Townsend.

"Busy. Our source within the castle seems to believe something big is coming," he replied.

"Like what?" she asked.

"Well, our source says there was a secret council meeting recently. The council only meets in secret when something big is going on and they don't want to cause a panic. First, the Blademaster hasn't been seen in weeks. Now secret council meetings. Something's up. I have my reporters running ragged trying to find something we can print," Mr. Townsend revealed.

Matthew felt uneasy. He wasn't sure if he should tell them about his mission. He decided to keep the fact that he was the new Blademaster to himself.

"Excuse me, Mr. Townsend. What exactly is your job?" Matthew asked.

"I'm the editor-in-chief of *The Daily Courier*. The largest newspaper in the seven kingdoms," replied Mr. Townsend.

"Oh."

"But I don't want to worry anyone until we can get more solid evidence," Mr. Townsend continued before looking back at his wife. "So, how was your day, sweetheart?"

"I did some gardening. That's where I got these potatoes. Then I cleaned the house and read some of that book I've been meaning to read for ages."

Mr. Townsend nodded his head as he ate more mashed potatoes. "What about you Kya?"

"I drew a bunch of pictures today. They're all in my room," Kya revealed.

"Well, you'll have to show me those pictures later," said Mr. Townsend.

"Okay," replied Kya.

"What about you, Ike? Anything interesting happen today?"

Ike's mouth was filled with food. He swallowed his food hard. "Uh … not really. I went to town for Mom, where nothing out of the ordinary happened, and then came home."

Mrs. Townsend shot Ike a death glare from across the table.

"And … there may have been some bandits, but we took care of them," Ike reluctantly added.

"Bandits?! How many were there?!" asked Mr. Townsend. He seemed very interested in his son's exploits.

Ike shrugged. "I don't know. Like five, six," he replied, his voice casual.

"Five! Six!" shouted Mrs. Townsend, surprised by this new information.

"And you two took them on all by yourselves? Very impressive boys, very impressive. I told you, Evelyn. Training with my father would pay off," said Mr. Townsend.

Mrs. Townsend glared at her husband.

"Uh … that was very dangerous, boys. You need to be more careful. You could've been seriously hurt," replied Mr. Townsend, correcting himself.

Mrs. Townsend just sighed. After that, Mr. Townsend changed the subject. Matthew sat and watched as Ike's family sat around, happily eating and chatting with each other. He couldn't remember the last time he had a meal like this, even with his mom.

"It's time for bed, Kya," Mr. Townsend annouced after dinner.

"But, I'm not even tired!" she complained.

"Come on. Let's go," ordered Mr. Townsend. They got up from the table. "It was nice meeting you, Matthew." He shook Matthew's hand.

"It was nice meeting you, too, Mr. Townsend," he replied.

Mr. Townsend and Kya left the dining room and headed upstairs.

"Dinner was great, Mrs. Townsend," Matthew complimented.

"Thank you, Matthew. I'm glad you enjoyed it," she replied. She stood up and, with a wave of her hands, the dirty dishes began to stack themselves before they floated off into the kitchen.

"Well, it's getting late. I should probably get going," said Matthew as he got up from the table and put his backpack on.

"Would you like some dessert or something?" offered Mrs. Townsend.

"I'm fine," Matthew replied.

"Where are you heading to?" Mrs. Townsend inquired. She sounded concerned.

"I'm gonna try to get closer to Stormhaven before I set up camp," answered Matthew casually.

"Set up camp? Like sleep in a tent?" she asked.

"It's a really nice place."

"Nonsense, you can stay here for the night. We have more than enough room," insisted Mrs. Townsend.

"But—" Matthew began.

"It's no use trying to argue," interrupted Ike.

"Well, okay," accepted Matthew.

"Can he sleep in my room?" asked Ike.

"If he doesn't mind," said Mrs. Townsend.

"Sure," replied Matthew.

"Hey Mom, can I have some dessert?" asked Ike.

"No!" Mrs. Townsend sternly snapped.

Ike was shocked at her reaction. "What?! Why not?" complained Ike.

"That's for those five or six bandits," she mockingly replied.

Ike frowned. He then got up from the table and said, "Well, I'm going to bed, then. Follow me."

Ike led Matthew up four flights of stairs to Ike's room. Once they were in Ike's room, Ike told Matthew to hold on and then left the room.

Ike's room was at the top of the house just beneath the attic. It was small with a vaulted ceiling, as well as a bed, a desk, a trunk, and a wooden wardrobe. A small circular window faced the expansive front yard.

The door opened. It was Mrs. Townsend.

"Here you go. Fresh sheets and a pillow."

"Thanks for letting me stay here," said Matthew as she handed them over.

"It's no problem."

Ike returned to his room with a cot. "Excuse me, Mom," said Ike.

Mrs. Townsend backed out of the room to allow Ike through. Ike set the cot down in the only available space.

"There you go," said Ike as he flopped on his bed.

"Well, goodnight you two. Don't stay up too late!" she warned.

"Alright, we got it. Night, Mom," Ike replied.

"Goodnight," said Matthew.

She then closed the door and headed downstairs to her bedroom. Matthew set his things down and began to put the sheets on the cot.

CHAPTER 10

MATTHEW IN THE BIG CITY

"Hey, that's an interesting sword you have," said Ike. Matthew again felt very uneasy. He didn't like lying, especially since he had been so nice. "Uhhh … thanks," he replied.

"Where'd you get it?" asked Ike.

"Uh, from my dad," Matthew lied.

"Cool."

"… Where did you get *your* sword?" Matthew inquired, desperate to change the subject.

"I made it," Ike answered casually.

"You made it?" Matthew replied, surprised.

"Yeah. I've made lots of stuff like swords, shields, armor, you name it."

Matthew walked over to Ike's sword, which was leaning on his desk. He unsheathed and examined it. It was a simple double-edged steel broad sword. It was incredibly sharp, surprisingly heavy, and well-balanced. He needed both hands to wield it, while Ike effortlessly wielded it with one. "It's really good," commended Matthew.

"Thanks, I named it Peacekeeper. Every sword must have a name. All the best ones do," he said, proudly.

Matthew put the heavy sword back down.

"Mom says I should look into getting an apprenticeship with a blacksmith," mentioned Ike.

"You sound unsure about that."

"I don't know. I like making stuff, but I don't know if I wanna do it forever, ya know. My parents really want me to get serious about something like my older siblings."

"Older siblings?" Matthew asked.

"Oh yeah, it didn't come up at dinner. There are five of us. My oldest brother Dominic, my oldest sister Samara, my other older brother Cedric, then there's me, and you already met Kya, the youngest. Do you have any siblings?"

"No. It's just me."

"Lucky you, no expectations from older siblings to live up to," lamented Ike.

"What do they do?"

"Well, Dominic works with my dad at the newspaper as a reporter, Samara's a lieutenant in the human royal navy, and Cedric is an assistant professor at some school for sorcery."

"Wow, they all seem to be doing well for themselves," Matthew replied, impressed.

"Yeah, I guess. Honestly, I'm worried I'll be the one failure and let everybody down," sighed Ike.

"I'm sure you'll do great."

"Thanks. Ugh … it's getting pretty late. We should get some sleep. You're going all the way to Stormhaven."

"Yeah," replied Matthew.

They both got ready for bed and went to sleep. Matthew woke up the next morning.

"Mom made breakfast," Ike annouced as he finished getting dressed. After putting on his shirt, Ike left the room and went downstairs.

Matthew got up and got dressed. He made up his cot, put on his backpack, and went downstairs. As Matthew came down the stairs the smell of breakfast hit him.

"Good morning," announced Mrs. Townsend as Matthew sat down at the table next to Ike.

"Good morning," he replied. On the table were several plates filled with sausage links, scrambled eggs, hash browns, and toast. Some of which were already missing. Matthew grabbed a plate and began to help himself to the food on the table. After breakfast, he stood up from the table and put on his backpack.

"Well, I think I've been enough of an inconvenience, I should go. Thanks, Mrs. Townsend for everything," he said with great appreciation.

"It's been no problem, dear. Oh, before you go, take this." Mrs. Townsend handed Matthew a brown paper bag and smiled. "It's some leftovers from yesterday's dinner."

"Thanks, I really appreciate it. See ya around, Ike,"

said Matthew.

"See ya around," Ike replied.

Matthew then stepped into the dining room, put on his shoes, and walked out the front door. Outside it was warm with a slight breeze blowing through the air. Matthew decided to head back to Goldcrest. After a few minutes of walking, he heard something behind him.

"Hey, Matthew!"

Matthew turned around. It was Ike running and shouting at him. Ike caught up to him.

"What's wrong? Did I forget something?"

"You forgot me. I wanna come along," annouced Ike. He was wearing a headband to keep his hair back, a heavy leather chest guard, his sword on his right hip, and a packed bag on his back.

"I don't know what you mean," replied Matthew. "I'm just going to Stormhaven. Nothing out of the ordinary is happening."

"That sword. I remember where I recognize it now. It is the Blade of the Elementals, only carried by the Blademaster himself. You're the new Blademaster."

Matthew looked around to see if anyone heard. "All right, all right, you caught me. I'm the Blademaster. I don't wanna announce it to everyone just yet."

"Oh, man. This is awesome. You must be on some kind of quest for the council. You gotta let me come with you. You've seen what I can do. I can help," Ike pleaded.

"Well ... I do need all the help I can get ... welcome aboard."

"We should probably get going. My mom doesn't exactly know I left yet and I don't wanna stick around until she does."

"Good point," said Matthew as he summoned the stagecoach. They embarked for Goldcrest. Once they reached Goldcrest, they took the northern gate toward Stormhaven.

"How far is Stormhaven from Goldcrest?" asked Matthew.

"Not too far. At this rate, we'll get there before this afternoon. You've never been to Stormhaven?" Ike asked.

"I'm not exactly from here."

"So … where are you from?"

"It's a long story," replied Matthew.

"Well, we've got a long trip," replied Ike.

With that, Matthew told him about everything that had happened to him so far.

"Wow. That's crazy."

"Crazy's an understatement," replied Matthew.

"Well, Stormhaven is pretty incredible. Pretty much all the best stuff is in Stormhaven. You can even see some of it already." Ike pointed to the sky. Off in the distance above the trees in the forest, there was a massive stone castle on a hill with large, pointed spires. He could also see the tops of various buildings and the tall spires of the cathedral. "We're almost at the gates," said Ike.

The two rode for several minutes more until they reached the gates of Stormhaven. The gates of Stormhaven were enormous—several stories tall. The white stone walls of the city were taller than the trees in the thick surrounding forest. The large wooden and metal doors were open with many people entering and leaving the city. Armored knights on horseback stood off to the sides by the doors. Matthew put the stagecoach back in its chest and he and Ike entered the city on foot.

Inside the city was more crowded and chaotic than anywhere Matthew had been before since he'd been here. Matthew and Ike stood on the sidewalk as hordes of different species of people walked around them. They were surrounded by some of the tallest buildings he had seen since being here. The streets were cobblestone and filled with people riding all sorts of exotic creatures. Some were even pulling carts. The air was filled with people talking, speaking different languages, and trying to attract customers into the stores or merchant stands. Store windows lined the streets selling food, weapons, armor, strange ingredients, and strange creatures for pets, among many other things.

"Where are we now?" shouted Matthew, trying to talk over the roar of the crowd.

"This is the market district. Where do you wanna go?" shouted Ike. He thought for a moment before digging in his pocket and pulling out a scrap of paper.

"Can you take me here?" he asked, handing Ike the piece of paper.

Ike opened the paper and looked it over. "Follow me."

Matthew followed him as he led them several blocks to a street trolley. They rode the street trolley out of the busy market district and into a new district. They exited the trolley and walked several more blocks. This new district was a lot calmer than the market district. Instead of all the stores and restaurants like the market district, they were homes, parks, small trees, and grass. It was a lot less chaotic than the market district and the sidewalks were less crowded.

"What district is this?" asked Matthew.

"This is New Town." Ike led Matthew to a brownstone townhouse. "Well … this is it," he said as he handed Matthew back the paper.

Matthew went up the stairs and knocked on the door. After a few moments, the door opened and there stood a tall seventeen year old girl with brown hair and blue eyes. She was Alice's older sister Viola.

"Umm…Hello?" she asked. Like Alice, she had an accent.

"Uh…Hi, I'm looking for Alice. Is she here? We're her friends."

Viola turned inside the house and yelled "Alice! Some of your friends are at the door." She then walked off, leaving Matthew standing in front of an open door.

After a few moments, Alice came to the door. She was barefoot and wearing a knee-length, light yellow sundress. Her long, thick blond hair fell past her shoulders. She was holding in her arms a little reddish-brown kitten with a pink ribbon around her neck.

"Matthew?!" she said with great surprise.

"Who's at the door, sweetie?" asked a woman's soft

voice from inside. The woman walked over to Alice. She was in her late thirties, tall and skinny with fair skin, shoulder-length brown hair, green eyes, and glasses. She didn't have an accent like Alice or Viola.

"Oh. Hi there! You must be some of Alice's friends. Please come in, come in," she welcomed, gesturing for them to enter. They entered the house into the living room. She guided them over to one of the couches in the living room. The living room was fancily furnished and clean with artwork on the walls, several bookshelves, two leather tan sofas, and a wooden coffee table between them. Framed painted portraits of Alice and her family were on the walls and the mantle of the large fireplace beside the two sofas.

"Would you boys like something to drink? It's pretty warm outside today. We have water, lemonade, and cranberry juice," she offered.

"I'll have some lemonade, please," said Ike.

"I'll take one too. Thanks, Missus—um?" said Matthew.

"Please, call me Mrs. Liddell " she replied before going into the kitchen.

Alice sat on the couch across for Matthew and Ike. She remained silent. After a few moments of awkward silence, Mrs. Liddell came back into the room carrying two glasses of lemonade garnished with lemon slices. She placed the two glasses in front of Matthew and Ike.

"It's nice to finally meet some of Alice's friends. We don't seem to get many visits from them," she said, smiling.

Alice grew annoyed. "Can you give us the room,

please?" She spoke in a stern tone of voice. Silence hung in the air for a few moments.

"Alright, I'll just leave you to it, then." Mrs. Liddell turned and went upstairs.

"Your mom seems nice," Matthew began.

"She's my stepmother," Alice corrected, seeming slightly irritated.

"Oh."

An awkward silence once again descended upon them. Ike began to drink his lemonade.

"Uh … you don't seem happy to see me," observed Matthew.

"Well, I must say I'm … just simply surprised is all," she replied. For now, she seemed back to her normal self.

"So … do you still wanna come along?" Matthew asked the question slowly.

"Well, when you said you wanted me to come along, I thought you would've come by after a few days or a week at the most. But it's been well over a month!" Alice replied.

"I didn't know your offer had an expiration date."

Alice smirked. "It's nothing like that. It's … complicated. I thought you had already gone off on your adventure. What were you doing for all that time?"

"Well … a lot's happened. It's a long story, but I haven't gone on my quest yet. I wanted to see if you still wanted to come, first," Matthew replied.

Alice placed her kitten down, got up from the sofa, and walked over to the empty fireplace. She looked at the various framed portraits on the mantle for several moments, then at one portrait in particular. It was the oldest one on the mantle: a small portrait of a family. The portrait consisted of a man with brown hair and brown eyes with his arm around a woman with long blonde hair with blue eyes and a black ribbon in her hair. Both were in their mid-twenties. The man had his other arm on the shoulder of a little girl with long brown hair and blue eyes while the woman held a small baby no more than a few months old, with short blonde hair and blue eyes.

"I'd love to come along with you … if you'll still have me," Alice said, turning around to face Matthew.

"Welcome aboard!" he excitedly replied.

"Man, this lemonade is delicious!" exclaimed Ike. Alice and Matthew both looked at Ike. "What? I kinda zoned out there for a minute," Ike added.

"I believe we haven't had the chance to acquaint ourselves. My name is Alice, a pleasure to meet you," Alice said, extending her hand to Ike.

"I'm Ike," he replied as he shook her hand.

"Well, I must prepare for our adventure. Wait for me at the corner. I shall be along momentarily." Alice ran upstairs.

Matthew and Ike continued to sit on the couch. "Are you going to finish that?" asked Ike.

Matthew slid the glass over to Ike. After he finished the lemonade, they got up and left the house.

Alice entered her room at the end of the upstairs hallway. It was a small room, but very neat and tidy. There was a bed, a dresser, a vanity table with a large mirror, a window seat covered in a pile of various stuffed animals, and a bookshelf filled with books—so many books that many were stacked up on the floor next to it. Alice went into her closet and began to pack her bag. Suddenly, she remembered her stepmother. She stopped packing her bag and walked back down the hall. She entered her father and stepmother's bedroom.

Mrs. Liddell was sitting in a chair by the window reading a magazine.

"My friends are going camping this weekend, I wish to join them," Alice announced.

"How long will you be gone?" asked Mrs. Liddell.

"Oh, It's just for a few days. Since it's summer break and we haven't done anything or had anything going on, I figure it wouldn't be a problem."

"Well, Alice, this weekend I thought we were supposed to spend some time together. You know … we never really spend time together, just the two of us."

"But it's summer break. I'd rather prefer to spend it actually having fun. I mean you understand, right?" Alice reasoned

"Oh," Mrs. Liddell said softly. "Are there going to be any adults there for supervision?"

"Sure," Alice replied.

Mrs. Liddell sighed. "Fine, you can go with your friends. I'll tell your father when he comes home."

"Great. Thank you," said Alice, smiling. She then turned and left the room to continue packing.

At the corner of Alice's street, Matthew and Ike

waited for several minutes before Alice emerged from her house. She was wearing a white blouse with small flowers on it, with jeans, a black ribbon in her hair, and a large backpack.

"Alright. I guess onward to the cathedral now," annouced Matthew.

They walked for several blocks to the street trolley and rode it into the Cathedral District. The Cathedral District was similar to New Town, but slightly more crowded. There were homes, businesses, trees, parks, and fountains. At the edge of the Cathedral District was the Stormhaven Cathedral itself. The white stone cathedral, viewed up close, was massive: stained glass windows, impressive stone steps, and tall towers. It was surrounded by well-manicured grass and trees.

"Wow. It's even bigger up close," noted Matthew.

"Why have we come to the cathedral?" asked Alice.

"I need Aleron's box and I think it may be here," Matthew replied.

"But Aleron's box has been lost for centuries."

"That's what I said," interjected Ike.

"The story said it was hidden away. All we have to do is find it and I'm guessing our best bet is here. The priest who hid it once lived here. There must be some clue of its whereabouts," reasoned Matthew.

"Perhaps, but it sounds like a long shot," Alice doubted.

"That's what I also said," Ike replied.

"Come on guys. If we don't find anything we'll think

of something else," Matthew insisted.

The three of them entered the cathedral. They searched the cathedral for hours. They even talked to several of the priests and monks in the cathedral but to no avail. Eventually, they gave up the search, left the cathedral, and sat on the front steps.

"Well … that could've gone better," said Ike.

"Perhaps it actually is lost. Even the priests seem rather certain of it," suggested Alice.

"Maybe. Ugh. I really needed to find that box. My whole plan kinda hinged on it," replied Matthew.

"I'm sure we can come up with another plan," encouraged Ike.

The three of them sat on the cathedral steps thinking of a plan.

"Maybe the box is in another church?" suggested Ike. "Somewhere much lower profile, probably nearby to keep an eye on things."

After several moments of silence, Alice leapt to her feet. "I got it! Ike, you're brilliant."

"I know, but what are you talking about?" he asked.

"The box! I think I might know where it is," said Alice.

"But how?" asked Matthew.

"I'll explain on the way," she insisted. They got up from the stairs and followed Alice. They walked several blocks until they reached another trolley station. They rode the trolley to the market district.

"So what's going on?" asked Ike.

"Well, perhaps you're right. I think we were looking in the wrong place. The Stormhaven Cathedral seems like such an obvious place to hide it, so you don't hide it there. You would hide it somewhere a lot less obvious but still close enough so you could keep an eye on it," explained Alice.

In the market district, they exited the trolley and left the city. After they left the city, they headed through the forest. After being led through the forest by Alice they came upon a small, run-down wooden building. The wooden building was surrounded by a rusty iron rod fence. Next to the wooden building, there was a small graveyard. The graveyard was overgrown with tall grasses covering most of the gravestones. Alice tried to open the rusty iron gate, but it was so rusty the gate didn't swing open anymore.

"A little … help would be much appreciated," she demanded.

Matthew and Ike went over to the gate and began to push on it. After a few moments, they managed to push the iron gate open just enough for them to squeeze through. Then, they walked up the old wooden steps to the front door. Alice approached the door and gave it a few light knocks. The force from Alice's light knocks made the old and creaky wooden door open.

"Hello …. is anybody here?" asked Alice.

There was silence. The three of them entered the building. Inside the main area were several rows of old wooden pews. On the far side of the room, there was a wooden podium and a wooden table behind it. There was also a door next to the wooden table. There were multiple, large, stained glass windows on the front, left, and right walls. Streaks of sunlight shone through the windows, illuminating the room. It also exposed just how much dust was hanging in the air. On every surface, there were cobwebs and a thick layer of dust. It looked like no one had been here in ages.

"Where exactly is here anyway?" asked Matthew, looking around.

"Allow me to introduce you to one of Stormhaven's first churches." Alice gestured at the empty room.

"Where did you find out about this place?" asked Ike.

"I read about it in a book. It was called *The History of the Order of Light: Through the Third and Fourth Ages*. It's quite a fascinating read. Lots of beautiful artwork," boasted Alice.

"You'll have to float that by me sometime," said a sarcastic Ike. Alice smirked.

"Well, let's look around," said Matthew.

They began to search the main area as the old wood floor loudly creaked beneath their feet.

"I hope this place doesn't collapse," worried Ike, feeling uneasy.

CHAPTER 11

INTO THE MOUNTAINS

"What are three children doing in here?"

An old man appeared, suddenly and unexpectedly, from what looked like the other side of the wooden table. The three of them jumped in surprise.

"Sorry. We didn't think anyone was in here," replied Matthew.

"Well, there is. This isn't a place for children. I'm going to have to ask you to leave," demanded the old man, who was wearing old and tattered robes.

"Sorry," said Matthew.

"If you don't mind me asking, why are you here?" inquired Alice.

"I'm here to make sure people don't destroy this

place."

"But you're just one old man. Why doesn't the king send real guards if this place is important?" asked Ike.

"His majesty can't spare the men," the old man replied.

"Why doesn't the king want to protect this place?" asked Alice.

"His majesty has more important matters to attend to."

"More important than protecting this place!? This is a piece of history!" Alice replied, offended.

"Apparently. Now please leave."

"What's so special about this place that it needs protecting?" asked Matthew.

"Despite its current condition, it is still a historical landmark," replied the old man.

"You'd think they'd want to keep their historical landmarks in better shape," Ike mused, looking around at the terrible shape the building was in. Matthew thought to himself for a few moments.

"Ya know something … I think Alice is right," asserted Matthew.

"Pardon me?" he asked.

"I think the reason the king didn't send guards is that you didn't tell the king what's really here. If he knew, he would send extra security. And if he did that then it would attract too much attention. You already have the Stormhaven Cathedral as a perfect red herring. This place is already the perfect hiding place. It's unsuspecting, it's close, there's even someone here to watch over it." Matthew gestured toward the old man.

"I've had enough of your questions and accusations. There's nothing here. It's time to go." The old man's voice was firm but calm.

Matthew's face dropped. "Oh." He was surprised to learn that he was wrong.

"Well, if nothing's here, a little look around can't hurt," suggested Ike as he began to walk toward the old man. The old man began to glow with strong, yellow energy as he clenched his fists. Ike stopped walking toward the old man and put his hand on the hilt of his sword.

"Wait! Stop!" interjected Matthew. The old man unclenched his fists and Ike took his hand off his sword.

Matthew walked up to the old man and drew his sword. "Look, I'm the Blademaster. I really need the box for a very important reason. People are getting hurt. It's the only thing that can stop whoever is behind these attacks," he pleaded.

The old man stood there for a moment. Finally, he let out a sigh. "Very well, come with me."

Matthew, Ike, and Alice began to follow the old man until he turned and stated "Your friends will have to stay here."

Matthew turned to his friends and nodded to them. He then followed the old man around the table. On the other side of the table, there was a hidden stone staircase. The old man led Matthew down the staircase into the basement. The basement was mostly empty except for some more wooden pews and stacked wooden crates in the corner covered in cobwebs. In another corner was a small cot. The walls of the basement were made of stones. The old man walked over to the far corner of the room. He pressed one of the bricks with his glowing hand and a few of the bricks moved to reveal a small opening. He pulled a small wooden chest out of the opening and walked over to Matthew. He opened the chest and handed a rolled-up scroll to Matthew.

"I need Aleron's box. What is this?" asked Matthew.

"It's a map. It will lead you to the box."

"Oh, alright," replied Matthew. He then turned and began to ascend the stairs.

"Before you go," started the old man. "You must remember to keep this map a secret. If the map or the box fell into the wrong hands again, it could be the end of all of us. It was hidden away for a reason."

Matthew stopped and looked at the old man. "Don't worry, I'll keep it safe, and I'll return it when I'm done," promised Matthew, putting the map in his bag.

The old man nodded and Matthew continued up the stairs. When Matthew came back up the stairs, Ike was sitting on one of the pews with Alice standing next to him with her arms folded.

"How can you sit there? This place is really quite filthy," she complained as she observed all the cobwebs and the dust particles swirling in the air.

"I wiped the seat off before I sat down, what's the problem?" Ike replied. Alice sighed in response.

Matthew walked over to Ike and Alice. "Let's go," he

said.

Ike got up from the pew, brushed himself off, and followed Matthew and Alice out of the church. They walked through the forest and headed back toward Stormhaven.

"Can we see the box?" Ike asked, curious.

Matthew stopped walking. He reached into his bag, pulled out the rolled-up scroll, and handed it to Ike. Ike unrolled the scroll and looked it over. Alice walked over to Ike to get a look at the scroll.

"It's a … map," she observed.

"A not very good one. Nothing is labeled and there are just outlines of the continents," added Ike.

Matthew walked over to Ike and Alice looking at the scroll. "Oh, there's some sort of marking over here. This must be where the box is," directed Alice.

"Wait a minute, I got an idea," said Matthew. He pulled out the golden book from his bag and began flipping through it. He found a world map in the book and sat it down on the grass.

"Let me see that map," he asked. Ike handed the map to Matthew. He compared the map in the book to the map that was given to them.

"So the box must be somewhere … over here," he said. He compared the spot on the scroll to where the spot would be on the world map.

"It's in … the ocean?!" he said.

"Pardon me, that can't be right," doubted Alice.

Matthew once again compared the spot on the two maps.

"Maybe that old man tricked us, giving us a fake map," Ike suggested.

"No, I'm sure this really is the map. He stressed keeping this map a secret," explained Matthew.

"Perhaps the box is underwater," suggested Alice.

"Or maybe it could be an uncharted island," suggested Ike.

"Oh my. That could be possible. Who possibly knows how many uncharted islands could be out there?" reasoned Alice.

"Okay, so how do we get there?" Matthew asked.

"Perhaps we can go to Stormhaven Harbor, inquire about chartering a boat," replied Alice.

"We don't have the money to charter a boat. Besides, can we really trust those people? We need someone who can take us there for cheap, no questions asked," Ike suggested.

"Where are we supposed to go, then?" asked Alice.

"How about…Albatross Point," Ike suggested.

"Albatross Point? … Albatross Point?! Oh dear! You'll never find a more wretched hive of scum and villainy. How do we know we can even trust them?" complained Alice.

Ike nodded in agreement. "Good point, but I'm all ears for any other suggestions."

Alice looked at Matthew. "What do you think, Matthew?"

Matthew was silent for a few moments. "Where exactly is Albatross Point?"

Ike put his finger on the map in the golden book.

"We are here, by Stormhaven." Ike then traced his finger up the west coast. "To here. Just on the other side of the Iron Peaks Mountains. If we can catch the train to Anvilholde, we can travel the rest of the way. It should only take a couple of days to get there with your carriage."

"I guess we don't have much of a choice. I have to get this box," Matthew declared.

"Well, we should head to the train station, then," said Alice.

Matthew put the scroll and book back into his bag. They headed back through the forest and back to the gates of Stormhaven. They headed through the Market District to the trolley. They took the trolley to the Castle District, which was similar to New Town and the Cathedral District. The massive stone castle of the king loomed over the district, with more armed guards patrolling its streets.

In the Castle District was Stormhaven Station. The train station was a large stone building with enormous stone columns and glass windows. They entered the station. The train station was made up of a large long hallway with stone floors and a curved ceiling. Large iron chandeliers hung from the ceiling. There was a massive four-sided clock in the middle of the room, and on the right side of the room were rows of wooden pews where people sat waiting for their train.

On the left side of the room, there were three ticket booths with small metal bars that were built into the station's stone walls. There was also a little café with some people sitting at small tables, in a roped-off area next to the ticket booth. The first ticket booth had a wooden sign with the word "CLOSED" painted on it, and the second ticket booth was busy, so they walked up to the third booth. At the third booth was an old woman with long gray hair. She wore a small pair of glasses on her nose.

"Hello, my good lady. We would like three tickets to Anvilholde," said Ike.

"That will be six bronze, please," replied the old woman. Alice and Ike each pulled out two bronze.

Matthew reached into his bag and pulled out the coin pouch Sterling gave him. "All I have is gold coins," he said.

Alice pulled out two more bronze coins and put them on the ticket booth. The old woman raked the bronze coins into her hands and put them in a locked iron box below the ticket booth counter. The old woman pulled out a booklet and tore out three tickets. She signed and stamped all three, and then she handed them to Ike. The three of them then moved out of the way of the next customer.

"Umm … thanks for that," said Matthew.

"Oh, It's quite alright," reassured Alice.

Ike handed Alice and Matthew their tickets. "The platform is down here," Ike said, then led them down the hall to the train platform.

On the platform, there were several people already waiting for the train. Ike walked over to an empty wooden bench and sat down. Alice sat next to him on the bench while Matthew stood beside them.

"How long until the train gets here?" asked Matthew.

"It shouldn't be too long. The train runs several times

a day. It looks like we just made the last trip today," replied Ike pointing to the clock post on the platform. They waited on the platform for several minutes until they hear the loud horn of the train.

Suddenly, a large copper steam train pulled into the platform with a long line of compartments behind it. The train came to a complete stop as white steam plumed from the tracks beneath it. Moments later, the doors opened.

A male Hairn wearing a conductor's uniform exited the train. A crowd of passengers followed him.

After all the passengers got off the train, the conductor shouted, "Now boarding!"

"Well, let's go. I want to try to get a good seat," insisted Ike.

They walked over to the fourth train car and got in line with other people trying to board the train. The train car was long and dotted with windows and curtains. Above the windows was a long rack the length of the car for item storage with two burgundy linen benches facing each next to the window. On the train, Matthew and Alice followed Ike down the aisle as people around them found seats, sat down, and put their things in the racks above the windows.

"How about here?" asked Ike in front of some empty seats.

"Sure," replied Matthew.

Ike quickly took off his sword belt and sat in the seat on the left. Alice put her bag on the rack above the window and sat in the seat across from Ike. Matthew put his bag beside him and sat next to Ike.

"Have you guys ever been to this place … Anvilholde?" asked Matthew.

"Only once before," answered Alice.

"Couple times," said Ike.

After everyone found a seat the conductor came aboard and closed the door.

"Here we go," said Ike as the train began to pull out of the station.

"Please, have your tickets ready," shouted the conductor as he came down the aisle.

"How long is this train ride?" asked Matthew.

"Just a few hours," answered Alice. The conductor went row by row, down the train car, clipping tickets. After the conductor clipped everyone's tickets he moved to the next car. The car became livelier once the conductor left.

"You never told me what you were up to all this time after you left Gerda's Inn?" asked Alice.

"Oh … well, after I left Gerda's Inn I met my uncle," revealed Matthew.

"Your uncle? You have family here? What's his name?" asked Alice, shocked.

"Apparently, I guess Bernhart knows him. Sterling Jacobs," said Matthew.

"Sterling Jacobs?! *Thee* Sterling Jacobs?! Sterling Jacobs is your uncle?!" asked an excited Alice. People on the train started to look at them from the commotion.

"Keep it down, will you?" Matthew whispered.

"My apologies," said an embarrassed Alice.

"You know him?" he asked.

"Yes … well … no, I've never actually met him before, but I have certainly heard about him. I've read some of his books on magic. They say he's one of the most powerful sorcerers in the world," Alice replied.

"He trained me for a month. Then, after that, I headed to Goldcrest where I met Ike," said Matthew, pointing with his thumb at Ike. "Then we came to Stormhaven to meet you."

"It seems you were quite busy," she replied.

"What were you up to after I left?"

"Well…" she began, "first, I returned home. My dad was incredibly worried since I was a day late from my aunt's house. I told him about the black knights, you, Bernhart, Gerda, and that's why I was late. I decided to leave out our little adventure in wonderland. No need to worry him any further, the black knights worried him enough. Then I read a lot of books while I waited for you to come. There's this charming little second-hand bookshop in Stormhaven's Old Town that I just postively adore. There are just so many fascinating old books to read there. So many of them are filled with just the most wonderful pictures. I wished more books had pictures. I think all books should have pictures. I also practiced my violin and I got a new kitten. Her name is Dinah."

"You play the violin?" asked Matthew.

"My dad was quite insistent about me doing something at school. He wanted me to have an extracurricular activity, to be more involved. That and he didn't want me sitting around reading all day. I've gotten plenty good at the violin, played in a few recitals," she bragged.

"My mom would give her left arm to get me more into reading," Ike chimed in.

"Then what does interest you?" Alice asked.

"I call my interests the three S's. Steel, Snacks, and Sleeping," Ike replied with pride.

Matthew and Alice both began to laugh. Suddenly a female Hairn, pushing a cart and wearing a similar uniform to the conductor, stopped in front of their row. "Anything from the cart?" she asked.

"What do you have?" asked Matthew.

"Pretzels, peanuts, popcorn, and assorted fruits," said the woman.

"I'll take the pretzels," said Ike. The woman handed Ike a small paper bag of pretzels. "Anything for you two?"

"I'll take some pretzels, too," said Matthew. The woman handed him a bag of pretzels.

"I'll take an apple, thank you," said Alice. The Hairn woman handed Alice her apple before continuing to push her cart down the aisle.

Matthew and Ike began to eat their pretzels while Alice looked out the window. The train was still going through the forest. Ike was munching on his pretzels.

"These pretzels are making me thirsty. I wish we had some of that lemonade Alice's mom made. It was delicious," he remembered.

"She's not my mother!" Alice snapped. Matthew and Ike exchanged glances. Alice quickly realized what happened and corrected herself, her voice calmer. "She's my stepmother."

She began to eat her apple, and they all fell quiet as the train headed out of the forest and into the snowy Iron Peaks Mountains. Finally, the train pulled into the Anvilholde station. There were dozens of people standing on the open-air train platform. They were all wearing light jackets. When the train came to a complete stop, the Hairn conductor walked up the aisle, opened the train door, and stepped onto the platform.

Everyone picked up their things and exited the train. Alice waited for everyone else to leave and then stood up to gather her things. She went down the aisle, followed by Matthew and then Ike. They stepped off the train and onto the station platform.

There was a slight chill in the air and the sun was starting to set behind the snow-peaked mountains that surrounded them in the distance.

"Is this Anvilholde?" asked Matthew as they exited the train station.

"No, this is Ironbrook," annouced Ike. Matthew looked out at the small mountain village of timber-lined buildings just down the hill from where they were standing. "That's Anvilholde." Ike pointed to the highest and closest snow-peaked mountain, which loomed in the distance.

"I wish I had brought a jacket. It's chilly in the mountains." Ike rubbed his arms.

Matthew pulled out the chest and from it the coach spilled. The three of them climbed aboard.

"Anvilholde," commanded Matthew. The coach began to roll forward.

"I'm starved," complained Ike.

"Didn't you eat earlier?" asked Alice.

"Yeah, pretzels, not like a real meal," complained Ike.

"I'm sure we can find something in town."

The carriage pulled up to the gates of Anvilholde around dusk. The gates of Anvilholde were enormous and carved into the mountainside. It had a large wooden and steel gate that was drawn up allowing entrance into the city. Just outside the gates, there were several merchant stalls. The three of them exited the coach.

"Someone's selling sausages over there," said Ike before rushing off. Matthew and Alice hurried behind him.

"Three sausages, my good lady," ordered Ike.

The Hairn woman behind the market stall handed Ike three sausages on sticks.

"I got this," declared Matthew as he pulled out a gold coin and handed it to the woman. The woman repeatedly thanked Matthew and shook his hand.

"What was that all about?" wondered Alice, as the three of them left the stall and Ike handed her a sausage.

"I paid for the sausages," Matthew explained, taking his sausage from Ike.

"How much did you give her?" asked Ike.

"A gold coin."

"Matthew, the food would've only cost one silver," said Alice.

"How many silvers is a gold coin?" asked Matthew.

"Three," replied Ike.

"Oops. But she seemed really happy," said Matthew.

Matthew, Alice, and Ike now entered the gates to the city. The city of Anvilholde was much different than Stormhaven. The biggest difference was that the entire city was carved inside a hollowed-out mountain. Despite the city being inside a mountain, it didn't feel claustrophobic. The ceiling was several hundred feet high with lots of open areas. Most of the buildings were carved out of the very walls of the mountain though there were free-standing buildings. The streets were stone tiles with lampposts holding glowing crystals to illuminate them. The city was made up of several large ring levels going deeper into the mountain. On the ceiling, there was an enormous glowing crystal chandelier bathing the entire city in a gentle white light.

"We should probably get some supplies for our journey to Albatross Point while we're here," suggested Matthew.

"Okay, what do we need?" asked Ike.

"Umm…Just get whatever you think we'll need," handing Ike and Alice some of his gold coins.

"Aye, captain," replied Ike.

"We can meet back right here," suggested Alice.

"Where is 'here', exactly?" asked Ike. They looked up at the building awning under which they now stood.

"It's … the Anvilholde post office," read Alice.

"Okay, meet back in an hour … or less," said Ike.

Ike and Alice then headed down the sidewalk. Matthew stood there on the sidewalk in front of the post office thinking where to go, when suddenly he thought about

Sterling.

He reached into his bag and pulled out the purple crystal Sterling had given him.

CHAPTER 12

UNDER THE BRIDGE

Matthew laid the crystal flat in the palm of his hand and cleared his throat.

"Umm … hello, Sterling. Are you there?" he voiced into the crystal. He then immediately heard, the sound of shattering glass, coming from the crystal.

"Crap!" responded Sterling from the other side of the crystal.

"Hello, Sterling," Matthew repeated louder.

"Just a minute!" shouted Sterling, followed by the sounds of moving furniture and more breaking glass.

"Crap … got it, hello?" answered Sterling. Sterling's face appeared on the crystal.

"Hey Sterling. Is this a bad time?" he asked.

"Hey, no, I had just forgotten where I had put this

thing. What's going on?" asked Sterling.

"I just wanted to update you on my mission," he said.

"Oh, alright," replied Sterling.

"Well, we found a clue to the box's location and now we're on our way to get it. We're in Anvilholde now."

"Anvilholde? We?" Sterling sounded surprised.

"Um … yeah, I met some people. They're helping me."

"Well, that's good. It's a big job."

"Has anything happened since I've been gone?" asked Matthew.

Sterling fell silent for a moment. "There's been another incident, but it wasn't as bad as the one you got caught in. The town's guard managed to get it under control. It seems these attacks are happening pretty much at random now. Please, don't go off doing something dangerous in an attempt to rush things. Be smart. Be careful," warned Sterling.

"Okay."

"Look, Matthew, I gotta go. If you have any more questions or concerns, I'm just one call away."

"Okay. See you later."

Sterling waved and his image faded away on the crystal. Matthew felt uneasy. He had no time to waste. People were in danger.

"Matthew … Matthew, is that you?" asked a German-accented voice. Matthew looked around in confusion.

Suddenly, he spotted who was calling him. It was Bernhart. He was sitting in his cart, which he had pulled over in front of the post office.

"Bernhart!?" said Matthew, surprised.

"Ah, hello there my friend." Bernhart hopped out of his cart and walked up to him.

"Hi, Bernhart. What are you doing here?"

"I was shopping for ingredients for some soup I was preparing. What brings you to Anvilholde, my friend?"

"Just gathering supplies for the quest," answered Matthew.

Alice and Ike returned carrying a few bags. "We're back," announced Ike.

"Bernhart?" exclaimed Alice.

"Hello, again," greeted Bernhart.

"Bernhart! How lovely to see you again," she replied.

"Ike, this is our friend Bernhart," she introduced.

"Hi," replied Ike.

"Well, it was nice meeting you again, Bernhart, but we have to get going. Long journey ahead," hurried Matthew.

"You plan on traveling now? It's pretty late. You can stay with me for the night if you need a place to stay," Bernhart suggested.

"That would be quite lovely but, we don't want to put you out," enthused Alice.

"Oh nonsense, it's no trouble at all," assured Bernhart.

"Alright." Ike shrugged. Ike and Alice picked up their bags and headed over to the cart. Matthew stood there for a moment.

"Everything alright?" asked Alice from the back of

the cart.

He wondered if he should tell them what Sterling told him. "Nothing, let's go." He walked over to the cart, climbed in and sat next to Ike.

"Let's go home, girl," said Bernhart as the ram began to pull the cart. They rode down the street to the gates of Anvilholde. Outside the city it was night. Hairn guards patrolled the perimeter with lanterns. They rode back down the Anvilholde mountain pass and headed the opposite way they had come before. They rode through the nippy mountain air under the stars, until they came to Bernhart's home. His home was a small, wood-framed cottage with a wooden barn next to it. He pulled the cart up to the front of the barn and hopped off the front seat and unhooked his ram from the front of the cart. The ram walked forward into the barn. They grabbed their things and hopped out of the back of the cart. Bernhart walked over to the front door of his cottage and unlocked it.

Bernhart's cottage was made up of a large room that acted as a living room, dining room, and kitchen. The main room had three other rooms—a bathroom and two bedrooms—connected to it. The group entered Bernhart's home, which was dark except for one oil lamp next to the door. Ike closed the door behind them. Bernhart walked over to the wall and lit the fireplace, illuminating the living room. The living room was cozy and filled with rustic furniture. There were portraits and various other knick-knacks on the walls.

"Please make yourselves at home. I'm going to get

dinner started." Bernhart walked over to the kitchen area.

Alice sat down on the couch in front of the fireplace. "What a lovely home you have, Bernhart," she said. Ike sat down next to her while Matthew took a seat in a chair next to the couch.

"Danke," Bernhart replied as he loaded ingredients into a large, cast-iron pot. He closed the pot, walked over to the fireplace, and placed the pot over the fire. He then sat in the chair on the other side of the couch.

"So, how do you guys know each other?" asked Ike.

"Remember, I told you about that burning village. He helped us escape," Matthew replied.

"Oh yeah," said Ike.

"Hey, where's Sonja?" asked Alice.

"Who's Sonja?" asked Ike.

"Bernhart has a pet bear," answered Matthew.

"Wow, how'd you get a bear for a pet?"

"You know something, that's a good question," Matthew mused.

"Sonja's in the barn. It's where she sleeps. It was thirteen years ago. I remember it was a particularly rough winter. Roughest winter I'd been through in ages. Food was very scarce that season. One day while hunting, I spotted an elk. Well, you could imagine my joy. I was nearly starving to death, and here was this elk. It was like it was sent from the gods. I'd managed to wound it. I was tracking it through the forest until I came across a clearing with a cave. In the snow, a brown bear was standing next to the downed elk I had wounded. The bear had most likely been awakened early from its hibernation, attracted by the bleeding, and finished it off. I needed that elk. It was the first decent hunt I had in months, so I attempted to scare the bear off. It didn't work. I shot at the bear's feet with my crossbow. It just made the bear angry and it charged me. I nearly lost my life to that bear but I managed to kill it. As I went to collect the elk, I heard a small cry come from inside the cave. It was a bear cub. I knew she would never survive alone during the winter, so I decided to take her in and we've been together ever since," said Bernhart. He then got up from his seat and stirred the food in the pot.

"Oh Goodness, That's incredible," said Alice.

"Well, the food is ready." Bernhart scooped the soup into wooden bowls and handed them to everyone. After eating dinner, they sat around talking with each other for hours.

"It's getting late. Alice, you can use the guest room and I have some extra blankets for you two to sleep out here," said Bernhart.

"No problem," replied Matthew. Bernhart got up from his seat, went into his room for a few moments, and returned with a stack of blankets and pillows. He handed them both a pillow and some blankets.

Alice got up from the couch and yawned. "Good night, everyone." She gathered her things and went to the guest room.

"Well, goodnight fellas," said Bernhart.

"Goodnight," replied Matthew.

"Night," added Ike.

Bernhart then went to his room. Matthew and Ike spread the blankets over the couch and prepared for bed. Matthew lay under the covers as the fire in the fireplace began to die. He closed his eyes to fall asleep.

Matthew awoke to the smell and sound of bacon crackling on a cast iron griddle. Bernhart was cooking breakfast over the fireplace. He sat up on the couch. Ike and Alice were already dressed, up and about.

"Good morning," Alice announced as she walked by behind the couch. Matthew turned around to see her. She placed a basket of fruit on the wooden table. Ike was setting the table while eating an apple.

"Guten Morgen," said Bernhart when he noticed Matthew was awake. "Breakfast is almost ready."

Matthew got up from the couch and got ready for the day. He folded up the blankets and sat down.

"Breakfast is ready," announced Bernhart. He raked the food off the griddle and onto a plate, then placed it on the table. They all sat around the table to eat. There was a pot of porridge in the middle of the table with a jar of honey and a small bowl of blueberries. They each scooped the warm porridge into their wooden bowls and passed around the fruit and bacon.

"So, where are you all off to this morning?" asked Bernhart.

"We're heading north," answered Alice as she put honey on her porridge.

"Heading north. To where in particular?" asked Bernhart.

Matthew, Ike, and Alice exchanged glances with each other. "That's classified. Important council business," replied Ike.

Bernhart softly chuckled. "Very well. You know, Matthew, your father was secretive about his missions, too."

"You knew my dad?"

"I'd met him a few times. I thought I'd told you this. Anyway, he also never spoke about his missions. I don't know if the council asked him not to or if he just preferred not to. Has there been any new information about him?" Bernhart scooped some more porridge into his mouth.

"No. I haven't heard anything," Matthew answered solemnly.

"This porridge is delicious. Where did you get it?" Alice asked, desperate to change the subject.

After breakfast, they packed their bags and stood outside Bernhart's home. "Well, good luck on the rest of your journey," said Bernhart. He shook everyone's hands.

"Thank you for having us, Bernhart," said Alice.

"Thanks again," said Ike.

Alice and Ike stepped off Bernhart's porch and walked a few feet away.

"Feel free to come by anytime Auf Wiedersehen.," declared Bernhart.

"Okay, thanks," said Matthew as he turned to walk away.

"I'm sure your fathers okay," Bernhart assured.

"Thanks," Matthew repeated. He joined Alice and Ike and summoned the stagecoach. They headed off. Bernhart's cottage was in the direction they had to go, anyway.

"Are we going in the right direction?" Alice asked as they rode along. They had been traveling for almost two hours.

"Let me see that map," asked Ike.

Matthew took out the golden book and handed it to him. He flipped to the back of the book where he found a map.

"See, here's Anvilholde. Here's the Iron Peak Mountains, and here's the road we're on now." Ike moved his fingers across the map. He then flipped the book to a page with another map—this time, a world map. "We then head to the coast to Albatross Point." He handed back the book to Matthew.

"Alright. We're on the right track," declared Matthew.

They continued down the road for a few hours. Eventually, they began to descend from the mountains and into a light forest shrouded in a light fog. They continued to travel until they heard loud voices up ahead.

"Come on, let's go!" demanded one impatient voice.

"No way!" replied another voice.

"It'll be alright. Let's just find another way around," a third voice spoke.

"We don't have all day! Let's go!" ordered the first voice.

"No way!" replied the second voice again. The owner of the second voice ran down the road toward them. Suddenly, a small tan goat penetrated the fog and approached Matthew, Ike, and Alice.

"Help!" pleaded the tan goat.

The stagecoach immediately came to a stop. "What's wrong?" asked Alice as she hopped off the driver's seat.

"There's a monster over there," warned the tan goat.

"Don't worry, we can handle any monsters," boasted Ike. He climbed off the driver's seat.

"You'll help us?" asked the tan goat.

Matthew sat in the driver's seat in silence, stunned by the talking goat.

"We'd be happy to assist," Alice assured.

Matthew climbed off the driver's seat and put the stagecoach back into its chest. The four of them walked back down the road where they were met by two other goats standing in front of a massive brick bridge. One goat had long black-colored fur and was the biggest of the three. The other goat was white and was smaller than the black goat, but bigger than the tan one.

"There you are," worried the black goat, walking up to them.

"Hey, these people said they'd help us," announced the tan goat.

"Whatever, let's just go," insisted the white goat.

"Alright, let's go," said Ike.

The group headed across the bridge. After a few minutes, they could no longer see either side of the bridge due to the thick fog surrounding them.

"What was that?" asked the tan goat, stopping to look around. Everyone else stopped as well.

"I didn't hear anything," said Matthew.

"Me neither," added the black goat.

"Please, not this again. Let's keep moving," complianed the white goat.

"We'll be alright, as long as we stay together," Alice reassured the tan goat. The goat nodded to Alice and the group started to move again.

A sudden unease feeling washed over Matthew. Moments later, the shadow of a large figure rocketed over the side of the bridge, up into the air. The shadow landed in front of them with a crash, shaking the bridge.

"Monster!" shouted the tan goat. He ran to hide behind Alice.

Matthew, Ike, and the black goat jumped forward to confront the monster.

The troll stood eight feet tall. It was a gorilla-like creature with horns. Its long, wild, and matted dark green fur covered everything but its face, chest, and inner arms. Its face was covered with pale green skin, yellow eyes, and two large tusk-like teeth that protruded from its lower jaw.

"There's a toll to cross this bridge. Pay up," demanded the troll.

"Uh … okay. How much?" asked Matthew.

"One hundred gold coins."

"What?! We can't afford that!" complained Ike.

"Well then. Looks like you'll be forced to make a swift exit from my bridge."

Matthew and Ike drew their swords. The bridge wasn't large enough for Matthew, Ike, and the black goat to properly maneuver around the troll. They were certainly at a huge disadvantage. The troll bared his sharp teeth and prepared to pounce when suddenly Alice stepped forward.

"Hold on, Hold on!" she interjected, holding up her hands. "Must we resort to violence?"

"What do you have in mind instead?" asked the troll.

"A wager. If I win, you let us all across the bridge safely."

"Hmm. And if I win?"

"Umm…. What do you want?" asked Alice.

The troll put his massive hand on his chin and thought to himself for a moment.

"If I win, I get to eat you all. It's been a while since I've had children to eat."

"Uhhh … Alice," Ike began.

"Deal!" Alice accepted without hesitation.

"Alice!?" asked a worried Matthew. Alice turned to face them. "I've got this. Trust me."

"What's your wager?" asked the troll.

"I'll ask you a question and then you can ask me one. The first one to stump the other wins," Alice declared.

"Fine, ask your question."

Alice thought for a moment. "I am not alive, but I grow. I don't have lungs, but I need air. I don't have a mouth, but water kills me. What am I?"

The troll fell silent for several moments. "Easy, fire," answered the troll.

"Fine, ask your question," she replied.

"Alright." The troll was quiet for a minute. "I'm always there, some distance away. Somewhere between land or sea and sky, I lay. You may move towards me, yet distant I stay. What am I?" asked the troll.

Alice thought for a few moments. "The horizon," she replied.

The troll scoffed. "Ask your next question."

Alice paced back and forth on the bridge for a few moments. "Oh … I've got one. What flies when it's born, lies when it's alive, and runs when it's dead?"

The troll thought for several moments. He thought longer than he had for the other ones.

I got him, Alice thought. "Do you give up?" she asked the troll, smirking.

"Snow … it's snow," answered the troll. He sounded pleased with himself and his answer wiped the smirk from Alice's face.

"Very well, ask your question," she grumbled.

The troll pondered for a minute. "This old one runs forever, but never moves at all. He has no lungs nor throat, but still a mighty roaring call. What am I?"

Alice thought about it for several moments. She had nothing. Alice walked over to the side of the bridge and looked out at the landscape. Even though they were making their way out of the mountains, the bridge was still pretty high up. Alice looked out on the picturesque foggy mountain and forest landscape. There was even a waterfall off in the distance.

"Well?" asked the Troll. His face was growing into a smirk.

"Just a moment. I gave you time to think," she replied. Alice acted calm even though on the inside, she was quickly beginning to panic. She turned back around and stared at the landscape. Alice was desperate for something to jog her memory or give her a clue.

"Time's up," declared the troll. His face slowly broke out into a toothy grin.

A pit formed in Matthew's stomach. The Goats exchanged looks of panic and worry.

Suddenly, it came to her. "A waterfall!" Alice shouted, spinning around to face him. "It's a waterfall."

The troll's look of self-satisfaction drained from his face. An expression of anger and frustration replaced it. "Ask. Your. Question." The troll spoke through gritted teeth.

"That wasn't even that hard," Alice lied. She then paced back and forth for a few moments.

"What is never late, can go anywhere, fits in one's pocket, but can't be touched?" asked Alice.

The troll fell silent for several moments. "Well?" asked Alice.

"Wait a minute," said the troll, putting up his hand. He began to pace back and forth on the bridge, muttering to himself. His face of annoyance, frustration, and anger transformed into one of shock. Alice folded her arms and smirked.

"Well?" she asked again.

The troll continued to mumble to himself. "Time's up. I win," declared Alice.

The troll quickly turned and leapt across the bridge at

Alice and loudly roared in her face. Alice turned pale white. He balled up and raised his massive fist to her like he was about to effortlessly punch her off the bridge. Alice stood there, frozen with fear.

The troll simply lowered his hand and turned to the side of the bridge. "Get off my bridge." He then hoisted himself off the bridge and disappeared into the fog beneath.

The color returned to Alice's face as she breathed a sigh of relief. "Come everyone, move along now," she said, quickly moving forward. The others stood in place, still shocked. "Off the bridge! Now!" she shouted, this time with more force.

The group fled to the other side of the bridge. Once they were safe on the other side, they stopped at a fork in the road.

"This is where we part ways, humans," stated the white goat. "Thank you for helping us!" exclaimed the tan goat. He jumped around Alice happily.

"I don't think we can ever repay you for helping us," thanked the black goat as he walked up to them.

"Yeah ... you really ... helped us out of a jam. Thanks," added the white goat.

"It was all Alice," acknowledged Matthew.

"She came through for us all," added Ike.

Alice began to blush from all the praise. "Oh please, It was nothing, really." She waved everyone off.

"Let's get going boys, long journey ahead of us," stated the white goat. He began to walk down the road to the left.

"Goodbye!" replied the little tan goat as he and the black goat went after their brother.

Matthew, Ike, and Alice headed down the road to the right. After several minutes of walking, Ike asked a question.

"Hey Alice, what was the answer to that riddle?"

"Pardon?" asked Alice.

"You know. What is never late, can go anywhere, fits in one's pocket but can't be touched?"

Alice shrugged. "Oh … that … I don't know, I just made it up," Alice admitted with a smile.

"You cheated?" asked Matthew. He looked surprised. Ike burst out laughing as they continued their way down the road.

"What?" asked Alice. "It worked, didn't it? He was going to eat us, remember?"

"Fair enough," Matthew replied as he summoned the stagecoach.

CHAPTER 13

THE SWAMP OF FEARS

"**P**lease don't tell me we're going through there?!" asked Ike.

Matthew, Ike, and Alice all sat in the driver's seat of the stagecoach. It had been several hours since they parted ways with the three Billy goats. They had finally made it out of the mountains and were one step closer to their destination, Albatross Point.

"Yeah. What's wrong?" asked Matthew.

"What's wrong?! What's wrong is that's the Swamp of Fears," Ike annouced worriedly.

"The Swamp … of Fears?" Alice repeated, her tone sarcastic.

"I expected Matthew to have never heard of it, but you, Alice? For shame," countered Ike.

"Just tell us what's wrong. Why can't we go through there?" asked Matthew.

"Alright, alright," replied Ike, putting up his hands in surrender. "My older brother, Dominic, once told me this story. About fifty years ago there was this village near here where children had been constantly and mysteriously disappearing for decades. Every time a child would go missing, the whole village would search for them. I'm talking everybody, like all the villagers and militiamen. They'd put up wanted posters, offered rewards, used tracking spells and dogs, but they would always never find anything. Then out of nowhere, after going missing for several days, the missing children would just wander back into the village from the nearby woods. The children were now all old and wrinkly with grey-haired. When the villagers would try to question the kids about what happened to them or where they were the whole time, they got nothing. The children were now so old they could barely speak and their memories had faded, just like an old person. They could barely walk or feed themselves anymore, they were so old now. This apparently went on for decades, all until one night. One night while patrolling the village, a member of the village's militia heard some strange noises coming from one of the houses. The man went to investigate the strange noise when he saw strange lights coming from the basement of an old lady who lived there. The man saw an old woman performing some kind of ritual on a tied-up child. She was a witch who was draining the child of their youth. The man quickly left and returned with the entire militia and several villagers.

They tried to confront the woman, but she was too powerful for them. She managed to escape the village but the villagers were hot on her trail. They managed to corner her in the nearby swamp and charged in after her. To save herself, she cast a spell on the swamp, forcing all who enter it to witness their greatest fears. The few who managed to make it back out of the swamp alive forbade anyone else from going in there after her. Soon after, the tales of what happened quickly spread around the kingdoms. Beware of the Swamp of Fears. They say the witch still lives there, to this day, draining unsuspecting victims of their youth, intent on living forever," said Ike.

Matthew and Alice were unmoved by his story. "And you honestly believe all of this?" Alice asked unconvinced.

"Yes … no … look. I don't know if the story is real or not, but we shouldn't go through that swamp. Haunted or not, let's just go around it. It'll just add another day at the most," reasoned Ike.

"We don't have time for this. Let's just go through it. It's only a few hours. We have the stagecoach, we'll be okay," replied Matthew.

"He's right. If we just stick together we'll be alright," Alice reassured.

Ike sighed. "Fine. Let's just get through this as fast as possible," he continued.

The three of them continued down the road as they officially entered the swamp. Ike refused to ride through the swamp outside, so he rode inside the coach while Matthew and Alice sat in the driver's seat. As they traveled along the road, the stagecoach began to slow down until it came to a stop.

"Something the matter?" Alice asked. Ike opened the door of the stagecoach and stuck his head outside.

"What's going on? Why have we stopped?" he paniked.

"I don't know," Matthew replied. Matthew climbed out of the driver's seat. He saw the wheels of the stagecoach slowly spinning in the thick mud of the swamp. "Well, looks like we're on foot from here," said Matthew. Alice climbed out of the driver's seat while Ike exited the stagecoach. Matthew put the coach back in its chest.

"I gotta bad feeling about this," Ike grumbled.

They continued on foot through the swamp. The path they were on narrowed as swampy pools of water ran alongside them. The swamp was cold and the once sunny skies turned a uniform grey as a light mist cloaked the ground. The swamp had little plant life besides tall grasses that gathered around the murky pools, a few floating plants, and a scattering of trees. As they continued, the path became so narrow that the trio had to walk in a single-file line: Matthew in front, Ike in the back, and Alice in the middle.

The loud, sudden cry of a crow startled them. They all jumped.

"What was that?!" panicked Ike.

"Over there," said Matthew pointing to a crow sitting high in a nearby tree. The crow let out another loud cry before flying off.

"Well, that was ominous," Ike smirked.

"Let's just keep moving," replied Alice.

The three of them continued to travel through the swamp for an hour.

"Should we take a break?" asked Matthew.

"I'm alright. I just want to get out of here as soon as possible," said Alice, holding herself.

"What about you, Ike?" asked Matthew.

They turned around, but Ike had disappeared.

"Ike? Ike?!" called Matthew. He tried to sound braver than he felt.

"Ike? This isn't funny," called Alice, her voice beginning to shake. Their voices echoed in the swamp for a few moments before falling silent again. Now, all they could hear were the ambient noises of the animals and insects of the swamp.

"Oh Dear, what do we do now?" Alice's voice was shaking.

"We have to stay together. As long as we're together we have a better chance of finding Ike and getting out of here," Matthew said calmly.

Matthew and Alice continued down the road. As they traveled, the dirt road in front of them began to disappear from view. It was submerged in ankle-deep, muddy water and tall, thick foliage. Matthew and Alice waded through the foliage as it thickened. Matthew drew his sword and attempted to cut a path through the tall grasses. He made it to the other side and back to the dry dirt road. Matthew turned around, waiting for Alice to come through.

After a few moments, Alice didn't emerge from the

foliage.

"Alice?!" he called.

There was silence. Matthew was alone.

"Matthew! Alice!" called Ike, walking through the misty swamp. "I knew coming through here was a bad idea." Then, in a mocking tone of voice, he said, "*It's only a few hours. We have the stagecoach. If we just stick together, we'll be fine.*"

Ike continued to walk until he came to a clearing. There, he heard a familiar voice.

"Oh, there he is," annouced a voice.

Ike instantly recognized the voice.

"Mom?" He was stunned. Ike's mother was standing there in the swamp. He ran to her. "Mom!? How did you get out here? By the way, I'm sorry for running away. I should have told you, but we're trying to save the world," he continued.

His mom looked unenthused to see him.

"What does it matter anyway, Ike? You've always been a disappointment anyway," she replied calmly.

"What?" Her words cutting him like a knife.

"You were never going to amount to anything, unlike your siblings," she calmly continued.

Ike stood there, still stunned, trying to form a sentence. Ike's father emerged from some nearby foliage.

"I told you, Evelyn, he's going to be dependent on us for the rest of his miserable life," he added.

"Dad!?" said Ike bewildered.

"Well, there's always Kya. Hopefully, she won't be

such a huge failure like this one," his mom said, gesturing to Ike.

"Well, four out of five isn't bad," his dad replied. As he said this, the rest of his siblings walked out of the foliage.

"You can't expect him to live up to us. I mean just look at him," sneered Dominic. Dominic was in his late twenties. He was tall with brown skin and short black curly hair.

"I'm just glad we're finally being honest with him. It's time he learned the truth," added Samara. She was in her mid-twenties. She was slightly shorter than Dominic and was a bit stockier. She had brown skin and brown eyes with long curly hair.

"I just like to pretend he doesn't exist," shrugged Cedric. He was in his mid-twenties. He was taller than Samara but shorter than Dominic. He was also stockier than them both, with brown skin and short black hair.

"Why are you all saying these things?!" Ike asked. They approached Ike, closing in on him until they surrounded him completely.

"Because it's time we were finally honest with you and that you're honest with yourself, Ike. You're a disgrace to us and this family," his mom declared, her voice still calm.

"Frankly, I'm embarrassed to call you my son," his dad added, sounding just as calm.

Ike drew his sword. "Shut up!" he shouted. He swung through all of them in a single, fluid motion. His family evaporated into mist. He stood there, alone again, in the swamp.

Alice continued through the swamp on her own. As she walked, she waved her hands at the buzzing insects flying around her.

"Matthew! Ike! Oh dear," she called, her voice shaking.

A new path, flanked by tall trees, was set before her. As Alice continued to walk down the forested path, she began to notice they were draped in white. As she continued to walk, she noticed the white was actually thin webs on the trees. Alice kept her head down and held herself as she continued forward. The webs on the trees became thicker and more plentiful. Soon, Alice came to a clearing shrouded in white. It was surrounded by trees and smothered in thick, silky white webs. The webs draped from one tree to the next, creating something around the clearing that resembled a fence. The ground was covered in thick webs, making it harder for her to even walk.

The air was filled with the sound of rustling leaves. Alice took a deep breath to gather her nerves and quickly moved to the other side of the clearing where her exit was blocked by heavy ropes of webs. Desperate to escape, she began to claw at the webs to create an opening. Suddenly, the hair on the back of her neck began to rise and she quickly swung around. She spotted a large spider, the size of a dinner plate, having descended from the trees. Its legs twitched as it hung in front of her face. In a moment of shock and instinct, she immediately batted the spider away from her so hard it flew across the clearing and splattered on a tree trunk.

The sound of rustling leaves immediately turned to silence. Dozens of large spiders began descending from the treetops. Alice cried out in panic as she franticly attempted to bat away as many of the spiders as she could, but there were too many of them. The spiders began wrapping her in a cocoon as another spider, the size of a small car, made its way down from the treetops.

Alice struggled but the webs were too strong and sticky. As the giant spider began to close in on her, when she noticed she could see her breath. Suddenly, a blonde-haired woman in white appeared. She flew down and, with a blast from her hands, began to freeze the spiders. The spiders crawled off Alice and became preoccupied with the flying blonde woman. Alice was still trapped in a web cocoon. It was beginning to harden due to the extreme cold, but was still too tough for Alice to break free.

Suddenly, Alice's stepmother, Mrs. Liddell, appeared overhead. She began to franticly claw at the cocoon Alice was trapped in. Mrs. Liddell managed to pull Alice free from the web cocoon. Once freed, Alice and Mrs. Liddell hurried down the path, while the flying blonde woman continued to battle the hordes of massive spiders around them. The two of them franticly clawed at the frozen webs to create an exit. Eventually they created a hole large enough for one of them to crawl through.

"Go Alice, hurry!" Mrs. Liddell shouted at Alice. She began to crawl through the hole they created.

Alice made it safely through the hole. Instead of following her Mrs. Liddell had already run to help the mystery woman, who was now overrun with spiders. Safe on the other side, Alice had finally managed a good look at the other woman who had also helped her. She was an older woman with long blonde hair and blue eyes. She locked eyes with Alice and smiled as the spiders began to climb all over her body. Then, she exploded in a blast of extreme cold. It knocked Alice several feet back, and she landed in the normal swamp.

Alice scrambled to her feet and fled down the road. Tears began to fall from her eyes.

Matthew continued down the path. He had been wandering alone for what felt like hours. After some time, he spotted a man standing in the road.

Matthew was torn. He remembered Ike's story, but he was desperate. He grabbed the hilt of his sword and walked up to the man. The man turned around. Matthew recognized the man immediately. It was his father, Leon.

Matthew had only seen his father in a picture given to him by his mother. The man in front of him had the appearance of an older man in his late thirties, but there was no mistaking who it was. Matthew was stunned.

"Dad?" he asked tentatively.

Leon was tall and handsome. He was slim but muscular, with brown skin, brown eyes, and short black hair. His possessed a clean-shaven face.

Leon looked over Matthew. "How did you find me!?" Leon interrogated.

"Excuse me?" asked Matthew.

"I thought that when I left you with your mother, I wouldn't have to see your miserable face again," he replied.

Matthew gritted his teeth. "Well, you can just go back to whatever hole you crawled out of. I'll find my way outta here myself," he replied.

"Well, you're doing a bang-up job so far. Tell me, where are your little friends? Gonna get them killed following you," retorted Leon.

"I've got a job to do, no thanks to you. So, you can do what you're best at and leave me alone," Matthew snapped as he walked past Leon.

"I guess I shouldn't be surprised you turned out like this. Your mother certainly did a piss poor job of raising you," replied Leon.

Matthew was fuming. He quickly drew his sword and swung it at Leon. Leon instantly blocked with his own sword. The two locked blades.

"I guess I hit a nerve there, momma's boy," mocked Leon.

"Shut up!" Matthew shouted. He jumped back, changing his sword into the Sword of Wind. He sent a quick barrage of wind blades.

Leon blocked the barrage and leaped at him with a heavy overhand swing. Matthew responded with a swing of his sword, swinging as hard as he could, and sent a powerful gust of wind. The wind knocked Leon out of the air and onto his back. Matthew used his sword to create a tornado and sent it down the path toward Leon. Leon got to his feet and, without effort, cut the tornado in half.

Matthew changed his sword to the Sword of Water and launched himself at Leon. Leon blocked him and went on the offensive with a flurry of attacks. Matthew tried his best to counter them, but several attacks got through, cutting his cheek, his shoulder, his forearms, and his thigh. Matthew could barely feel the pain—he was running on adrenaline. Leon then delivered a swift kick to the stomach. It sent Matthew stumbling back several feet. Matthew fell to one knee, his left arm wrapped around his stomach, his right arm holding his sword.

"Pathetic. Is that the best you've got, momma's boy?" Leon stood over Matthew and mocked him.

Matthew took his right arm and swung his sword as hard and fast as he could. He pulled all the water out of a nearby pool of swamp and blindsided Leon before he could react. The water hit Leon so hard that it launched him into a nearby tree. The tree broke in half. Leon, upon making contact with the tree, evaporated into mist.

Matthew got to his feet. His stomach pained him and his cuts began to sting. Luckily, they weren't very deep. He sheathed his sword and continued down the path until he came to a large clearing with a dead end.

"Great," grumbled Matthew.

Something began to rustle nearby. Matthew drew his sword and Ike stumbled out from the bushes.

"Ike?!" he asked surprised.

"Matthew! Man, am I glad to see you," said Ike, rushing over to him.

"Wait! This could be another trick." Matthew stopped

in his tracks.

Ike slowly stuck out his hand and poked Matthew in his chest a few times.

"I'm real," Matthew asserted. Ike went in for a hug.

"Jeez, man. You look like you've been through some stuff," replied Ike.

"I don't want to talk about it. Have you seen Alice?"

Ike shook his head no. Alice made a sudden appearance and stepped out from the nearby foliage. She was wiping tears from her eyes until she looked up and saw them.

"Matthew! Ike!" Alice shouted with excitement. Smiling, she ran over to them.

"Wait! How do we know you're real and not some trick?" hesitated Ike. He put up his hand to block her. Alice's face dropped.

"But, It's me … really." Alice whimpered, almost on the verge of tears again.

Matthew and Ike looked at each other. Ike cautiously moved toward her as he attempted to poke Alice in her chest. She quickly slapped Ike's hand.

"Okay, you're real," said a relieved Ike.

"My, what a pretty sight," spoke a woman's voice.

Matthew and Ike drew their swords at the sound of the voice. The trio looked around.

"Up there,"observed Alice. She pointed to a woman sitting high up in a tree. She was a woman in her late fifties, wearing rags. She had long, wild black hair with streaks of grey.

"It's the witch!" shouted Ike, pointing at her.

"Ike. Don't be rude!" responded Alice, then whispered to him. "You want to get on her bad side if she is?"

"What brings three children into my swamp?" demanded the woman.

"Um … we're just trying to pass through. I'm sorry, we didn't know anyone actually lived here," replied Matthew.

The crow landed on the woman's shoulder. "Even adults know to steer clear of this place. You must be either very brave or stupid to enter here," the woman retorted.

Matthew, Ike, and Alice remained silent.

"My little friend here has been watching your progress." She continued gesturing to the crow. The crow let out a loud cry.

"Are you the one behind what we've been through, what we've seen?" Ike accused in anger.

"No. This swamp always has a way of showing people what they need to see. Anything you saw here was of your design," she replied.

"Well … we'd like to leave now … please … thank you," requested Alice. She was peeking out from behind Matthew.

"Once you've dealt with what the swamp has shown you, then you can leave," the woman said with a laugh.

"We've already done that," Matthew replied.

"Well, since you've already survived what the swamp showed you, you can leave anytime you want to. You're already on the right path," she replied. She pointed to the path they were already standing on. The path now continued off into the distance.

"Um … okay. Thank you," said Alice. The woman nodded.

The three of them were about to head off when Ike said, "I guess you aren't the witch from the story who steals her youth from unsuspecting kids, after all."

The woman replied "I only do that when I get too old. Do you think I look old?" The woman began to touch her slightly wrinkled face. She smirked at the three of them.

"Uhhh—" Ike began as he quickly pushed Matthew and Alice down the road.

The rest of the trip out of the swamp was relatively silent.

They boarded the driver's seat of the stagecoach and traveled down the road to Albatross Point. None of them had said so much as a word since they escaped the swamp.

After a few hours of traveling, Matthew finally broke the silence.

"Do you guys mind if we stop for a break?"

"Alright," Alice replied. Ike nodded in agreement. The three of them pulled over on the side of the road and went inside the stagecoach.

Matthew and Ike sat at the large wooden table in the dining room. "Oh dear, you're injured. I can patch you up, if you'd like," suggested Alice.

"It's not as bad as it looks," he said as he winced, touching the cut on his cheek.

Alice rolled her eyes and pulled some medical supplies from her bag. She began to tend to his wounds. After

Matthew's cuts were dealt with, Alice sat on the opposite side of the table to rest.

CHAPTER 14

SAILING AWAY

After a few minutes of awkward silence, Ike spoke. "So, no one wants to talk about what happens in the swamp?"

Matthew and Alice continued to stare off into space, lost in their own thoughts.

Ike sighed. "Well, I guess I'll go first," he said. "I saw my family in there. Matthew … I haven't been entirely honest about why I wanted to come with you. Part of the reason I wanted to come with you was because I figured if I helped you—if I did something important—I wouldn't feel like an embarrassment to my family. Like I'm everyone's shadow. But during the time that we've traveled together, you've become my friends. I don't want you to feel like I'm using you for my own reasons. I'm sorry."

Matthew was silent for a few moments before he answered. "It's alright. I don't know if I would've made it this far without you."

Ike formed a weak smile. "I'm with you till the end, man," boasted Ike.

The room fell silent again. "I supposed … I'll go next … I saw my mom in the swamp. She saved me … from giant spiders," Alice uttered.

"That sounds nice. Well, except for the part about the giant spiders," replied Ike.

"At least, I think it was my mom. I never really got a chance to meet my real mother. I've only ever seen her in pictures. She was a witch and died when I was a baby. But when I saw her there, I just knew it was her," asserted Alice.

"What happened to her?" asked Matthew.

"She died at the battle of Highstar. She was a hero. My dad says I look just like her and this black ribbon is all I have of her … But the strangest thing was, I saw my step-mother, too. She also helped me."

"Why is that strange?" asked Ike.

"Because … I haven't the faintest idea why she showed up. We've never really been particulary close."

"Maybe that's not how you really feel," suggested Ike.

Alice fell silent for a few moments. "I'm afraid of replacing my real mom. I don't even have any memories of her, like Viola. I was far too young. I don't want to … abandon her. To replace her with someone else," admitted Alice.

"Maybe that's the point of it. You don't have to

choose between them," suggested Ike.

Alice went quiet again before she spoke. "Perhaps you're right. The reason I wanted to come along with you, Matthew, was to try and be a hero just like my mom, but I don't feel like much of a hero now," lamented Alice. Tears started to trickle from her eyes.

"Are you kidding me!?" Ike raised his voice.

Matthew and Alice jumped but remained silent. "Without your help, we probably wouldn't have found that map or gotten across that bridge, you've been a big help, Alice," Ike declared, standing up.

Alice sat there for a few moments. She wiped the tears from her eyes and formed a slight smile. "I suppose you're right. Thank you," she replied weakly.

Matthew remained silent. "Matthew, what did you see in the swamp?" asked Alice.

"You seemed the worst off of any of us," added Ike.

"I don't want to talk about it," replied Matthew.

"Come on, Matthew," encouraged Ike.

"You can tell us anything, we're your friends," reasoned Alice.

"Just drop it," he said firmly.

"No!" Ike replied. He walked over and sat next to Alice at the picnic table.

Matthew got up from the table and walked up the stairs and into one of the bedrooms, where he closed the door. Ike sighed.

"Oh dear, what do we do?" Alice asked.

"Well, we wait until he wants to talk, and then we

need to just be there for him," Ike replied.

After an hour, Matthew emerged from the bedroom.

"If you guys are hungry … I got some sandwiches," he offered.

"Thank you," replied Alice. Matthew shared his sandwiches with Ike and Alice and they had lunch. "We should probably get going," he annouced.

The three of them exited the stagecoach, got back in the driver's seat, and continued down the road. By the time the three of them reached Albatross Point the sun was beginning to set.

Albatross Point was a small inland island connected to the mainland by a long stone bridge. It was once a small port town before it was damaged by a storm and left abandoned. The town found new life as a haven for adventurers, bounty hunters, and pirates alike. They crossed the stone bridge into the town and continued to walk along the boardwalk. The boardwalk was filled with shops and bars. There were dozens of ships of various sizes docked in the distance. The trio stopped at the wooden railing of the boardwalk, above the beach.

"So, I guess we look for a ride now," said Ike.

Matthew stared out at the ocean as seagulls flew overhead and the smell of the ocean filled his nose. "We should split up. We'll cover more ground that way," he reasoned.

"Be discreet, we don't want to raise any suspicions. Let's meet back here later," Alice suggested.

Matthew and Ike nodded in agreement. The three of them headed off to find someone willing to offer them a ride. After a few hours, Alice returned to find Matthew standing on the boardwalk where they had agreed to meet alone. He stared out at the dark ocean, watching the waves crash against the beach.

"Any good news?" Alice asked with hope.

"No," he replied flatly.

"Oh."

Matthew continued to stare at the ocean.

"Where's Ike?" she asked. Matthew shrugged.

"Well, he should be here by now. Shouldn't we go try and find him? What if he's in trouble?"

He sighed. "Alright. Calm down."

They headed down the boardwalk looking for Ike. After several minutes of searching, Alice spotted him.

"There he is." She pointed through the window of a tavern. Matthew and Alice entered the tavern. Ike was sitting at a round wooden table with a large pile of coins in the middle. Several people were sitting around the table as well. One of the people sitting at the table was shuffling a deck of cards and began to deal them to Ike and the other players sitting at the table. Matthew and Alice made their way through the crowd of onlookers over to Ike.

"Ike, what's the meaning of this?" she asked.

"Oh, hey guys. I'm in the middle of a game right now," replied Ike.

"You're supposed to be looking for a ride, not gambling," grumbled Matthew.

"Relax, I got a plan." Ike looked over his cards. The other players looked over their cards and glanced around at each other. Ike played several rounds of cards for what felt like hours, losing a few hands but winning others. The other players sitting around the table would leave the game after losing enough of their money. The empty chairs were quickly filled by new challengers from the crowd gathered around the table. Ike along with another man sitting at the table had managed to do quite well for themselves. The man was wearing a feathered tricorn hat with a navy-blue coat.

"You're quite good at this game," commented Alice. She stood next to Ike at the table.

"Thanks."

"As fun as it's been taking all y'all money, this is gonna be my last hand," said the man in the tricorn hat. The goblin sitting at the table shuffled the cards and began to deal them out to the players. They spent a few moments looking over their hands.

"I open," announced a man at the table. The man looked over his cards again before taking five gold coins from his pile and tossing them in the pot.

The goblin sitting next to him looked over his cards. "I fold," replied the goblin, putting his cards face down. Next to the goblin, a woman was sitting next to him.

"I'm out," added the woman. Next to the woman was an Orc, who also folded. After looking over his cards, he folded, too.

"I call," announced Ike. He tossed five gold coins from his pile into the pot.

The man looked at his cards again. "I raise," replied the man in the hat. He then tossed three platinum coins into the pot.

Ike looked over his cards. "Looks like it's too rich for your blood," smirked the man in the hat as he began to reach for the pot.

"Hold it," replied Ike. "I raise." Ike pushed his pile of coins into the pot and took his sword from his waist. He placed it on the pot.

"Oh Ike, not your sword!" Alice pleaded. The man reached over and grabbed Ike's sword. He partially unsheathed the sword to inspect it. He then closed the sword and put it back on the table. Ike and the man looked at each other for several moments.

"Nice sword. I'll be happy to take it from ya," boasted the man. The man pushed his coins into the pile and revealed his cards. The onlookers erupted in cheers.

"Those are pretty impressive," replied Ike. "If only I didn't have this."

Ike spread out his cards on the table. The onlookers erupted into even louder cheers. Ike raked the pile of coins into his bag while the other players, disappointed, rose from the table. The onlookers dispersed as Ike hooked his sword back to his waist and raked the coins into his bag.

"Most impressive," cheered Alice.

"Thanks," replied Ike.

"How does this help us find a ride?" Matthew asked.

"Relax," Ike repeated. "It's all a part of the plan. Tomorrow, phase two begins."

"Any chance we'll be let in on this plan?" asked Alice.

"All in good time."

Alice looked at Matthew. Matthew shrugged. Ike rose from the table and they all left the tavern. They headed back out to the outskirts of town where they summoned the stagecoach again for the night.

Matthew, Alice, and Ike ate dinner and got ready for bed. Matthew sat at the dining room table, staring off into space. Ike and Alice sat in the sitting room. Ike was teaching Alice how to play cards before bed.

"I saw my dad in the swamp," Matthew mumbled. He spoke softly but was clenching his fists tightly.

"Pardon Me?" asked Alice from the other room.

"You're going to have to speak up," added Ike.

Matthew sighed. "I saw my dad in the swamp." He spoke louder so that they could hear him from the other room. Ike and Alice immediately put down their cards, stood up from their seats, and walked over to the wooden table where Matthew was seated. Alice sat beside Matthew and Ike sat across from him.

Matthew began to unclench his fists. "Well … I actually fought him. That's how I got all those cuts. At least, I think it was him. I never actually met him before. All I have is an old picture of him that my mom gave me, but I'm pretty sure it was him." He stared at the table before continuing.

"When I met my uncle, Sterling, he told me that it was my dad who was the Blademaster before me, and one of the ways the sword passes to a new wielder is through the death of the last one. He's already been missing for several weeks now. and at first, I tried to stay positive. But what if he really is dead, and I never got to meet him? I never got to do any of that father-son stuff. Or what if he's alive but he doesn't want to see me? What if that's the whole reason he left in the first place? What if I'm not what he expects?" Matthew's voice began to tremble as his eyes began to water. "Part of the reason I even accepted this sword, and all this, was to try to find him. Now … I'm scared."

"I'm very sorry," said Alice, placing her hand on Matthew's forearm. "We hadn't the faintest idea you were feeling like that."

"Well, you still got us, man. We'll always be there for you," replied Ike with a smile.

Matthew quickly wiped the tears from his eyes.

"Well, I may not know if he's alive or not, but I know he won't be disappointed in the person you've become. And if he is … well then it's you who should be disappointed in him, because you are one of the best people I've ever met." smiled Alice.

"Thanks, guys," said Matthew. He wiped the rest of the tears from his eyes.

Ike and Alice got up from the table and hugged him. After a few moments, Matthew began to hug them back. He formed a weak smile.

"Do you feel better after talking about it?" asked Ike.

Matthew nodded. Alice smiled.

"We should probably get some sleep. We got the rest of Ike's secret plan tomorrow," repliedMatthew. He gave another weak smile as he stood up from the picnic table.

"Okay. Well, good night," annouced Alice. She then

headed into one of the bedrooms.

"Goodnight," replied Matthew.

"Night," said Ike. He patted Matthew on his shoulder and headed into the other bedroom. Matthew followed Ike into the other bedroom and grabbed a cot to sleep in. Matthew fell asleep with ease.

The next morning, Matthew, Ike, and Alice got ready for the day ahead.

Matthew entered the bathroom and began to remove his bandages. His cuts had completely healed—like they were never there in the first place. He ran his hand over his cheek. *That's weird*, he thought. Matthew exited the bathroom and headed downstairs to where Alice and Ike were sitting.

"Welp. Looks like we're out of food," announced Ike.

"Well, maybe if someone didn't do so much snacking, we wouldn't have run out of food so fast," complained Alice.

"We could sit around all day and point fingers about how this happened—" began Ike.

"You ate our food," interrupted Alice.

"Or, we can just eat back in town. I'll even pay," Ike suggested.

"Very well," accepted Alice.

"Sounds good," replied Matthew. The three of them packed up the stagecoach and headed back across the stone bridge into Albatross Point. In town they found a tavern and ordered breakfast. After breakfast, the three of them stood on the boardwalk.

"So … what's phase two of this plan?" asked Matthew.

"Right there!" Ike said, pointing to a small shack on the edge of the boardwalk.

"So, your plan was to rent a sailboat?!" she asked.

Ike smirked. "Yes … I'm guessing based on your tone that you disapprove."

"What about trying to find someone to take us?" asked Matthew.

"We couldn't find anyone, remember? And you said time is of the essence," Ike replied.

"Do you even know how to sail a boat?" asked Alice.

"My sister taught me a thing or two. She's in the royal navy," replied Ike.

"Do you even know how to navigate on the seas?" asked Alice.

"We'll figure it out. We have a map, a compass, and the stars. How hard could it be?" suggested Ike.

"Well, I guess it could work," reasoned Matthew.

Alice sighed. "alright. If we're going to do this, we'll need much more supplies in case something happens."

"Okay. I'll get the boat and you guys get the supplies. Meet back here," decided Ike.

He entered the shack while Matthew and Alice headed off for supplies. After an hour, Matthew and Alice returned to the front of the shack.

"Where is Ike? He said to meet back here." Alice was holding several bags in her hands. Matthew shrugged. He was holding a small wooden crate.

Ike walked up to the two of them standing in front of the shack. "The boat's over here, guys," said Ike.

Matthew and Alice followed Ike to the boat down by the docks. "Here she is! It was the biggest one they had. Cost me most of my winnings, but whatever," he said.

It was a midsize wooden sloop sailboat, just big enough to comfortably fit the three of them. They boarded the ship and stored their supplies below deck.

"Let's have a look at that map," asked Ike.

Matthew pulled out the maps and handed them to Ike. Ike studied the maps for several moments with the compass. "We're here and we have to get here, so we head southwest," reasoned Ike as he moved his finger along the path on the map.

"Alright, let's set sail," said Matthew.

Following Ike's orders, Matthew and Alice helped him unfurl the ship's large and tall sails. Matthew drew his sword and changed it to its wind form. He generated wind gusts, pushing the boat along while Ike steered the helm. They continued far out to sea until they could no longer see the Albatross Point shore.

As their sailboat swiftly sailed amongst the waves, Alice went below deck. The below deck was small. There were two small, circular windows on each side of the room. There was some rope, metal lanterns, two long wooden benches with a small storage chest on each side, and some circular life preservers.

After about an hour, Matthew spoke. "My arms are getting tired. Can I stop?"

"Yeah. You can rest for a while. The natural wind should continue to carry us from here," replied Ike. Matthew stopped generating the wind and the sailboat slowed down a bit, catching the natural breeze in its sails. Matthew put the sword down and sat on the ship's wooden bow.

"Are we still heading in the right direction?" asked Matthew. Alice came up from below deck and sat next to Ike.

"Alice, can you hold this?" asked Ike.

She got up and took control of the helm. Ike examined the maps and the compass he had. "We're still heading in the right direction, but I can't tell you how much further though," replied Ike. "Just keep heading southwest, Alice. I'm sure we'll see the island, eventually."

Alice steered the ship for a time while Matthew and Ike played cards. After a long while, Matthew took over steering duty and the three of them ate lunch. They continued to sail until the sun had set. Matthew and Alice lit several lanterns on the ship as Ike steered. The night sky was beautiful and the moon illuminated the dark ocean. Matthew had never seen so many stars before.

"How do we know where we're going?" he asked.

Ike looked down at the compass. It was visible beneath the light of a nearby lantern.

"We're still headed in the right direction," replied Ike. They continued to sail and had their dinner.

"We should probably sleep in shifts, so someone can make sure we stay on course," suggested Alice.

"Alright," agreed Matthew.

"Fine by me. I'll just continue the first shift," said Ike.

"I'll take the next shift. I'm a morning person, any-way," offered Alice.

"I guess that's me with the third shift," said Matthew. He didn't complain—he wasn't a morning person.

Alice and Matthew went below the deck. The two of them attempted to set up makeshift beds on the wooden benches since they couldn't sleep in the carriage. They used the ponchos below deck, some life vests, and a few blankets. Some they already had and some were from below deck. After making herself comfortable, Alice fell asleep. Matthew rolled around for hours trying to get comfortable until he finally fell asleep, too. He awoke the next morning when the boat began to sway, rougher than before, and found Ike asleep below deck in Alice's makeshift bed. He got up from the blankets and went above deck.

Alice was standing on deck holding the helm. "Good morning," she greeted Matthew as walked up and stood beside her.

"Morning. How's everything going?" he asked.

"Well, the sea seems to be getting a bit rougher. But so far, so good. Still haven't spotted this island yet," she answered.

Matthew opened the golden book and examined the map and the compass. "I don't know how close we are, but it seems we're still heading in the right direction."

"I hope so," she replied.

Matthew and Alice ate some sandwiches for break-fast. Off in the distance, they spotted dark clouds. As they continued to sail toward their destination, the sunny blue afternoon sky shifted to a sad grey. Increasingly grey clouds covered the sun. The wind picked up and the boat's swaying roughened.

"I guess we're nearing our destination," assumed Matthew.

As they continued to sail under the cloudy grey skies, a soft rain began. Matthew took over steering duties from Alice after a while. She went below deck and returned with ponchos for the two of them. It was becoming harder for them to stay on course. They put on their ponchos as the rain picked up, and continued to sail along.

Matthew put the maps in his bag to keep them from getting wet. As long as they kept heading in the same direction, they would reach their destination. The rain grew heavier while the wind whipped and the sea became more aggressive. The rocking of the ship must have awakened Ike—he emerged from below deck.

"What's going on?!" Ike shouted over the wind.

"We must've hit a storm! We should turn back!" shouted Alice.

"There usually aren't storms of this caliber this time of year!" shouted Ike. He threw on a poncho.

"What if we're getting closer?" shouted Matthew.

"What!?" Ike and Alice shouted in unison.

"Maybe the storm is a part of the island. Keeps people away," Matthew shouted.

Ike and Alice looked at each other with concern.

"Ike! Take the helm!" shouted Matthew.

THE SECRET OF THE ISLAND

Ike quickly made his way over to Matthew, being careful to not fall overboard from the thrashing ship. He tightly grabbed the helm with both hands using all his strength to stay on course.

"What are you going to do?!" shouted Alice.

"I'm gonna try to keep us from tipping over!" shouted Matthew.

"Hold on!" she screamed, grabbing some nearby rope. "Everyone tie this around your waist!"

They tied the rope around their waists. Alice tied the rope's other end to the ship. Matthew carefully got up from his seat and drew his sword. He then concentrated and changed the sword into its water form. As they continued forward, it began to rain even harder. The wind whipped harder, the waves became taller, and lightning strikes lit up the distant sky as thunder boomed.

Matthew used the sword's water form to stabilize the water around the ship the best he could, while Alice used a bucket to franticly scoop excess water from the ship. The boat rose and fell over several large waves, each larger than the last, until there was finally a lull.

"Looks like the worst of it is over!" shouted Ike over the wind and rain.

Matthew was hit with a bad feeling. "Something's happening!" he shouted, looking around.

"What?! What is it?!" shouted Alice.

Matthew spotted it. "Wave!"

"What?! Where?! I don't see anything!" shouted Ike.

Matthew pointed in front of them. Before them was a wave so massive they couldn't see where it stopped or began. The wave was at least ten times the size of any of the waves they had faced before.

"That's a wave?!" shouted Ike.

"Oh dear, what are we going to do?!" Alice cried.

"We're gonna die!" screamed Ike.

"I've got an idea!" shouted Matthew.

"What are you going to do?!" Alice asked him.

Matthew, soaked from the pouring rain, carefully made his way to the bow of the ship. He took his sword in both hands and pointed it at the massive incoming wave. Matthew began to slowly inhale and exhale. He focused hard at a spot on the wave directly in front of their boat.

He pictured it in his mind: a tunnel of water penetrating the wave.

The boat sailed closer. It was now engulfed in the shadow of the massive wave. Matthew focused so hard on the spot in front of them, that he couldn't seem to hear or see anything besides the spot on which he was focused. The boat crept forward as a hole began to form in the wave. The hole grew large enough for most of the ship to sail through. Matthew successfully forged a tunnel of water through the wave. Their ship entered the tunnel.

"Wow!" gasped Alice, peering around at the tunnel of water.

"Whatever you're doing, keep doing it," Ike intructed Matthew.

Matthew gritted his teeth. He felt an intense burning sensation in his muscles and his head began to pound. "I don't know how much longer I can keep this up!" He closed his eyes tight. It was a feeling similar to keeping a muscle flexed for a prolonged period of time.

"We're almost there. Just a little longer," encouraged Ike.

"You can do it, Matthew!" cheered Alice.

Matthew continued to grit his teeth and hang on, but fatigue was rapidly setting in. His head pounded and his arms began to shake. Matthew's muscles burned and ached as he attempted to hold the tunnel together. The far end of the tunnel behind them began to collapse, creating a wall of rushing water that was headed toward them. The rushing wall of water behind them pushed the ship out of the tunnel before it collapsed, sending a bunch of water into their faces. Matthew fell back onto the ship's front deck.

Exiting the tunnel, bright sunshine and a clear blue sky greeted the trio. The raging storm had seemed to come to a complete stop, and seemed to be completely separate from the sunny island in front of them—almost like it the storm and the island were divided by a curtain.

Matthew wiped the water from his face. He felt dizzy and lightheaded. Every last one of his muscles ached. "Note to self, never do that again," he thought.

Matthew laid on the bow of the ship for several minutes until he recovered enough to move. Several yards ahead was an island with a small mountain in the distance. A dense jungle covered the mountain. Their momentum from carried their ship, gently, across the clear and calm blue water. Their ship entered the island's lagoon until it landed and beached itself upon a sandy, white shore.

The three of them sat up, soaking wet. They were stunned by what they had just made it through, and what they were staring directly at. Matthew got up from the floor, untied the rope around his waist, and hopped over the side of the ship. He grabbed a fist full of the beach's white sand.

"I guess we're here," he sighed, letting the sand fall through his hand. Alice pulled back the hood of her poncho. Her soaking wet, blonde hair stuck to her face. "Curiouser and curiouser," she mused, looking at the island.

The sunlight was strong and was make Matthew hot, so he removed his poncho and tossed it back on the ship. Ike got up from his seat.

"Is this it? Are we alive? Did we make it?" he asked, pulling back his hood.

"I think so. I'm gonna take a look around," said Matthew.

Alice rung out the water from her hair and slicked it back, while Ike rung out his green headband. Alice and Ike got up from the ship, ready to go along.

"You guys should stay with the ship, in case we need to get outta here fast," suggested Matthew.

"Okay," shrugged Ike. He walked over to the mast and sat down with his back against it and his arms behind his head.

"What?! You can't go out there alone. It could be dangerous," suggested a concerned Alice. She then looked over at Ike for backup. Ike's eyes were already closed as he began to make himself comfortable under the mast. Alice just sighed and dropped it.

Matthew smiled and gave Alice a thumbs up. She returned the gesture before he turned and headed into the nearby jungle.

Matthew had no idea where he was going. The map he was given, unfortunately, didn't tell him what to do once he reached the island. He decided to head out and first investigate the mountain's island on the island to investigate first. The island's sunlight was strong but at least his wet clothes were starting to dry. As he traveled through the jungle he noticed how eerily quiet everything was. There were no sounds of wind blowing, waves crashing, birds chipping, animals, or insect sounds. The only noise he could hear came from the sound of his own footsteps through the thick foliage of the jungle. He continued through the thick jungle foliage until he finally came to the base of the mountain. It was across a clearing with some stone ruins. In the grassy clearing, several large white stone columns were forming a circle around a small cavern.

The stone columns were all in various states of ruin with some still standing and some laying completely on their sides, or cracked in half. They all had some amount of moss and foliage growing on them. He got that bad feeling again but pressed on. He walked up to the entrance to the caverns in the middle of the ruins, where there was a broken stone column resting across the entrance. He managed to move the heavy stone column away from the entrance and entered the caverns. Near the entrance, there was an unlit wooden torch on the wall. The look of the torch was that it hadn't been lit in decades. In front of him was nothing but total darkness, so he grabbed the torch from the wall and lit it with a box of matches that he and Alice had purchased in Albatross Point.

Matthew followed the path inside the cavern, deep underground, until the path expanded into a large underground cavern. There was a massive hole in the ceiling where the sunlight from outside came through and water leaked from the ceiling. Thick plants were growing on the ground. More white stone columns could be found scattered around the cavern in various states of ruin. The sunlight entering the cavern from the ceiling wasn't enough to properly light the cavern. He found a large, metal brazier in the corner of the room. Matthew used the fire from his torch to light the brazier. The brazier sprang to life. Combined with the light coming from the ceiling, it was enough to fully illuminate the contents of the cavern.

It was a spacious cavern with many stalactites and stalagmites. Matthew began looking around. The box had to be here somewhere, he thought to himself. Suddenly, he noticed something in the far corner of the room. Matthew took his torch to check it out. In the corner was a brown, tattered-robed skeleton sitting on the floor, clutching a tan sack in its arms. Matthew spun around. He noticed four other similarly robed skeletons sprawled out on the cavern floor, obscured by the thick plant life on the ground.

He turned back around to the skeleton holding the sack and attempted to pull the sack from its arms. The sack wouldn't budge. Matthew sat his torch on the stone floor and pulled at the sack with both hands. This time he managed to free the sack from the grip of the skeleton. The force of Matthew ripping the sack from its arms caused the skeleton to slump over to the floor.

"Sorry about that," Matthew apologized.

The cavern began to shake violently. He grabbed the torch from the floor and with the sack in hand, sprinted for the exit. He made it back to the entrance of the cavern where he put out the torch and sat it back on the wall before rushing back out to the island sunlight.

Matthew head for the beach but then stopped. He untied the string around the sack and opened it. From it he retrieved a wooden box. It was small enough to fit in both hands. The box was smooth and had various strange symbols carved on each of its faces. A sudden and strong bad feeling washed over him, and the entrance of the cavern exploded. Stone debris flew toward him. Matthew ducked behind a nearby stone column for cover.

Out of the cavern emerged a massive stone golem, made from the white stone columns around the ruins. The golem had yellow energy seeping from the cracks in the columns. He peered around the column to get a better look at the golem. The yellow energy of the golem reminded him of the old man's energy.

"This must also be a part of the security for this box. Why can't anything be easy?" Matthew reasoned.

He quickly put the box back in its sack and tied it to his belt. "I could probably sneak off to the beach and sail off before this thing notices me," he thought.

Just then, the golem's arm smashed through the column he was hiding behind. Matthew narrowly managed to avoid being crushed.

"Welp, new plan," he thought. He stuck out his hand and his sword appeared in its wind form. The golem furiously swung its large stone arms at him. Matthew quickly dodged the golem as he searched for an opening. He used a slash of air to sever one of the golem's arms. The golem immediately stopped its attack on Matthew. The stone column then rolled up the golem's side, back in place of its once-severed arm, before it resumed its attack.

Matthew whipped up a wind vortex with his wrist and pushed the golem back into some nearby columns, which crumbled on top of the golem. The golem jumped out of the rubble and attacked him with a heavy overhead attack. Matthew blocked the attack with his sword. He struggled with the immense weight of the stone golem but gathered enough strength to push the golem back. He swung at the golem again, trapping it inside a small tornado.

The wind's speed caused the stone golem to crumble. The tornado dissipated, leaving the golem in a large pile of rubble on the ground. He looked over the pile to see if the golem had been defeated. After a few moments, the pile of rubble began to stir and the golem reformed.

Matthew began to spin the sword by the chain on its hilt. The trees around them began to violently sway and some of the nearby stone columns collapsed. The golem, newly reformed, trudged its way over to Matthew but was slowed by the powerful wind he was creating. With a great swing, Matthew released the full power of the wind in a condensed slash. The golem was cut in half, along with the remaining stone columns and several trees. Its upper body fell to the ground and collapsed into rubble.

"Surely that worked," he thought.

The rubble began to stir again. This time, the rubble of the nearby columns began to roll toward the golem. While the golem began to reform, Matthew took the opportunity to run back into the jungle and head for the beach. He sprinted as fast as he could before finally emerging at the jungle's edge. He was back on the beach.

Matthew spotted their ship. It was still docked in the sand, but was farther down on the beach. He had exited the jungle much farther from it than he hoped. Matthew ran toward the ship.

At the sight of him, Alice got up from her seat aboard the ship. "Matthew's back," she announced with excitement.

Ike was still sitting under the mast with his eyes closed. Suddenly, the massive stone golem emerged from the jungle and sprinted behind Matthew.

The golem, having absorbed the rest of the stone columns, was now much larger than before. It lunged at Matthew with its new spear-like left arm made from a broken column.

"Matthew! Behind you!" shouted Alice.

He quickly spun around to face the golem. Before he could react, however, Ike used his sword to safely guide the attack away from Matthew with his sword and into the sands of the beach.

"Who's your new friend?" Ike asked Matthew.

"Didn't catch his name," Matthew replied.

Because of the force of its attack, the golem's spear-like arm was now stuck in the sand. Ike cut off the golem's stuck arm with a flick of his wrist. Matthew and Ike attempted to take advantage of this, but the golem swung its hammer-like right arm at them. Ike jumped out of the way of the attack.

Matthew was sent flying into the jungle. The golem's cut-off arm quickly rolled itself over to the golem and back on its left arm. Matthew lay in the grass for a few minutes, dazed and with a throbbing pain in his chest. He tried to shake it off the best he could and returned to the beach to help Ike. Matthew finally emerged from the jungle as Ike dodged an overhead swing from the golem.

"Matthew! Are you okay?" Alice screamed from the boat.

Matthew untied the sack from his belt.

"Catch!" he shouted as he threw the sack over to Alice. Alice caught the sack and set it down on the floor of the ship. Matthew and Ike continued to battle with the massive stone golem. Matthew managed to cut off the golem's right arm with a slash of wind, but the golem simply reformed its arm from the rubble.

"This is going nowhere fast," Matthew complianed, dodging another attack from the golem.

"I'm open to ideas," Ike replied as he cut the golem's leg column.

"Can you move it closer to the water? I've got an idea," he said.

Ike nodded. He changed the sword to its water form and ran over and stood in the water. The golem repaired its leg and continued its onslaught of attacks on Ike. Ike franticly blocked and parried its attacks while slowly pacing backwards toward the water. When the golem got close enough, Matthew used the ocean water to create a thick whip of water and grabbed the golem's right arm and held it in place.

"Cut it off!" shouted Matthew.

Ike swiftly moved to cut the right arm off at the shoulder. After separating it from the golem's body, Matthew used the whip to fling it far into the ocean. The golem began to attack Ike with its left arm, but he grabbed it with another water whip. Ike removed it once again as Matthew flung it into the ocean.

"Let's finish this!" shouted Ike. He charged the golem and, in one swift motion, cut the golem in half at its waist. The force of the cut sent the golem's torso and head into the air. Matthew immediately sent a whip that punched a massive hole in its massive chest, and flung it far out to sea. The golem's legs collapsed into a pile of rubble on the beach.

"It looks like that worked. I'm starting to get the hang of this sword," boasted Matthew.

Ike sheathed his sword and walked over to the ship. Matthew walked over to the ship to join them. The two of them climbed back on the ship. Alice rushed over to him.

"Are you okay?" she asked.

Matthew rubbed his chest. It was still painful. "I'll live."

"Well, I'm glad all that's over," she said.

"So, did you find the box?" asked Ike.

"Yeah. I threw it to Alice."

"Oh, that's what that was?" Alice asked. She reached for the sack Matthew threw her. She untied the string around the sack and pulled out the box. "Wow! I can't believe you actually found it!"

"Huh, I thought it would be bigger," Ike replied.

"I couldn't have done it without you guys. We should probably head back to Albatross Point," said Matthew.

"Ugh, I'm in no hurry to go back through that storm.

I only just finished drying out," Alice complained.

"Maybe we should make camp here?" suggested Ike.

"There could be more of those golems. We should get outta here while we still can," said Alice.

"How are we gonna get out of here?" Ike asked.

"I'm on it," Matthew replied. He used his sword to raise the water around the ship, pulling the ship backward from the shore. Once in enough water, Matthew rotated the ship and guided it back to the sea.

The three of them put their ponchos back on and braced to enter the rough surrounding storm. Matthew again used his sword to stabilize the ship as Ike manned the helm. Using the large waves to push their ship away from the island, they managed to head back to sea without incident. They continued to sail until the dusk began to settle in.

"It's getting late. We should take shifts steering again for the night," mentioned Ike.

"Oh dear, I don't know if I can do that again. I barely got any sleep last time," complained Alice.

Matthew agreed with her. He was growing tired from his constant use of the sword, made worse by the fact that he also hadn't slept or ate well.

"Hey! What's that?" Matthew pointed to a large, dark object on the horizon.

"You think it could be an island?" asked Ike.

"Let's check it out. Maybe we could set up camp there," said Matthew.

Ike steered the helm in the direction of the object.

As they sailed closer to the object, they noticed it wasn't an island. It was an entrance to an enormous cave.

"It's a cave?" asked Matthew as they sailed closer.

"We could stay here till the morning," said Ike "This place gives me the creeps." Alice looked at what looked like the wreckages of dozens of other ships along the edges of the cave. They continued to sail until they spotted the end of the cave far off in the distance.

"It smells postively dreadful in here. How are we supposed to sleep here?" asked Alice holding her nose.

"It's not ideal, but it's only for a few hours," said Matthew. He was trying to stay positive and was too tired to care.

"Hey, guys, what's all that?" Ike pointed at the top of the cave. Over the entrance of the cave were several massive rows of what appeared to be sharp rocks, with more remains of a wrecked ship stuck on the ceiling. The cave was poorly lit, so it was hard to tell.

"It kinda looks like … teeth," mused Matthew.

Ike got up from the helm, walked to the bow of the ship, and tossed the anchor overboard.

"What kind of cave has teeth? Don't you mean stalactites?" asked Alice.

"Don't stalactites form everywhere, and not just at the opening?" Matthew pondered to himself.

A deep, loud noise, like a foghorn, rumbled through the cave. The trio quickly grabbed their ears.

The walls of the cave began to rumble and shake.

"I don't think this is a cave!" shouted Alice.

CHAPTER 16

THE CAVE AND THE WOODCARVER

Suddenly, several rows of massive, sharp teeth emerged from the water and headed toward the other rows at the top. It triggered a wave that came roaring toward them.

Ike frantically pulled the anchor aboard the ship. Alice moved to the helm while Matthew used his sword to power the ship toward the exit. The water rushed toward a massive black opening that appeared at the back of the cave. The force of the rushing water was too much for Matthew and his sword to overpower, and the ship slid back toward the opening at the rear of the cave. Ike turned around to and saw the rushing water tumbling into the unknown.

"Oh, we're gonna get sucked in!" shouted Alice.

Matthew gritted his teeth and swung the sword with

both hands. A huge blast of water propelled the ship forward, but Matthew passed out from the strain. He propelled the ship with enough force that it managed to hop over three rows of teeth—but the cave had already closed.

The ship flew into a dark crevice. Matthew awoke slow. His vision was blurry and spinning. Alice was looking over him. Her face was lit by the flame of a nearby lantern. Everything else around them was pitch black. Matthew tried to rise to his feet.

"Easy, take it easy. You passed out." Alice placed her hands on Matthew to steady him.

"Where are we? Where's Ike?" he asked.

"Well, we're still in this cave or whatever this place is. Ike went off trying to find a way out of here," she answered.

Suddenly there was a loud and unforeseen scratching sound from the side of the ship. Matthew called his sword to him as Alice lifted the lantern to get a better look. Ike climbed back over the side of the ship.

"Oh, you're back! Please tell me you found a way out of here?" Alice asked, her voice hopeful.

"Well, there's some good news and bad news. The bad news is I don't think we can fix the ship," Ike replied.

"What's wrong with the ship?" Matthew asked.

"The mast is broken and massive rocks—or teeth— are piercing the ship below deck," explained Alice.

"So, I'm pretty sure I'm not getting my deposit back," Ike complained.

"Ike, focus," Alice reminded. "What's the good news,

then?"

"I found someone I think can help us," he revealed.

"Someone else is here?" asked Matthew.

"Who are they?" Alice asked.

Ike shrugged. "I don't know. Some old guy and his kid. But he seems to have an idea about how to get out of here, so I say let's hear him out."

Matthew and Alice looked at each unsure, but they had no other options. "I suppose it's worth a listen," Alice replied.

The three of them gathered their remaining possessions and descended the rope to the ground below. Down on the cavern floor, there were the shattered remains of various wooden ships.

"Ugh! There's water down here!" complained Alice as she landed in cold, shin-deep water.

"Yeah, sorry about that, but there are some dry spots around," replied Ike. Ike lifted the lantern to illuminate the surrounding area. "This way."

He led them through the maze of wrecked ships, pools of water, and jagged rocks. After several minutes of walking, they came to a rope ladder. "Here we are. Head on up," said Ike.

Alice climbed the rope ladder, followed by Matthew and Ike. The rope ladder was a long way up, almost to the ceiling of the enormous cavern. Matthew finally reached the end of the rope ladder and climbed over the side of the ship onto the deck, followed by Ike. This ship was bigger than their own and was wedged in the ceiling.

"Hello! We're here! Where are you?!" shouted Ike.

The deck was a mess. It was strewn with various wooden barrels and crates, and lit by several candles and lanterns.

"Just a moment," replied Geppetto.

A man in his sixties emerged from behind a curtain. He was short and wore glasses on his large round nose. He wore a bright and dirty blonde wig that clashed with his thick grey mustache. His clothes were dirty and torn—it was clear that he had been here for a while.

"Ah! Welcome back! And I see you brought your friends. Salve," said Geppetto, who spoke with an Italian accent. He rushed over to shake Matthew's and Alice's hands as he introduced himself.

The sound of objects, hitting the floor behind the curtain, startled them. "Son, what are you doing back there? We have guests. Be polite," called Geppetto.

From behind the curtain emerged a small boy. The boy walked up to Geppetto, timid, and hid behind him. Now that he was closer, Matthew noticed something was off about the boy. He was made of wood.

"This is my son, Pinocchio," Geppetto introduced.

"Salve," greeted Pinocchio, giving a slight wave from behind his father.

Pinocchio was a wooden marionette the size of a small child. He had a detailed, carved wooden face, painted black hair, and blue eyes. Pinocchio wore loose-fitting dirty clothes and shoes.

"Geppetto, these are my friends I told you about,

Matthew and Alice." Ike gestured toward them.

"Hello. A pleasure to meet you both," replied Alice.

"Hi," said Matthew.

"So now that we're all here, how are we gonna get out?" asked Ike.

"Well, did you get the answer to the question I asked you earlier?" Geppetto asked.

"Yeah, our sails seem to still be in one piece," Ike replied.

"Molto bene, grazie," said Geppetto excitedly.

"What exactly is the plan?" asked Matthew.

"The plan is to take your sails and attach them to our ship. Our ship is fine, we just have nothing to power it and we can't exactly row it back to the mainland," Geppetto responded.

"You believe this will work?" asked Alice.

"Our sails may be a bit small for a ship this size, but between it, Matthew, and all of us rowing, it should work," answered Ike.

"Great, well let's get started," replied Matthew.

Matthew, Ike, and Geppetto got to work carefully removing the sails from their ship and attaching it to Geppetto's ship. Meanwhile, Alice watched after Pinocchio.

Once they had attached the sails to the new ship, Matthew asked, "How are we gonna get this cave to open?"

"Oh, this isn't a cave. It's a creature," answered Geppetto.

"What kind of creature is this big?" asked Alice.

"It is a fearsome sea monster known as the Terrible

Dogfish," answered Geppetto.

"So when it opens its mouth again, we cut the supports holding the ship in place and sail to freedom," explained Ike.

"Well, by my calculations, we still have several more hours before the dogfish will return to the surface. You're welcome to join us for dinner in the meantime and a short rest afterward. We were just about to eat," offered Geppetto.

"That would be lovely, thank you," accepted Alice.

"I could eat," replied Ike.

"Please have a seat anywhere and make yourselves comfortable."

Alice sat on a nearby crate and Ike and Matthew sat on two nearby barrels. Geppetto went behind the curtain and brought a large pot and set it on a crate covered by a cloth. Geppetto passed everyone a wooden bowl and spoon.

"Help yourselves," offered Geppetto, lifting the lid off the pot. Everyone began to fill their bowls.

"Where ever did you get this food?" asked Alice.

"One good thing about being stuck here is that there's plenty of fresh seafood in the pools," replied Geppetto.

Matthew was surprised by how hungry he was and even more surprised by how good the food tasted.

"How did you two end up here?" asked Alice.

"I was searching for my son, Pinocchio. I got caught in a storm and I thought I found a cave where I could rest, but it was this creature. I was nearly swallowed whole but I was thrown from my boat and got caught between its teeth. I've been stuck here for a month, using debris from the wreckage to survive before my Pinocchio washed up," explained Geppetto.

"How do you know when this creature will return to the surface?" asked Matthew.

"From what I noticed during my time inside the creature, it appears to have breathing problems and must return to the surface every so often, usually once every several hours. It varies, but it can't stay underwater forever," Geppetto explained.

They all ate their fill of Geppetto's seafood stew.

"While we wait for the creature to resurface to escape, we should probably get some rest if you would like. It could be a long trip to the coast. That is not optional for you, Pinocchio. Let's go," said Geppetto.

"But Papa, I'm not tired," Pinocchio argued. His wooden nose suddenly extended three inches.

"Come on, time for bed," declared Geppetto. He pointed to the curtain. Pinocchio grumbled.

"Perhaps some sleep is a splendid idea," yawned Alice.

"Good idea," agreed Ike.

Geppetto supplied the three of them with hammocks, made from fishing nets he scavenged, to sleep in alongside Geppetto and Pinocchio's net hammocks. After putting Pinocchio to bed, Matthew, Alice, and Ike followed suit. Geppetto extinguished most of the candles and lanterns around the ship and went to sleep. Matthew, Ike, and

Alice struggled to get comfortable and fall asleep. Eventually, their fatigue won out and they faded to sleep.

Everyone awoke in shock as the ship started to violently shake.

"Oh Dear! What's happening!?" Alice panicked.

"The creature has opened its mouth. It's time to see if our plan will work," annouced Geppetto.

Everyone exited the room and ran out to the main deck. They began to cut the ropes that tethered the ship to the ceiling. After the ropes were cut, the ship was still wedged to the ceiling.

"It must be stuck in there better than I thought," worried Geppetto.

"I'm on it," boasted Matthew.

Matthew began to spin the sword, in its wind form, at the ceiling. The vortex pushed against the ceiling.

"Come on, come on," groaned Matthew. He focused as hard as he could while sliding back.

After a few moments, the ship began to creak and slink forward. The ship continued forward until its weight pulled it from the ceiling. Eventually, the ship gave way and came crashing down.

Matthew swiftly aimed his spinning vortex at the now-flooded bottom portion of the terrible dogfish's mouth in an attempt to soften their landing. The ship landed with a huge splash as everyone landed on the deck with a big thud. The momentum of the landing began to push the ship toward the entrance of the dogfish's massive mouth. A deep loud noise, like a foghorn, sounded. The walls of the creature began to rumble.

"I think that woke it up!" shouted Ike.

"Quickly, we must hurry out of here before the creature swallows us whole," announced Geppetto as he sprinted from the deck floor and tossed makeshift paddles for everyone. They all franticly paddled out of the dogfish's mouth. Matthew changed his sword to its' water form. He hurriedly gathered as much water as he could to form a wave, and pushed the ship toward the mouth. The terrible dogfish's teeth began to peak out from the water.

"We're cut off!" shouted Geppetto.

Matthew forced more water into his wave. He forced the ship safely over the creature's jagged teeth and into the early morning ocean. The force of Matthew's wave carried the ship along, aided by everyone's paddling. Eventually, everyone stopped paddling for long enough to notice that the terrible dogfish had disappeared beneath the waves some time ago.

"Looks like we made it out in one piece," declared Ike.

"Where do we go now? We're in the middle of the ocean," asked Matthew.

"Not to worry. We have this," stated Geppetto. He pulled from his pocket a large bronze compass as everyone gathered around him. Geppetto lifted the lid of the compass.

"How's a compass going to help us? We don't know where we are," asked Matthew.

"This is no ordinary compass, children. This compass only points to Stormhaven City. I knew I couldn't navigate out at sea so I brought this to lead me back home after I found Pinocchio," answered Geppetto.

"Well, what are we waiting for? Let's get going," sa Ike.

They unfurled the makeshift mainsail from their rental ship and headed for Stormhaven.

The sun was beginning to set by the time their ship pulled into Stormhaven City harbor, where they were first greeted by the massive stone Stormhaven lighthouse. The Stormhaven harbor was massive, filled with ships of various sizes that were already docked, heading out to sea, or pulling into the dock. Due to the smaller size of the ship, they had to dock on the outskirts of the main harbor docks.

After docking, everyone gathered up their things and exited the ship. Geppetto and Pinocchio stood on the dock for a few moments.

"I owe you three my dearest thanks for saving us. There were times I feared the worst for my son and me. I thought we were going to be stuck inside that beast for the rest of our lives. Grazie millie," thanked Geppetto.

"Grazie," added Pinocchio.

"We never would have made it out of there if it wasn't for your help as well," replied Alice.

"We all helped each other. No need to thank us," said Matthew. Ike nodded in agreement.

"Well, Grazie, anyway. Pinocchio and I are heading home, it's been a long month. I wonder what condition my shop is in? I hope to see you all again someday, under better circumstances, of course. If you're even in old town, please stop by my shop for a visit. Arrivederci," said Geppetto.

"Ciao," added Pinocchio. They both waved goodbye before heading down the dock toward the city.

"What do we do now?" asked Ike.

"We should head back to my uncle's house. We'll plan our next move there," Matthew replied.

The three of them headed down the wooden dock toward the city. The towers of Stormhaven City began to come into view over the harbor. The harbor was a major transportation hub and even this late into the day, the docks were still teeming with all sorts of activity. The trio made their way past the massive ships, the shops, the merchant stalls, and the restaurants. They finally managed to reach the city and found an empty spot to summon the stagecoach. Matthew removed the chest from his bag and opened it. The stagecoach poured from the opened chest and the three of them piled inside.

"Sterling Jacob's house," commanded Matthew. The stagecoach began to move forward.

"I'm quite exhausted. Going to lay down," Alice announced as she ascended the stairs and headed for a bedroom.

"Yeah. Sleep sounds good," replied Ike as he followed Alice up the stairs.

Matthew shambled over to the sitting room and sat down on the couch. Sitting there on the couch, he discovered how tired he was. His overuse of the sword had taken a major toll on his body. He gathered what strength he had left and headed upstairs into a bedroom, collapsed on the bed, and fell asleep.

Several hours later, Matthew awoke from his deep sleep. He looked out from the window in his room: it was dawn. The stagecoach was rolling through a town. He recognized the place as Goldcrest. Matthew used the bathroom downstairs and returned to bed. When Matthew awoke again, it was the middle of the afternoon.

He headed downstairs again and sat on the couch. After a while, Ike came downstairs and sat on the couch beside him.

"I needed that," yawned Ike as he widely stretched.

Soon after, Alice descended the stairs and entered the sitting room. She was wearing her pajamas and her blonde hair was matted to the right side of her face.

"We should probably stop somewhere to eat. We're out of food," stated Matthew.

"Okay," agreed Ike. Alice nodded in agreement. Ike and Alice went back upstairs to get ready to eat, leaving Matthew alone on the couch. He sat there, alone, for a few moments.

His journey was almost at an end. He hoped that the black knights hadn't gotten too out of hand. Every moment he wasted felt like he was putting more and more people's lives at risk—and he was getting antsy. Matthew got up from the couch and went upstairs to get ready.

After the three of them were ready for lunch, Matthew stopped the coach in one of the villages they were passing through. The three of them exited and Matthew sucked the stagecoach back into its chest.

"Pinewatch. We should be able to find someplace here where we can eat," said Ike as he looked around.

"My, this place has greatly improved since we last saw it. Well, considering it was on fire last time we saw it," said Alice.

Alice's words jogged Matthew's memory. He remembered this village, as well, and a feeling of unease washed over him.

"Let's just eat and go. We have somewhere we have to be," insisted Matthew.

The trio quickly found something to eat at a nearby stall that sold sandwiches. Matthew paid and they returned to the coach to continue their journey. Alice and Ike sat in the sitting room and played cards while Matthew headed upstairs. Matthew closed the door behind him and sat on the bed. He reached into his pocket, pulled out his crystal, and called Sterling. After a few moments, Sterling appeared on the crystal.

"Hello there! I remembered where I put this thing this time," greeted Sterling.

"Hey! We got the box and we're on our way back to your house. I guess we'll figure out what to do after that I guess," announced Matthew.

"Well, I'll be. You actually found it. That's amazing! I'll ask the council if they have any new info for your quest. From what I've heard, the black knights really seem to be on the move. Their activities are spreading to some of the neighboring countries now," reported Sterling.

"Alright," replied Matthew. Now he felt worse.

"But, it's nothing too bad right now, just a minor nuisance. I'm sure you'll handle it soon," added Sterling when he noticed Matthew's shifting mood.

"Thanks," Matthew said half-heartedly.

"Is there anything else you want to talk about before you arrive?" asked Sterling.

"No. that's it," replied Matthew.

"Alright. Well, I'll see you when you get here. Good luck," said Sterling.

Sterling's image faded from the crystal. When the coach finally arrived at Sterling's house, it was nighttime. Sterling's house was lit by two lanterns on the front porch. The coach pulled up to the front porch and came to a complete stop.

Matthew, Ike, and Alice packed up their things and exited the coach. Matthew put the coach back in its chest and used the large silver knocker on the front door. After a few moments, the door opened. "Hello there, welcome back! Everyone come in, come in," said Sterling, gesturing for them to enter. Sterling closed the door behind them and they stood inside the great foyer. Ike and Alice looked around in wonder.

"Is it—" Ike began.

"Larger on the inside? Yes," Sterling answered as he entered the foyer. "Well, I believe introductions are in order. Sterling Jacobs." Sterling extended his hand.

"Ike," replied Ike, shaking his hand.

Alice's face lit up. "I'm Alice Liddell. It's a pleasure,

no an honor to be meeting you. I've read several of your books," she exclaimed, shaking Sterling's hand with enthusiasm.

"Umm, well, it's always nice to meet a fan. Are you a witch, by chance?" asked Sterling.

"Unfortunately, no, I'm not a witch. I wish I was. My mother was a witch, you see. She owned a few of your books. I guess that's why I've always found magic and sorcery so fascinating," Alice gushed.

"Well, that's great. Are you guys hungry? Did you eat already? I was just about to sit down for a meal," asked Sterling.

"We haven't eaten in ages," replied Alice.

"I can always eat," announced Ike.

"I guess," exhaled Matthew.

"Great. Follow me," said Sterling.

He led them into the dining room down the hall. There on the dining room table was a spread of roast beef, potatoes, salad, bread, and drinks. The four of them took a seat at the table and began to eat. Alice asked Sterling question after question about magic and sorcery, while Ike and Matthew ate in silence. Matthew wasn't very hungry, but he ate what he could before he excused himself from the table.

Matthew took his bags and returned to the room he stayed in the last time he was there. He got ready for bed and slipped under the covers. Matthew lay there in bed, restless for a few hours, before he gave up on trying to sleep and headed to the library.

CHAPTER 17

LOST AND FOUND

Matthew entered Sterling's massive library and took a seat in one of the leather chairs in front of the fireplace. He slumped down in the chair and exhaled. His mind was racing, and he felt he needed to be doing something—but had no idea what he needed to do.

"I didn't know you were still up," said Sterling as he entered the library. He took a seat in the chair next to Matthew. Sterling sipped from his goblet and he placed it on the wooden end table next to his seat.

"We didn't get a chance to talk earlier. That Alice is … quite the inquisitive one. So, how's everything? Are you okay?" asked Sterling.

"We found the box."

"That's not what I asked."

"I'm fine but we're not finished yet. The jobs not done," Matthew replied.

"Well, since our last conversation, I spoke with the council and they do have some news that might help you."

Matthew's anxiousness began to grow.

Sterling continued. "Their scouts have managed to track a few of them to an old and abandoned mining town, Silverrun, much further south. It's probably just a few stragglers or scouts but it might be worth checking out. You might find some new information."

"Alright, we'll check it out."

"Where's the box? I would love to give it a once-over before you leave," asked Sterling.

Matthew went to his room and retrieved the box. He handed it to Sterling. Sterling looked at the box with careful consideration, examining it in silence for several minutes.

"I can't believe it's actually real. You were right all along. You're probably right about other things as well," Sterling said when he handed the box back to Matthew. "It's getting late, is there anything else you wanted to talk about?"

Matthew remained silent for a few moments before answering. "No."

"Alright. We can talk some more in the morning. I'm going to bed, good night."

Sterling rose from his seat and lifted his goblet.

"Night," replied Matthew.

After Sterling left, Matthew stayed seated in the library for a little while longer. Then he left and went to bed.

The next morning, Matthew awoke and got ready for his journey. His anxiousness had shifted to restlessness. He was now itching to get started—to finish what he had begun all those weeks ago. He packed up his things and went downstairs.

Matthew entered the dining room. Sterling, Alice, and Ike were already there eating breakfast.

"Good morning," greeted Sterling.

"Good morning, everybody," replied Matthew as he took a seat at the dining room table.

After breakfast, Matthew, Alice, and Ike headed outside followed by Sterling. Matthew removed the coach's chest from the bag and opened it. The coach spilled forth from the chest.

"Well, it was nice meeting the two of you. Good luck on the rest of your journey," announced Sterling.

"Thank you for everything. It was a pleasure meeting you," exclaimed Alice.

"Thanks," added Ike.

"Matthew—a quick word," whispered Sterling.

Alice and Ike looked at Matthew. He shrugged and turned toward his uncle while Alice and Ike entered the coach.

"What's up?" asked Matthew.

"I just want to remind you. Don't let any worries about completing your quest force you into making costly mistakes. Remember to always think before acting, alright?"

"I will."

"I thought so. Just a friendly reminder," replied Sterling.

Matthew walked back to the carriage and hopped in the front seat. "Silverrun," comanded Matthew. The carriage started to roll forward, traveling down the smooth dirt road. They had already left Hazelhill a few hours ago and were heading south.

Matthew reached into the bag he'd sat beside him and pulled out the golden book. He turned to the map section and found Hazelhill. He then scanned for the town of Silverrun. There was a tiny dot in the southern corner of the human kingdom territory's map. The coach continued south for several more hours, winding through the surrounding lush forests and farmlands of Hazelhill before turning into harsh and barren yellow pastures. Weeds and seedling trees marked the barren landscape. The wind blew through the ragged fields. He spotted the many ragged ruins of abandoned farms and homesteads as their coach continued south.

As the coach rose over the crest of another hill, Matthew spotted the remnant of the town off in the distance. It was surrounded by a sea of yellow grassy fields. Matthew stopped the coach, opened the coach's door, and stepped inside.

Inside, Alice was sitting on the couch reading one of Sterling's books, while Ike was napping on the couch next to Alice. Alice lifted her eyes from the book she was reading.

"Have we arrived?" asked Alice.

"I think so."

Alice closed her book. "Ike. We're here."

Ike sprang awake. The three of them exited the coach.

"Over there." Matthew pointed to the cluster of buildings on the horizon.

"We'll go the rest of the way on foot. That way we can spot any black knights before they spot us," said Matthew. Alice and Ike nodded in agreement. The three of them attempted to make their way closer to Silverrun, as stealthily as they could, but the baron yellow fields and broad daylight made it difficult. They made it to the closest building and leaned against the wall. Silverrun consisted of roughly a dozen wooden buildings in various states of disrepair.

There were six buildings on each side of a dirt road that was overrun with weed growth, and another building directly in front of the road. The buildings on each side of the road were one or two stores. The building directly in front of the road was the biggest in town and stood three stories. Matthew peered around the corner of the building. The town was empty and silent.

"Let's look around," Matthew whispered. Alice and Ike nodded. The three of them crept around the abandoned buildings. They looked for the black knights, but the town was empty.

"There's nobody here," said Ike surprised.

Matthew looked around again. He remained quiet as he listened to the surrounding area. It was quiet except for the blowing wind and buzzing insects.

"Let's try these buildings," suggested Matthew. "I'll

check out the ones on the left, you guys can check out the ones on the right."

The three of them split up to search inside the buildings.

Matthew turned and entered the nearest building. It was missing a door. Unfortunately, he found nothing of any interest in any of the buildings on his side of the road. They were all empty. He figured that everything that had any importance or value was either taken when the place was first abandoned, or taken over the years by bandits or scavengers.

The buildings were filled with dust and cobwebs. Several of the windows were cracked or broken altogether, with grass and weeds growing from between the wooden floorboards. Matthew exited the final building on his side of the road. Ike and Alice had yet to return from their search, so Matthew turned his attention toward the large building in front of the main road between the two rows of buildings. Matthew headed down the road, went up the creaky wooden porch steps, and entered the building.

Like the other buildings, it was empty and filled with dust, cobwebs, and broken windows. Matthew stood in what appeared to be the foyer, and he began to look around. *This must have been the town hall or something*, he thought to himself. He climbed the rickety wooden staircase and searched each floor. He found nothing. When he made it to the top floor, Matthew looked out the front window over the deserted town. He spotted Alice and Ike exiting one of the buildings and entering the next one beside it. Matthew closed his eyes and tried to concentrate. He breathed, smoothly, in and out.

"Concentrate, reach out," he thought.

Matthew felt the sensation of a slight tingle. It came from behind him. He opened his eyes and turned to look out the back-facing windows and noticed something.

It was a person walking along a series of small hills near the town. He watched the person continue to walk until he disappeared around a hill. Matthew quickly headed to the first floor and exited the building. Alice and Ike spotted him leaving the building and walked over to him.

"Welp, we've come up empty-handed," Ike annouced.

"Tell us you've aleast found something?" Alice asked.

"I saw someone walking over there." Matthew pointed just beyond the row of buildings on the right.

"Let's go check it out," suggested Ike.

Matthew led them to the place where he saw the person walking. Nestled in the nearby hills just outside the town were the Silverrun mines. There was a mine entrance. It was all boarded up, with tracks leading out from the mine. A few mine carts sat on the tracks. From the looks of the mine carts, they hadn't been moved in years.

"It's the silver mines. The whole town was built because of them. I read that they ran dry decades ago. That's why everyone moved away and the town became abandoned," Alice explained.

Ike walked up to the mine entrance. He looked at the boards. Someone had painted the words "MINE CLOSED DO NOT ENTER" in red lettering. The paint was old, chipped and barely readable anymore. Ike gave one of the boards a slight tug. It was still nailed to the entrance.

He looked through the boards. It was dark but Ike could make out that the mines had collapsed several feet away from the entrance. "I doubt whoever you saw came from here," he said.

"They have to be around here somewhere," replied Matthew. He quickly headed off.

Alice and Ike continued to investigate the entrance. Matthew explored the surrounding region until the landscape started to flatten behind the hills. Behind the hills, there were trees and bushes—something that resembled a miniature forest. Matthew investigated the area until he came upon a massive hole in the hill.

He immediately returned to Ike and Alice. "I found something. There's a hole on the other side of the hills," he announced.

The three of them rushed back to the entrance.

"They made another entrance into the mines," Alice observed.

"Smart. An old mine makes for a great hidden base," replied Ike.

"Well, let's go inside," ordered Matthew.

"I beg your pardon?!" surprised Alice.

"We came here to put an end to these knights. We have to go inside," Matthew urged.

"We don't know what's waiting for us inside. We can't just charge in there," replied Ike. Alice agreed.

A bad feeling came over Matthew. "Someone's coming," he whispered.

The three of them hid in the nearby bushes. A black knight, pulling a wooden cart with barrels, came up the hill.

"I've got an idea," Ike whispered. He leaped from the bushes and subdued the knight. Matthew and Alice exited the bushes while Ike put on the black knight's armor.

"How do I look?" asked Ike.

"Brilliant," Alice smirked.

"Now you guys get in the barrels, and we'll just walk right in," suggested Ike. The three of them removed two of the barrels from the cart and poured out its contents behind a bush.

"What's this stuff?" asked Matthew.

"Ugh, It smells dreadful." Alice pinched her nose.

Ike examined the black substance. He rubbed it between two of his fingers. "It's black powder," he answered.

"Well, I can see that," replied Matthew.

"It's used for cannons, bombs, and explosives, mainly," answered Ike.

"Oh dear, if they have this stuff, that quite troubling ," worried Alice.

"That's why we're gonna stop them. Alright, let's go," stated Ike.

Alice climbed inside her now-empty barrel on the cart.

"Just a minute," replied Matthew.

He walked out of earshot from his friends and pulled the crystal from his pocket.

"Sterling. Are you there?" he asked.

Sterling's face appeared on the crystal. "Hello there.

Is everything alright?"

"We're fine. It looks like the black knights are here in Sliverrun. There in the abandoned mine."

"Are they still there?"

"It looks like it," Matthew replied.

"Alright. Stay put. I'll put in a word to get you all some backup. You shouldn't go in alone. That could be dangerous. You're not ready," cautioned Sterling.

"Yeah, alright."

Sterling's face faded from the crystal. Matthew walked back over to the cart and climbed in his barrel.

"Alright, let's go." Matthew sat down inside his barrel.

Ike pulled the cart into the mine. "It's dark and I don't know where I'm going," Ike whispered as they ventured deep into the mines.

"Just keep going," Matthew whispered.

Ike continued forth, following the old mine rails until he spotted light at the end of the tunnel. It was a lit torch on the wall. Ike stopped at the lit torch on the mines wall. The path before him was illuminated by torches. He followed the lit torches until he came to a large, open space that was crawling with black knights. The knights looked comfortable and were lounging about. Several of them sat at tables, playing cards, drinking ale, and talking. The space had a large open hole with a path spiraling down the hole. Ike pulled up to the wooden fence that walled off the edge.

"Hey! You there!" shouted a voice.

Ike quickly spun around. A black knight walked up the spiraling path to Ike.

"You're late. We've been waiting on you," complianed the knight.

"Umm … sorry. I wanted to make sure I wasn't followed here, ya know. Better safe than sorry," replied Ike.

"Yeah, I understand," the knight agreed. "Let me just check the merchandise,"

The knight walked up to the cart.

"Um, what?!" asked Ike. He moved fast toward the knight. The knight pulled up the lid on one of the barrels. Ike put his hand on his sword hilt. The knight reached in and took a fistful of black powder. He let the grains of powder slip through his fingers. Ike sighed and took his hand off his sword. The knight put the lid back on the barrel.

"Looks like we hit the jackpot," said the knight.

"What do you think it's for?" asked Ike.

"Hell if I know, they never tell me anything. Probably to just expand the mines or something. Just drop this stuff off in storage and relax for a bit, the boss is gonna be giving us our next task soon," directed the knight.

"Umm … where's the storage again? I forgot," asked Ike.

"Sixth tunnel down. You can't miss it," stated the knight as he walked off.

Ike made his way down the path, deeper into the hole, counting the tunnels he passed until he came to the sixth tunnel. The storage room was just a dead-end tunnel with wooden barrels, crates, and burlap sacks. There were several stands with armor and weapons. Ike looked around and saw no one.

"Coast is clear," whispered Ike.

Matthew and Alice popped out of their barrels and climbed out of the cart.

"Well, now that we're in, what do we do now?" Ike whispered.

"We should look for some information about what the knights are up to. Whoever's in charge is here somewhere apparently," Alice whispered.

"Alright, but we're gonna need disguises. This place is filled with knights," Matthew whispered. He walked over to the suits of armor that rested on wooden stands in the corner. Matthew and Alice put on some extra armor from storage. While the armor Ike was wearing was much larger than he was, he was the biggest and the tallest of the three. The armor still fit Ike better than either Matthew or Alice, both of whom were severely undersized—the armor loosely dangled from their respective frames. Matthew was in slightly better shape than Alice, who was practically drowning in her armor.

"It's heavier than it looks," said Matthew, struggling to adjust to the weight. He had never worn armor before but was getting used to it.

"Alice, are you okay?" asked Ike.

"I'll ... manage," she grunted.

"We should split up," suggested Matthew.

"What!?" shouted Alice.

"Shhhh," interjected Ike.

"We'll cover more ground that way. I'll search the upper tunnels. You guys search the lower tunnels. Meet back here in an hour when done," decided Matthew.

"I don't think that's a good idea—" Alice began, but before she could finish the sentence, Matthew ran down the tunnel in front of them, leaving the storage room. Alice sighed and looked at Ike. Ike nodded and the two of them exited the storage room.

Matthew made his way back up the spiral tunnel, searching the tunnels as he went. He tried his best to be as inconspicuous as possible. He couldn't risk starting a fight now.

"My dad might be in here somewhere," thought Matthew. He concentrated hard and attempted to let his senses guide him through the tunnels, but had no luck. He came to longer tunnels that seem to connect him to another part of the mine, with much wider and open tunnels with wooden supports and more lanterns on the walls. He had made it into the original mine.

He continued to work his way through the mine tunnels until he came to a large metal door guarded by two black knights. Matthew ducked behind some crates.

"I gotta get these guys to move," thought Matthew.

Matthew picked up a nearby rock and threw it down the tunnel.

"What was that?" asked one knight.

The other one shrugged. "Probably nothing."

Matthew threw another rock, this time with more force, down the tunnel.

"Okay. That was definitely something," complianed

the knight.

"Then go check it out if you're so worried," replied the other knight.

The first knight walked down the tunnel past the crates behind which Matthew was hid. Matthew summoned the Sword of Wind and commanded a powerful gust of wind that sent the knight crashing into the tunnel wall, knocking him out.

"What was that?" said the second knight. He rushed over to investigate but Matthew used his sword to slam him into the wall. Matthew dragged each knights behind the stack of crates and headed for the door.

Matthew knocked on the door. There was no answer. He opened the door and went inside. Inside was a makeshift office. There were desks, maps, tables, and bookshelves along the walls. He quickly began scanning the maps and documents on the desk. Unfortunately, he didn't know what he was looking for. He decided to look for any information about his dad. He scoured the table documents again before moving on to the bookshelves and the papers pinned to the wall.

Suddenly, Matthew heard a noise coming from the other side of the door. Matthew quickly looked around and spotted a large wardrobe in the corner. Matthew ran to it and hid inside.

Ike continued to make his way down the tunnel as Alice slowly waddled, under the weight of her armor, behind him.

"Can we please take a break?" she whispered.

"It's only been a few minutes, and we haven't found anything yet," whispered Ike.

"Yeah, but this armor is quite heavy."

Ike sighed. "Alright, follow me." Ike led her deeper into the mines until they came to a secluded, blocked-off tunnel. He looked around to see if they were alone.

"Coast is clear," whispered Ike.

Alice sat on a nearby crate and removed her helmet. Her face had turned bright red and was covered in sweat. Her blonde hair was stuck to her forehead. Ike lifted the visor on his helmet and looked around the room.

"It's some kind of makeshift jail or something," he suggested.

Alice wiped the sweat from her forehead and got up from the barrel. "Is anybody in here?" she asked.

Ike ran down the row of cells. "They're all empty. No one's here but it looks like someone was."

Alice walked over to the cell where Ike was standing. Ike then entered the cell. There was a blanket, a bucket, and a wooden bowl and spoon on the ground.

Ike and Alice heard a sudden noise from outside. Alice put on her helmet and Ike pulled down his visor. Together they exited the cell.

"Oh, sorry. Didn't know anyone was in here," said a black knight.

"Um, we were just leaving." Ike pushed Alice past the knight.

"Was anybody kept in these cells recently?" Ike asked the knight.

The knight shrugged. "I heard someone was held here a few months ago, but nobody since then," replied the knight.

"Okay. Thanks." Ike continued pushing Alice down the tunnel.

As they left, the knight noticed the strands of blonde hair that stuck out from the back of Alice's helmet.

GHOST TOWN SHOWDOWN

Matthew continued to hide in the wardrobe as three knights huddled over a large desk filled with documents. Two of the knights wore the same armor Matthew had seen a million times. The third knight's armor was quite different, still black like the others, but with larger plate armor.

"And from our latest reports, we already have men in positions here, here, and here, just waiting for the signal. We've also met our recruitment goals for this month, double that of last month, I think she'll be quite impressed," concluded one of the knights.

"That'll be all," interrupted the larger knight. "We'll discuss this more later."

The two knights gathered a few documents from the

table and left the room.

"You can come out now. I know you're here," annouced the knight who stayed behind.

Matthew hesitated for a moment but exited the wardrobe.

"Surrender! Whatever it is that you're doing here is now over!" Matthew demanded. He tried to sound braver than he felt.

"Surrender? And why would I do that?" The knight turned to face him.

"Because I'm here to stop you. Now, surrender!" Matthew drew his sword and pointed it at the large knight.

"So, you actually did have the sword? A mere child?!" The knight began with surprise. "After I dealt with the last one, I thought I'd have more time before I'd have to deal with another one. But at least this time, I'll make sure that sword doesn't slip away from me again."

"Alright, you asked for it," growled Matthew. He unsheathed his sword, pulled out Aleron's box, and attempted to use it.

Suddenly, it dawned on him. He didn't know how to open Aleron's box.

"Come on, come on." Matthew panicked trying to open the box. He franticly rotated the box in several directions. The box was firmly sealed shut.

"I've entertained this long enough," stated the knight. He began to draw his sword. Matthew thrust the box back in his bag, while the large knight attacked with a heavy overhead strike. Matthew summoned his sword and their blades clashed, sending shockwaves through Matthew's body.

Ike traveled through the tunnels while Alice continued behind him with her slow waddle. Eventually, she stopped.

"What's wrong?" Ike asked.

"We haven't found anything and I'm quite exhausted. Isn't it time that we regroup with Matthew?" she whispered.

"Alright, fine, we can go back," he replied.

They made their way back to the storage room and waited for several minutes.

"Where's Matthew? Shouldn't he be here by now," she asked.

"Maybe he just lost track of time or found something interesting," Ike replied.

Matthew moved swiftly to avoid another one of the large knight's massive swings. The knight's sword landed with a blow, slicing a bookshelf in half. Matthew noticed that he was faster than the large knight. He began to remove what pieces of his armor he could to lighten his weight even more. Matthew continued to avoid the large knight's attacks while the knight sliced a table in half, followed by another bookshelf.

"How long do you intend to avoid me, coward? Stand and fight!" demanded the knight.

"Yeah? Take this!" Matthew harnessed his Sword of Wind, whipping up a gust of that sent the room's debris and papers flying toward the large knight.

While the knight was distracted, Matthew slipped out of the room.

Several black knights came around the corner. They were there to investigate the commotion. Matthew used his sword to send some boxes and barrels rocketing in their direction. He hit most of them, but one of them managed to shout "Intruder!"

He quickly followed up with a slash of air to finish the last knight. As he did so, the large knight exited his office in pursuit of Matthew.

"There's an intruder!" shouted a black knight as he ran past the storage tunnel.

Alice and Ike looked at each other with panic. The two of them quickly attempted to make their way back to Matthew before Alice's helmet was snatched from her head.

"I knew it! More intruders!" shouted the black knight.

Ike immediately slashed the knight across the chest and kicked him over the wooden railing down into the mine shaft. He began fighting with the knights around him, taking special care to protect Alice. Matthew used a gust of wind to rocket a nearby mine cart at the large black knight. He managed to dodge one mine cart but was clipped by the second one Matthew sent his way. Several black knights, emerging from behind the larger knight, charged Matthew. He spun his sword and turned the tunnel into a wind tunnel. The wind sent the knights flying.

When the larger knight had recovered, he and slowly made his way toward Matthew. He attacked Matthew with a slash of condensed air. Matthew responded with one of his own, but the two canceled each other out. In a blur, the larger knight managed to close the distance. Matthew managed to dodge a fatal blow only resulting in a cut to his upper arm.

Ike continued to manage the black knights on the wooden walkway at bay. Since the walkway was narrow, their numbers didn't amount to much since they had to fight him one at a time.

"What do we do!?" Ike yelled to Alice.

"I don't know!? … Behind us!" she shouted.

Ike swiftly cut down the knight he was facing before spotting the next two knights who were coming up the spiral wooden walkway. He used his sword to destroy the wooden walkway before turning to fight off the approaching knights.

"Come on!" Alice shouted as she hastily began to remove parts of her armor. She sprinted past the knights who were fighting Ike. Ike kicked another knight off the side of the walkway and ran after Alice, while a few knights jumped the walkway gap he'd created. Ike followed Alice deeper into the mines until they came across a mine cart.

"Get in!" he shouted. Alice hopped in and Ike began pushing the mine cart up to speed before climbing in. Together they rocketed away into the darkness of the mine tunnels.

The large knight continued to press Matthew, who was just barely able to keep him at bay. The narrow tunnels meant that the large knight couldn't use his incredible strength and wide strikes to pound Matthew. However, he was still able to chip away at Matthew—every so often managing to slip inside his guard and cut him. Meanwhile,

Matthew couldn't manage to do much damage to the knight in return.

"I need to change tactics," he thought.

Matthew changed his sword to its water form and sprayed a jet of water into the knight's face. The jet of water temporarily blinded the knight. He lifted one hand in a feeble attempt to block the water jet. He stopped attacking and coughed up water as it flowed from his large helmet.

Matthew turned around and darted down the tunnel until he came to a pile of rocks that blocked his path. He changed his sword to its wind form and blasted the rocks down the tunnel and outside the mine. Matthew ran to the light at the end of the tunnel.

He was outside.

Ike and Alice's mine cart continued to speed through the dark mine tunnels.

"I wonder where this leads?" asked Alice.

"Hopefully not off a cliff or something," worried Ike.

Ike spotted debris covering the tracks further down the line. He immediately yanked the mine cart's brakes and hopped out of the cart.

"Quick, help me clear the track! They probably followed us down here."

Alice jumped out of the cart and started moving rocks off the track. While Alice cleared the track, Ike found a fork in the track with a track switch. One of the paths was boarded up. Ike hurriedly removed the boards from the path. The track looked clear as far as he could see. Alice and

Ike had almost finished clearing the track when they heard wheels squeaking down the tunnel behind them.

"They're almost here!" she announced.

"I'll hold 'em off."

The black knights stopped their cart and jumped at Ike. Ike began to fight them as Alice panicked and rushed to finish clear the tracks of the debris.

"It's clear! Let's go!" she shouted, then she started to push the cart again. Ike heard the sound of more wheels coming down the line and, in one swift motion, cut down the black knights. He ran over to help Alice push the mine cart up to speed.

"Get in!" he shouted.

Alice climbed in. Ike reached for the track switch and switched to track to head down the formerly boarded up tunnel. Before Ike could climb in, a black knight had chased them down and swung at him. Ike pulled the sword from Alice's belt and blocked the attack.

"Ike!" Alice shouted in horror. The cart rocketed down the dark tunnel. Ike drew his broadsword and used both blades to cut down the black knight. Ike walked over to the track switch, switched the track back to the way he found it, and cut the switch in half—locking it in that position as more and more black knights caught up to him.

Ike brandished both blades and charged the knights.

Matthew was in an enormous stone mining quarry with a mix of wooden scaffolding walkways and large dirt ridges and paths. At the bottom of the quarry was a large, still-water pond.

"I gotta get to that water. It's my only chance," he thought.

As he attempted to make his way to the water below, an avalanche of rocks crashed through the ceiling in front of him.

"This has gone on long enough," the large knight threatened from the walkway overhead.

He walked down the wooden decline to where Matthew stood. Matthew swiftly unleashed a flurry of wind slashes. The large knight blocked a few but there were too many, too fast, and he took several of them. He used his sword to whip up a dust cloud to blind the large knight and ran down another wooden decline toward the water. Using the wooden scaffolding attached to the quarry wall, Matthew attempted to make his way to the bottom of the quarry. Suddenly, the large knight came crashing through the above wooden walkway. The two re-engaged in a sword fight. He continued to press Matthew with an onslaught of brutal attacks. He once again slipped through his guard, slicing him on his inner arms, upper arms, ribs, and thighs.

Matthew was trying his absolute hardest to keep the large knight from delivering a fatal strike. The large knight looked to be no trouble against him.

Alice's mine cart continued to speed through the dark mine tunnels. She had been going for several minutes since Ike had sent her off. Alice was crying, worried about what would happen to her friend. Her cart took a sudden hard turn into another tunnel with a light at the end. As her cart rapidly approached the light, she noticed that the exit was boarded up. She hurriedly ducked inside her cart as it crashed through the old wooden boards.

Alice raised her head from the cart to see the end of the tracks. They were headed toward a massive quarry. She promptly jumped out of the cart before it rocketed off the edge of the quarry wall. Alice rolled on the ground but caught herself just before she reached the edge of the quarry's scaffolding. She scrambled to her feet and observed her surroundings.

Alice spotted Matthew. He was engaged in a sword fight with the large knight, on the wooden walkways, several rows above her. Alice hurriedly made her climbed to reach him.

Matthew sent another slash of air at the large knight, who ducked and countered. Matthew jumped back and changed his sword to its water form. He sent a slash of water at the large knight, who attempt to cut through but most of it got him. Matthew followed that up with another wind slash and then another water attack. He rapidly alternated between his sword's water and wind forms to unleash a barrage of attacks.

This onslaught proved to be too much for the large knight to counter, sending him flying down the wooden walkway. The wooden walkway collapsed in part on top of him.

Matthew hurriedly continued to make his way to the water at the bottom of the quarry.

"Matthew!" Alice screamed.

He looked down and spotted her on a lower walkway. "Take this!" Matthew shouted. He hastily removed his backpack and threw it in Alice's direction. It landed on the walkway just below Alice.

"What was that?!" she shouted at Matthew.

"The box! Use the box!"

Alice nodded and urgently began to make her way down the scaffolding to reach Matthew's bag while he descended to another level of the scaffolding. He was headed for the water. The large knight was back on his feet and had now swung down, from the wooden walkway above, and kicked Matthew into the quarry wall. The knight instantly followed this with a swing that almost took Matthew's head off.

Matthew barely dodged it and the swing instead sliced deep into the quarry wall.

"I've had enough of you and that sword," the knight bellowed as he charged Matthew. They exchanged attacks until the knight maneuvered his blade inside Matthew's guard and forced his sword down, embedding it into the wooden walkway floor. He delivered a swift backhanded punch, followed by a fast kick to the gut, sending Matthew flying. He landed several feet down the walkway on the level's dirt ridge.

"Finally. This sword is mine," exclaimed the large knight.

He grabbed the sword with one hand, but it didn't move. The large knight tried again but the results were the same. The knight tried both hands but the sword still wouldn't budge. Matthew lay there in the dirt, dazed and bleeding. He mustered as much energy as he could to begin to stand. He lumbered to his wobbly legs but it hurt to breathe. He spotted Alice, who had managed to get to his bag and was now rummaging through it.

Matthew took a few deep breaths to gather himself. The large knight continued to struggle with the sword. Even with all his might, he couldn't move the sword an inch. He fell to his knees in disbelief. Matthew stuck out his hand for the sword. The sword began to wobble as it worked its way out of the floor and flew down the walkway into his hand. Matthew threw all caution to the wind and began to run and slide down the quarry's dirt inclines toward the water. The large knight quickly snapped out to see him making a beeline for the water and immediately moved to intercept him. The large knight began to fire air slashes at him as he slid down the dirt inclines. Matthew immediately moved his sword to block the incoming attacks but the attacks were too many. A few slipped in. They were just enough to knock Matthew off the side, and he fell the rest of the way to the bottom.

Alice finally managed to pull Aleron's box from Matthew's bag. She quickly made her way down the wooden declines. He rolled over to the edge of the pool of water at the bottom of the quarry. Matthew rolled over on his back to see the large knight in the air. The knight rocketed toward him and was ready to impale. Matthew used a massive whip of water to swat the large knight out of the air. It sent the large knight back several feet before he came crashing down. He hit the ground hard, forming a crater in the dirt.

The large knight rose again to his feet. Alice made her way to the bottom of the quarry and attempted to open the box, but it wouldn't open. She began to rotate the box and flip it over trying to open it any way she could but to no avail.

Matthew again struggled to his feet and pointed the sword's water form at the large still-water pool. He manipulated it into a magnificent column of water. He commanded the column to strike the large knight. The knight swiftly dodged the incoming water column and kept moving toward Matthew. Matthew promptly bent the column between them and kept the large knight at bay, turning the tide of the battle against the large knight.

The large knight did his best to fight Matthew. He sliced the water column and lunged at Matthew, over and over again, but the column of water would just reform and snaked around for a counterattack as if nothing had happened. The speed of the water occasionally broke through the large knight's guard and sent him crashing into the quarry walls—damaging his armor.

He attempted to strike at Matthew from afar with air slashes, but Matthew bent the column in front of him to shield himself from the attack. He began to slow from fatigue and the water in his armor weighed him down. His armor was dripping wet and covered in cracks and dents, and his breathing had become heavy. Matthew again sent the water column crashing into the knight. It made his muscles ache and burn; his head throbbed.

The large knight slammed into the wooden scaffolding on the quarry floor and fell to one knee. Alice continued struggling to open the box until the markings on the box began to glow. The wooden flaps on top of the box flew open and a beam of white light shot out. It struck the large knight.

The large knight screamed in agony as something—it appeared to be a ghost—was removed from him and sucked into the box.

He dropped his sword and fell on both knees. Matthew grabbed his sword in both hands and charged the large knight. He gathered a massive wave of water from the pond as he ran. The column of water crashed into the large knight so hard it created another crater, this time on the side of the quarry wall. The wooden walkways overhead began to collapse.

Alice ran for safety. Matthew used the water to shield himself from the falling debris above.

Then, he passed out.

"Matthew!" Alice screamed. She ran back towards the massive pile of debris, her eyes swollen with tears. She climbed over the collapsed walkways to find him and the large knight both laying face down in the dirt, unharmed by the collapsed walkways. She rolled Matthew over and put her ear to his chest.

"They're over here!" a voice yelled.

Alice instantly turned to look. A man was standing on top of the debris in leather armor. Alice was stunned as more people wearing similar armor began climbing over the debris. Then Sterling appeared on top of the debris.

"Sterling!?" Alice said. Tears streamed down her face.

Sterling swiftly ran toward them and put his hand on Matthew's chest. "Thank the gods, he's alive! Medic! *Now!*" he ordered.

A woman in leather armor kneeled next to him and placed her hands over Matthew's chest. Her hands began to glow with a faint yellow energy, as did Matthew's body.

"Sterling! Ike! He's still in there! He's somewhere in the mine!" Alice shouted.

Sterling put his hands on her shoulders to calm her. "We already have people in the mines. We'll find him," he said.

"Okay. He's stable enough to move him," stated the woman. Several of the surrounding people lifted Matthew onto a stretcher. Sterling waved his hand and a large pile of debris moved to clear a path. Matthew was carried off to safety.

"And who's this?" asked Sterling, noticing the unconscious large knight.

"I think he's the one behind all this. He's their leader," she answered.

Sterling nodded in the direction of the knight. Several soldiers walked over to check if he was alive. "He's out, but breathing," declared one of the soldiers.

"That kid sure did a number on him," added another, one looking him over.

The large knight was secured in iron shackles before someone began to heal him enough to move him.

"Let's get a better look at who our new friend is," said

Sterling. He walked over to the large knight and carefully removed his helmet.

He immediately dropped the helmet in shock.

"It can't be. Impossible!" he said.

The surrounding soldiers exchanged looks of shock.

"What!? Do you know him?" Alice asked.

Sterling slowly nodded his head.

"Who is it?" asked Alice.

"It's my brother. Matthew's father," he answered.

Inside the mines, several soldiers were still searching the dark tunnels with lanterns.

"Is anyone in here?" asked a soldier. They came across a lacerated black knight laying on the ground. A little farther in, they found another one. The farther they went down the tunnel, the more and more black knights they found littering the tunnels. All of them severely injured.

"What the hell? Who did all this?" asked one soldier.

Suddenly, the soldiers heard something slowly making its way towards them from farther down the dark mine tunnel.

"Halt! Identify yourself!" shouted a soldier.

The figure continued to shamble towards the soldiers. They drew their weapons. "Halt!" shouted a soldier. One soldier lifted his lantern to see the figure.

Ike emerged from the darkness. He was gravely wounded, covered in blood and lacerations. His armor was covered in cuts and dents, and his breathing was slow and heavy. Several arrows jutted out from his body. He was still holding two swords.

The soldiers were all horrified at the sight of him. Ike slowly approached the soldiers.

"Are … my friends … okay?" He struggled to get out the words.

"Yeah, we found them. They're okay," the soldier replied.

Ike immediately fell over and passed out.

CHAPTER 19

COMING HOME

Two days had passed since the battle at Silverrun. Matthew slowly awoke from his slumber in a soft bed. He was wearing soft white robes. He looked around his new surroundings. He was in a small, stone-walled room with wooden floors. Inside the room were a bed, a nightstand, two wooden chairs, and a tall wooden closet. He moved to get out of bed but his muscles ached and burned. It was hard to move.

He sat on the side of his bed for several minutes. After a while, he mustered his energy and exited the room. He entered a hallway lined with doors. The hallway was decorated with beautiful paintings. There were tables upon which sat vases of flowers.

As Matthew walked down the hall he spotted Alice,

Sterling, and a Sun Elf woman. They were coming down the hallway toward him.

"Matthew!" Alice exclaimed.

Sterling and the Sun Elf woman reacted in shock. The three of them rushed to Matthew's side.

"Matthew! You shouldn't be out here," complianed the Sun Elf.

"Let's go back to your room," suggested Sterling.

They helped Matthew back to his room where he took a seat on the bed.

"Now that you're finally awake, allow me to introduce myself. I'm Dr. Emberheart," said the Sun Elf woman.

She looked much older than the Sun Elf he had seen earlier, in her late fifties. She had orange skin and mono-chromatic green eyes. Her hair was dark brown with streaks of grey and she was wearing glasses and a white robe.

"Well, you must be feeling better, since you're already up and about. How are you feeling today?" she asked.

"Um … kinda sore. All over," he answered.

"Let's see how you're healing," the doctor replied. She unraveled Matthew's bandages. "My, you're healing quite well, even faster than our healers expected." She looked over his arm.

"If I'm healing so well, what's with the soreness?" he asked.

"You see, cuts, bruises, broken bones, they're all easi-ly fixed with magic. A little soreness is always to be expected when one undergoes the healing process. It's the body heal-ing itself. However, that sword of yours complicates things.

It puts a lot of strain on the body. Especially for someone as young as yourself. We can give you some medicine to ease the discomfort, but any lingering soreness should disappear over the next few days."

"Okay. That would be good, thanks," he replied.

"You're welcome," she said.

"How do you know about the sword?"

"Don't worry, doctor-patient confidentiality. Your secret is safe. I'll be back with your medicine and then you'll be free to leave."

She opened the door and left the room.

"Where's Ike? Is he okay? Where am I? What happened back at the mine?" Matthew asked.

"Ike is fine, he's down the hall. We're in Rivershade, it's west of Silverrun. You can see him after you're done here," Sterling replied.

Matthew felt much better knowing that Ike and Alice were okay. "What about the mine? What happened there?" he asked.

"You don't remember what happened?" Alice asked.

Matthew tried to remember. "Um. I remember fighting a large knight and Alice using the box. After that, I don't remember anything else." He thought about it a little more. "I also remember … I didn't find my dad in those mines. I'm sorry, Sterling. I just couldn't find him." Matthew's voice was sad.

Alice and Sterling looked at each other.

"Matthew, I have to tell you something," began Sterling. "That knight you fought—well, he … was your father."

Matthew sat up in confusion. "What? How? Why? Where is he now?" he asked.

"He's been taken to Stormhaven for healing and questioning. I'm sure we'll learn more about what happened in the coming days, but he's alive."

Matthew sat there in silence. The door opened and the doctor reentered the room holding a little bag.

"Hello, I hope I'm not interrupting anything?" she asked. The three of them shook their heads no. The doctor loosened the string around the little bag and pulled out a glass vial with dark purple liquid.

"Drink a little of this. After you've eaten something, to help with your soreness, okay?"

"Okay."

"Have a good rest of your day." The doctor handed him the vial and the bag. She then left the room.

"I should get dressed," he stated.

"Alright, your bag is in the closet. We'll be outside," Sterling replied.

Alice and Sterling left the room and Matthew changed into his clothes. He packed up his things and left the room. In the hallway, Alice and Sterling were down the hall standing by the door. Matthew walked over to them as Dr. Emberheart was leaving the room.

"He's all ready to see you now," announced the doctor.

"You two go ahead. I need to send word to the council about your recovery. I'll be in the lobby." Sterling walked down the hall while Matthew and Alice entered Ike's room.

Ike had just finished getting dressed. "Hey guys, ready to go?" asked Ike.

"Ike! You're okay," Matthew exclaimed.

"More or less," replied Ike. He rotated his arm.

"Good," declared Alice. She marched toward him and punched him in the arm.

"Hey! What was that for?!" Ike cried.

"For leaving me in the mines! Are you mad?! You could've been killed taking on all those knights by yourself!" She continued to angrily pummel him. Ike put up his hands to block her.

"Hey, I saved your life and everything worked out alright. I'm okay and you helped Matthew. So how about a thank you," Ike replied.

Alice frowned. "Thank you. But don't do it again."

"Saving your life? Or …" teased Ike.

"You know what I mean," snapped Alice. She gave him a few more punches.

The three of them left the room and headed downstairs to the lobby from the third floor. Sterling was standing in the lobby as the three of them approached.

"How are you feeling, Ike?" asked Sterling.

"Great, I'm all healed up. Better than ever," he replied.

"That's good to hear. Matthew, I've sent word to the council about your recovery. They'll probably want some kind of report on what happened. We should make our way to Stormhaven immediately," stated Sterling.

"Can I talk to you for a second?" Matthew asked.

He and Sterling walked out of Ike and Alice's earshot. "Can I take my friends home first? I can meet you in Stormhaven. Alice lives there anyway."

Sterling thought to himself for a few moments. "Alright, I have some things I can do before meeting you in Stormhaven. I'll see you there," replied Sterling.

"Thanks," he said.

"Please be sure to take it easy this time. I haven't forgotten you ignoring my advice last time."

"Sorry, for not listening."

Sterling waved him off. "You're still alive. That's all that matters, but next time, listen to my advice," he cautioned.

"No problem." Matthew walked back over to Alice and Ike, while Sterling vanished from the lobby.

"So, what's the plan?" Ike asked as they stepped outside onto the hospital sidewalk. Rivershade was a large town, similar to Goldcrest and Hazelhill, filled with lots of people and businesses.

"Well, I've already sent word to my parents. I told them I was heading back to Stormhaven. I'm quite sure they're worried, this whole thing took longer than I originally told them," announced Alice.

"Ugh, don't remind me. I'm not looking forward to dealing with my parents," replied Ike.

"I could give you guys a ride home. I'm going to Stormhaven anyway," Matthew suggested.

"That sounds positively lovely," exclaimed Alice.

"I'm in," annouced Ike.

Matthew reached into his bag and pulled out the stagecoach chest. He opened it up and the coach came pouring out. The three of them climbed into the driver's seat.

"Goldcrest," commanded Matthew. The coach began to roll forward down the street. "I want to take this time to thank you guys for helping me out. I couldn't have done it without you guys."

"We're quite aware," Alice teased with a chuckle.

"But you're welcome anyway," added Ike. Matthew smiled.

"We couldn't have done it without you either," smiled Alice.

The coach traveled over the large stone Rivershade Bridge and out of town. They traveled down the road for several hours until they spotted something off in the distance. It was the ruins of the town of Silverrun. However, it was different than the last time he'd seen it, several days ago. There was a large encampment of ten or more big, canvas tents next to the town. Matthew could spot people walking back and forth between the town and the camp.

"What's going on?" asked Matthew.

"They're from Rivershade. Sterling said the Rivershade militia and knights from Stormhaven are investigating the mines for any more information, sending it back to Stormhaven," replied Alice.

Matthew remained silent. He thought about his dad. The coach continued through the barren yellow pastures and abandoned homesteads of the south as they approached Hazelhill.

"I'm starving. I haven't eaten since breakfast," complianed Ike.

"Do we have any food?" asked Matthew.

"I afraid we ate all of our food before we made it to Silverrun and we didn't pack anything new," replied Alice.

"We're almost to Hazelhill. We can eat something there," suggested Matthew.

The sun had set by the time they had rolled into Hazelhill. Since it was late in the day, most of the businesses were closed but they managed to find an open food stall.

"How about there?" Ike suggested, pointing at a food stall. They stopped the coach and walked over. Ike and Matthew ordered turkey legs, and Alice ordered a turkey sandwich. Matthew paid the man and they returned to the carriage to continue their travels. After eating, Matthew drank his medicine. They headed inside the carriage to play cards for a while before retiring to bed.

The next morning, Matthew was the last to come downstairs. Alice and Ike were already down.

"You think we can get some breakfast somewhere?" asked Ike.

"Sure," agreed Matthew. The three of them traveled back to Hazelhill for breakfast. In town, they had breakfast at a local tavern before continuing their journey to Goldcrest.

The coach came to a stop several feet from the front of Ike's house.

"Well, this is me," he said.

Ike hopped out of the driver's seat and entered the coach. His things were already packed. Matthew and Alice climbed down from the driver's seat, as Ike exited the coach.

"Ugh, I'm not looking forward to this."

"I can go with you if you want," Matthew suggested.

"It's probably best if I go it alone. It's my mess. Hopefully, they've calmed down by now, especially when they hear how I helped save the kingdoms," Ike replied.

Matthew and Ike shook hands. "I guess … this is goodbye," lamented Matthew.

"You think that after everything we've done, you can get rid of me that easily? I don't think so," Ike boasted.

Matthew smiled. "I hope not."

"You can come visit anytime … after my parents calm down, that is," he reasoned.

"Alright," agreed Matthew. The two of them hugged.

"That goes for you too, miss," Ike added to Alice. Alice walked over to Ike and the two embraced. Alice nodded.

"Besides, who else is gonna have you guys' back like me, huh?" Ike bragged.

"Then, it's until next time," annouced Matthew.

"Until next time," replied Ike. Ike waved goodbye. He then turned and headed up the road to his parent's house.

Matthew and Alice climbed into the driver's seat of the carriage. "Stormhaven," comanded Matthew. The coach turned around and headed toward Stormhaven. The sun had begun to set as the coach rolled through woods toward the gates of Stormhaven. Matthew stopped the coach.

"Something the matter?" asked Alice.

"We gotta make a stop first." Matthew climbed down from the coach.

"Where?" she asked.

"That church. Do you remember where it is?" he asked.

Alice nodded. "Follow me," she led.

Alice and Matthew traveled through the woods until they reached the old church, a small wooden building surrounded by a rusty iron-rod fence next to an overgrown graveyard. The graveyard was covered in foliage.

"Is it possible this place looks worse than I remember?" he asked. Matthew pushed the rusted metal gate open enough for them to fit through. The two of them went up the creaky wooden stairs and knocked on the door. There was no answer. Matthew pushed open the wooden door.

"Hello?! Old man? Are you still here?" he called.

There was no answer. Matthew crossed the room, passed the rows of old pews, and walked over to the table at the front of the room. Suddenly, the old man rose up the stairs from the other side of the table.

"What are two children doing here?" asked the old monk.

Matthew and Alice jumped. "You need to start wearing a bell or something," Matthew complained.

"So. You've returned," the old monk said with a hint of surprise in his voice.

Matthew reached inside his bag and pulled out the sack. The monk's eyes widened at the sight of it.

"It actually exist. You actually found it."

"And I've come to return it. The scroll's inside. As you said, it was hidden for a reason." Matthew handed over the sack to the monk.

"Thank you," replied the old monk. He then turned and headed downstairs as Matthew and Alice exited the church.

It was nighttime when the coach finally pulled in front of Alice's Brownstone.

"We're here," said Matthew. He and Alice climbed down from the driver's seat.

"Huh, I guess you were right," she said.

Matthew looked confused. "About what?"

"We do make a good team."

Matthew couldn't help but smile. They hugged.

"You're welcome to come in. I'm sure dinner is probably ready by now," she suggested.

"I'm supposed to meet with my uncle after I'm done here. But rain check."

Alice smiled. "Very well ... until next time," she announced.

"Until next time," replied Matthew.

Alice headed up the stairs to her front door, giving him one last wave goodbye before knocking on the door.

Matthew climbed into the driver's seat and the coach began to roll down the street. He pulled his crystal from his pocket and held it in his palm.

"Sterling? Sterling, are you there? I finished with Ike and Alice," he said.

Sterling's face appeared on the crystal. "You can meet

me in the Castle District. It's the one with the big castle, you can't miss it. I'll be at the fountain in front of the castle," he told Matthew.

Matthew rode the coach down the cobblestone streets into the Castle District. Stormhaven almost seemed like a different city at night, with its light from the countless lanterns and lampposts. Matthew came as close to the castle as he dared before pulling the coach over by the fountain. He waited for his uncle.

A wave of sadness washed over Matthew. It had just now hit him: his friends were gone and he was all alone again. He didn't know if he could handle being alone again.

"Hey! Matthew," called Sterling. Matthew lifted his head and spotted Sterling. He was waving his arms and standing beside an enormous fountain before the castle.

Stormhaven Castle was a massive stone castle, with several large towers and stone walls. Matthew hopped out of the driver's seat and sucked the carriage back into its chest. Matthew and Sterling walked up to Stormhaven Castle's front gate. Sterling handed one of the heavily armored knights, who was standing in front of the closed metal gate, a piece of paper. The knight read over the piece of paper for a few moments.

"Open the gate!" shouted the knight.

There was a momentary silence and then the sound of heavy metal gears turning could be heard. They lifted up the heavy, metal gate.

Matthew and Sterling entered the grand castle's main hall. Inside, the castle was immaculately decorated. There were fancy paintings and sculptures, tables with vases, golden chandeliers suspended from the ceiling, and massive rugs lining the stone floors.

A woman in fine robes met them. "Hello, hello. His majesty is expecting you. Please follow me," instructed the woman.

Matthew and Sterling followed the woman up the large marble staircase and through the winding corridors and hall. Eventually, they reached a large oak door.

"One moment," said the woman. She then knocked on the door and waited a few moments before entering. They stood in the castle hallway for a minute before the woman returned. "His majesty will see you now," she said.

Matthew took a deep breath before entering the room. The door led to a circular stone staircase. Matthew climbed the stairs and entered an enormous circular study. The walls were lined with bookshelves and paintings, and there were multiple large desks covered in papers around the room.

"This way, child," called Tovan. Tovan ushered him into an adjacent room.

This room was a smaller circular room with seven large circular mirrors on the walls. The mirrors didn't reflect Matthew or Tovan. Inside each mirror was the reflection of each one of the council members.

"Now that we're all here, we can begin," annouced Tovan.

"Finally, some of us live in different time zones," complained Lizlee the Goblin Queen.

"Fair enough. It's quite late even here, so we'll try to keep this as brief as we can," said Tovan.

"What happened at the mines?" asked Miranda the Sun Elf empress.

"Um. The black knights were using the mines as a hidden base. Umm, their leader was there. I fought him. I guess he was my dad," he replied.

"This is also Leon's son," Tovan explained to the rest of the council.

"I never knew he had children," replied Kilchii the Orc chieftain.

"How did you manage to defeat him?" asked Lizlee.

"I had help from my uncle, and my friends, Ike and Alice. I also used Aleron's box."

The council erupted in chatter. "Aleron's box? Impossible," quipped Reinhardt the Hairn king.

"The box was lost centuries ago," added Tovan.

"Where is the box? Can we see it?" asked Kilchii.

"I don't have it anymore. I returned it. It's in safe hands."

"Where did you return it? You can trust us," reasoned Miranda.

"With all due respect—, to all of you, I promised to keep the location a secret and I don't go back on my promises," declared Matthew.

Asger the Kreath king erupted in laughter. "A true warrior and a man of his word. I like this one."

The other leaders tried to convince Matthew to tell them about the box but he refused.

"Perhaps the box should remain hidden. Better than to fall into the wrong hands," stated the Silvani Archdruid Sylvestris.

"Very well. Anyway, did the black knight's leader tell you anything?" asked Tovan.

"He didn't tell me much. He was too busy trying to kill me. Didn't my dad tell you anything?" he asked.

"He doesn't remember anything from when he was possessed. Between him, the knights we managed to capture, and the documents that were recovered, we just don't have much to go on," sighed Sylvestris.

"Then let's move on. We'll just have to be more vigilant next time," suggested Lizlee.

"I'll see to it that these black knights are properly dealt with. The black knights are a shameful reminder of my countries past and my father," Miranda fumed.

"Well if there's nothing else, this meeting is adjourned," annouced Tovan. No one said anything. "Very well."

The images on the mirrors faded away. "You are free to go unless you have something you want to discuss," Tovan then said to Matthew.

Matthew was silent for a few moments. "Um. Is my dad here? My uncle said he was brought to Stormhaven."

"Leon was here. After it became clear that he didn't have any information and wasn't a part of the black knights, we released him. He lives in Eastshire, just northeast of here. I'm sure Sterling knows of it," replied Tovan.

"Oh ... that's all," said Matthew.

"Very well, then. I trust you can see yourself out."

Matthew turned and left the room. He walked down the stairs and out the door.

Sterling was talking to the woman from earlier. Matthew walked up to the two of them.

"The meeting is over," said Matthew.

"Alright. So, what's next?" asked Sterling.

"The king said my dad left. He went home," replied Matthew.

"I can take you there if you'd like," Sterling suggested.

Matthew thought about it for a few moments.

CHAPTER 20

BIRTHDAY BASH

"**I** think I'm gonna go home and see my mom. I made her a promise I'd come back," he stated.

Sterling smiled. "That's probably for the best for now. There is peace now and you should enjoy that. You did well."

"Thanks. What are you going to do?" Matthew asked.

"I think maybe it's finally time I speak with my brother. Leave the past in the past. We have … much to discuss."

Matthew dug in his bag and pulled out the stagecoach chest and handed it to him. "I won't be needing this anymore," said Matthew.

Sterling took the chest. "Have a good trip. Feel free to drop by anytime." Matthew and Sterling hugged before Matthew pulled the golden book from his bag and opened it. The book's bright light engulfed Matthew, forcing his eyes closed.

Matthew opened his eyes. He was standing in his bedroom.

The aroma of cinnamon filled his nose: he was home. Matthew sprinted out of his bedroom. Elizabeth was sitting on the living room couch, watching TV in her pajamas.

"Mom! I'm back!" he exclaimed.

Elizabeth spotted Matthew standing in the living room and jumped to hug him.

"You're back!" she smiled, hugging him tight.

"I promised I'd come back," he said, proudly.

"You were right. I'm so glad you're okay."

"Mom … I found Dad."

"Found him? What does that mean?" she asked.

"Well, it's a long story, but he was in trouble and I saved him."

She walked over to the couch and sat down. "Did you … speak with him?"

"No." His voice was solemn.

"Oh, I'm sure there will be time for that later. Well … now that you're back, I want to hear all about what happened. Where did you go? What was it like?"

Matthew sat on the couch next to her. "It's a long story and it's pretty late," he yawned.

"You have a point. I'm just so glad you're back. Alright, first thing in the morning, over breakfast, how's that sound?"

"Sounds great."

It had been three weeks since Matthew's battle at the mines. He was sitting on his bed back in New Jersey.

"Matthew. Are you ready to go? We don't want to be late," Liz said from the living room.

He got up from the bed. "It's my birthday, they can't have it without me," he replied.

"Still, you know. It's always better to be early than late," his mom said, entering his room.

"Alright, I'm ready when you are."

"So, how does this work exactly?" she asked.

Matthew grabbed the golden book off his desk. "I don't know, actually. Just stand there and close your eyes. It's a bit bright."

He stood next to his mom while she closed her eyes. Matthew opened the book and a bright light engulfed them. Matthew opened his eyes and they were now standing in front of Gerda's Inn.

"Wow. This is incredible. Where are we?" she asked, looking around.

"Gerda's Inn," he said.

Matthew and his mom walked up the wooden steps across the front porch and inside the inn.

"Guten Tag, How many?" asked Gerda without looking up. She was focusing intently on the notepad on the podium by the front door.

"Hey Gerda, we're here!" said Matthew.

Gerda lifted her eyes from the pad. "Hallo Matthew!" She smiled. Gerda ran around the side of the podium to hug Matthew. "It's so good to see you. We didn't expect you two so early. Please, right this way," Gerda continued.

She led them through the dining room and into another connecting room. The room was large and in the process of being decorated, with a wide wooden table in the middle with large bright windows facing the forest behind the inn. There were smaller tables with tablecloths and chairs, each featuring a bouquet.

"Everything's already in the oven, so everything should be ready to go later this afternoon," said Gerda.

"That's great, Gerda. Thanks," he said. "Oh, Gerda. This is my mom." Matthew gestured at his mother.

"Liz," his mom said, introducing herself.

"Gerda." They shook hands.

"It's nice to meet you. Matthew tells me so many good things about you and how you gave him a place to stay," said Liz.

"It was nothing. It's so nice to meet the mother of the Blademaster. You must be so proud," replied Gerda.

"I always knew Matthew was going to do great things."

"Well, I've got to get back to the kitchen. If you two need anything, please don't hesitate to ask." Gerda smiled before turning and leaving the room. Matthew sat in one of the chairs while Elizabeth looked around the room.

"Wow, I know you told me she was short but, She's absolutely tiny!" Liz softly laughed.

"Mom?!" said Matthew.

Liz put up her hands in surrender. "She seems nice and I'm glad she helped you. This place is nice, too. I'm not gonna get a bill for all this out of nowhere, though, am I?"

"No, Mom. *The Daily Courier* is paying for everything in exchange for an exclusive interview with the new Blademaster," replied Matthew.

"Alright, just be careful. Don't feel like you have to do anything you don't want to. You can always talk to me or your uncle, or your dad about it first, okay?" advised Liz.

"I understand," replied Matthew. "Mom … I'm sorry about earlier. I'm sorry for being angry with you about not spending the summer together, and that I spent most of the summer here. That's not fair," he apologized.

"It's okay. Don't worry about it, I'd forgotten all about that. Besides, summer is not over yet and I have some time off coming up," she replied with a smile.

Matthew smiled. The door to the room opened and Bernhart entered the room.

"Happy Birthday!" he exclaimed.

"Bernhart!" replied Matthew walking, over to greet him. The two shook hands and Bernhart handed him a box with a bow.

"Bernhart, this is my mom," stated Matthew.

"Liz," she introduced.

"Ahhh … hallo, there. A pleasure to meet you," replied Bernhart as they shook hands.

"Remember? I told you he saved me and Alice, and he has a pet bear."

"A pet bear?" asked Liz.

"Ah, yes. I left Sonja at home. I'm afraid she not very fond of long trips," said Bernhart.

Gerda entered the room holding a tray of finger foods. "The first course is ready." She was followed by another waiter carrying more food. They set the food down on the table with plates and utensils. "Please, enjoy," said Gerda. She turned and left the room.

"Looks like we've arrived just in time," announced Ike. He entered the room followed by his parents Martin and Evelyn, his little sister Kya, and one other person Matthew hadn't seen before. Ike was holding a large gift basket wrapped with a large bow. "Happy Birthday!" said Ike, handing the gift basket to Matthew.

"Thanks. What's all this?" he asked.

"It's a gift basket from Honeyburrow Candy in Stormhaven. Best sweets in the kingdoms. I didn't know what you like, so the basket has a bit of everything. Like Chocakes, Caramellows, Gummi Dragons, Peanut Crumbles, Unicorn Stix, and all kinds of good stuff," replied Ike.

"Uh, I better take this. I don't want you to wind up eating it all at once," interjected Liz. She retrieved the basket from Matthew's hands.

"This is my Mom. Mom, this is Ike. He helped me a lot on my quest."

"Nice to meet you. These are my parents, my little sister, and my older brother," introduced Ike.

Ike's parents shook hands with Liz.

"Martin Townsend," said Ike's father.

"Evelyn," said Ike's mother.

"Dominic," said Ike's brother.

"Oh my. It's so nice to finally meet you. We had no

idea your son was the Blademaster. We were happy to help him," enthused Evelyn.

"Thank you for looking after Matthew. I really appreciate it," she replied.

"Oh, Matthew dear, please know we don't blame you for Ike's … decisions. We're sure you had nothing to do with it," Ike's mother reassured him with a warm smile.

"Okay," replied Matthew.

"Well, please help yourselves. I mean you're paying for everything, essentially," said Liz.

"It's no trouble at all. Between you and me, this whole thing can be written off as a business expense, anyway. Oh, Matthew, Dominic here will be handling the interview, but we can talk about that later, just enjoy your party," stated Martin.

"Thanks," replied Matthew.

Everyone walked off, leaving Matthew and Ike behind.

"Your mom's still mad about the whole running away thing?" he asked.

"You have no idea. I've been on twenty-four-hour lockdown since I got back. The only reason they allowed me to come was that you asked for me to be here," Ike complained.

"I couldn't leave you hanging. You did help the kingdoms avoid a war. It's the least I could do."

"I think that's the only reason why I'm not six feet under right now," Ike joked.

Matthew and Ike went over and grabbed some of the

appetizers on the table.

"Hey, you having a good time?" asked Liz.

"Yeah," said Matthew. He was now seated at a small table.

"Well, I got word that your dad's coming. Is that okay? I can tell him not to come if him being here makes you uncomfortable."

Matthew remained silent for a few moments. "It's fine, I guess."

"You know, it's ok to feel a bit … nervous about meeting him for the first time. I'll be right there with you, okay?" she reassured.

"Alright," replied Matthew.

The door to the room opened again. Alice and a tall man in his late thirties with fair skin, brown hair, and brown eyes entered the room followed by Gerda and a waiter carrying more trays of food.

"Alice is here," he said to his mom, desperate to change the subject. The two of them got up to greet them.

"Happy Birthday!" smiled Alice. She was doing a poor job of hiding something behind her back. "Here's your gift!"

Alice revealed a box. Matthew took the box in his hands. "Thanks. Alice, this is my mom," he introduced.

"Pleasure to meet you," said Alice, shaking Liz's hand.

"I'm Alice and this is my father," said Alice, introducing the man next to her.

"Lewis Liddell, pleasure," replied Alice's father. He shook Liz's hand.

Alice's dad, like his daughter, also had an accent.

"Dad, this is Matthew," said Alice.

"Ah, it's nice to finally meet the boy my daughter's told me so much about." Lewis shook Matthew's hand.

"Good things, I hope?" replied Matthew.

"Dad!" whined Alice. Her cheeks turned a mild red from embarrassment. Matthew smiled.

"Well, it was nice meeting both of you, have you eaten anything yet? The food is incredible," said Liz.

"I'm quite hungry," said Lewis. He headed off to the buffet table followed by Liz, leaving Matthew alone with Alice.

"What's this box?" he asked as he examined it closer. It looked like a small wooden file cabinet. It was painted like a starry night sky and had his name painted at the top with Alice, Ike, and Sterling's names on each drawer.

"It's a way for us to communicate after you've gone home. You can use it to send letters. All you have to do is just put it in the correct slot with their name," she said, excited.

"Oh, cool. Where'd you get this from?"

"I made it. Well, technically Sterling enchanted it to send the letters across planes of existence, but it was my idea, and I bought and painted the boxes," explained Alice. "I had one made for Ike and Sterling, too."

"Can it send anything bigger than a letter?" he asked.

"I'm afraid not. Sterling said anything bigger than a letter and the spell won't transport it."

"It's no big deal. Thanks again, Alice," replied Matthew.

"You're welcome," she smiled.

Matthew sat around with Ike and Alice as they ate. "Aren't you gonna eat something?" she asked.

"I ate earlier," replied Matthew. He wasn't very hungry.

The door to the room opened, and Sterling entered the room followed by Leon.

Liz immediately made her way across the room to intercept the two of them.

"My dad's here," he stated.

Alice and Ike quickly turned to look at him. Liz was talking with Sterling and Leon in the corner of the room.

"He came to your birthday, isn't that a good thing?" asked Ike.

"Yes. No. I don't know," uttered Matthew.

"I'm positive it'll be alright. You did save his life, after all. He probably just wants to meet you," reassured Alice.

Matthew remained silent. Liz walked over to the table where they were sitting.

"Matthew, we're gonna go upstairs for a little while, okay?" said Liz.

"Okay." Matthew got up from the table and followed his mother out of the room. They went up the stairs to the second floor. On the second floor, they entered the first room on the left. The room was a normal inn room with a bed, desk, chair, and dresser with an oil lamp.

Leon was standing in the middle of the room when Matthew entered. Elizabeth closed the door behind them.

"The innkeeper said we could use this room to talk privately," said Leon. The three of them stood there in awkward silence.

"Well, I guess I'll start. Matthew, this is your dad, Leon," Liz annouced, gesturing toward Leon.

Leon walked over to Matthew and stuck out his hand. "It's nice to finally meet you. Liz and Sterling told me so much about you," exclamed Leon.

Matthew shook Leon's hand. Leon got on one knee to look Matthew in the face. "Matthew, I want to apologize for not being there for most of your life, but there wasn't a day that went by when I didn't think about you. I know there's nothing I can say to make up for not being there all those years but I'd like to begin the process of moving forward with you. That is, if you'll let me?"

Matthew was silent for a few moments before answering. "Um … okay," replied Matthew.

Leon smiled and his eyes began to water. He stood up and hugged Matthew. Liz smiled and began to cry as well.

"I also owe you a big thanks for saving my life. When I had Sterling send you that book, and I managed to relinquish the sword before I blacked out a final time, I had no idea it would all work out as it did, but it's worked out even better than I could've imagined!" Leon said excitedly.

"Sterling sent me the book? You sent me the sword?" asked Matthew.

Leon nodded. "I managed to relinquish the sword to you before I was possessed. However, as far as the sword is concerned my decision to give you the sword is just a suggestion. I didn't know if you'd actually meet the requirements of the sword to actually be able to wield it. Very few people do—call it a shot in the dark. I couldn't let it fall into the wrong hands, so I sent it to you," said Leon.

"Why me?" asked Matthew.

"Well, why not? I'd hoped you'd be interested enough in meeting your old man to find me. If the sword went to someone else, who knows if they'd care enough to find me," said Leon.

Liz was shocked. "I can't believe this! Let me get this straight, you intentionally endangered our son, on a wild gambit, to save your own skin!?" she asked.

"Well, when you say it like that …" Leon replied, embarrassed.

While Liz was fuming, Matthew was thrilled to hear all of this. Not only was his father happy to see him, but he still thought about him after all these years.

"This is exactly what I wanted to avoid in the first place, all those years ago when you first got that sword, endangering our family! Matthew, give the sword back to your dad, right now!" she commanded.

"Uh, about that, Liz … he can't," admitted Leon.

"Why not?" she asked.

"Once I gave up the sword to him, I can no longer wield it anymore. It's his until he dies or gives it up," replied Leon.

"Dies?!" she repeated, horrified.

"Or gives it up," Leon repeated.

Liz felt lightheaded and sat down on the bed.

"I can't believe this is happening again! Matthew, give up the sword. Right now!" demanded said.

"Shouldn't that be his decision, Liz?" asked Leon.

"I wanna keep the sword," answered Matthew.

"See," said Leon.

"He's twelve! He's incapable of making this decision," she scolded.

"Technically, I'm thirteen now," corrected Matthew.

"This is not the time," she replied.

"Don't worry, Liz. I'll be there. I can train him myself. Would you like that, training with your old man?" Leon asked.

Matthew nodded.

"Sterling tells me you're a chip off the old block," Leon continued.

Liz sighed, defeated.

"Well, since it's your birthday, I've brought some gifts. There just outside in my cart," revealed Leon, wanting to change to subject.

Leon led Matthew and Elizabeth outside of the inn. He pulled off the canvas sheet at the back of his cart to reveal several crates and chests.

"First, for you, Matthew, since it's your birthday, I give you this," Leon announced.

He opened a wooden crate on the cart and pulled out a smaller wooden chest. He then handed it to Matthew. He opened the crate. Inside the chest was a long, black, oblong-shaped, rocky object with several cracks of bright blue in it, lying in some hay.

"Wow! Thanks … What is it?" he asked.

Leon scratched his chin. "Well, it's a cool-looking rock I found on a quest I went on. But this rock has brought me lots of good fortune since I found it which eventually led me back to you two."

Matthew thought the rock looked really cool and was happy for the gift. "Wow! Thanks."

Liz was far less impressed and rolled her eyes.

"And now for you Liz, this," continued Leon. He opened a large wooden chest. It was filled with gold coins and large jewels. Liz was stunned. She scooped a handful of gold coins from the chest and let them slip through her fingers.

"Think of it as … back child support," suggested Leon.

"Well, it's a start," she smirked, trying to calm down.

"We should get back to the party. I don't want to hold you up," said Leon.

The three of them reentered the inn and rejoined the party.

"Happy Birthday," Sterling said to Matthew when he entered the room.

"Thanks."

"I hope everything went well with Leon?"

"Yeah. It went well … I think. My mom's not really happy about me having the sword," said Matthew.

"Well, can you blame her? It's a tough and dangerous job as you found out," replied Sterling.

"I guess you're right, but I couldn't have done it without everyone's help," Matthew admitted.

"You've done well so far."

"Hey, Sterling. You're the one who sent me the golden book?" asked Matthew.

"I guess that means he's told you everything. Yeah, I did," revealed Sterling.

"Why didn't you tell me?" asked Matthew.

"Honestly—I didn't know it bothered you so much. Did it really matter if you found it in a truck or if I sent it to you? You managed to do the right thing regardless," replied Sterling.

"I guess that's true but no more secrets," grumbled Matthew.

"Alright," agreed Sterling. He gave a soft chuckle. "So how old are you now, anyway? Thirty-five? Thirty-six?" joked Sterling.

"I'm thirteen now," he replied with pride.

"That's good. I got you a gift." Sterling stuck out his hand and a small chest appeared. Matthew immediately recognized it as the chest that held the carriage. Matthew took the chest from Sterling.

"Are you sure?" he asked.

Sterling nodded. "I have a feeling you'll be using it more than I ever did. Plus, I can just teleport if I need to go somewhere," admitted Sterling.

"You can teleport?!" asked Matthew.

"You never noticed? I can do many things. I thought I told you that already," shrugged Sterling.

"Thanks, Sterling," said Matthew.

"No problem. Now, if you excuse me, those deviled eggs have my name on them." Sterling headed back to the buffet table.

Matthew felt much better after talking with his parents—like a load had been lifted off his shoulders. He walked back to Ike and Alice and told them about what had happened with his parents. Afterward, he went over to the buffet table to eat his fill.

Once everyone finished eating dinner, Gerda entered the room with a large birthday cake. Everyone sang happy birthday to Matthew. Afterward, Gerda cut up the cake for everyone and handed out slices. People finished their cake, said goodbye, and began to leave the party.

Matthew waved goodbye to his friends as they left. the party Gerda and the staff began to clean up after the party.

Finally, there was only Matthew, Elizabeth, Leon, Ike's father, and Ike's brother. Matthew sat at a table, alone, eating another slice of his birthday cake while Leon and Elizabeth talked at another table.

Dominic walked over and took a seat at Matthew's table. "Hey, Matthew. Are you ready to go?" asked Dominic.

Matthew finished shoveling cake into his mouth and nodded yes.

"Alright," said Dominic, who took out a notepad and pencil. "Okay, so I'm just gonna ask you some simple questions and you just feel free to answer them the best you can. I want the article to introduce the people of the kingdoms to the person who just stopped a costly war," said Dominic.

"Okay," replied Matthew.

"So, let's start with an easy one. Who are you?" asked Dominic.

"I'm Matthew Jacobs and I'm the Blademaster," said Matthew.

EPILOGUE

Prince Valen rushed down the enormous castle hall. He was at home in the capital city of the Sun Elf empire, Corona Bay.

Valen was a tall and handsome Sun Elf in his early twenties. His skin was orange, his eyes were monochromatic green, and his long, thick, auburn hair was kept high and tight in a top knot. His crimson and gold kimono robes rustled as he quickly made his way through the castle's halls. Valen came to a large wooden sliding door. He opened it and stepped inside.

The room was a small room with large painted wooden panels lining the walls and a wooden floor. The room was lit with a small brazier at its center. On the wooden wall panels was a beautiful painting of a landscape mural. Inside the room was his twin sister, the Sun Elf empress Miranda. She wore a long crimson and gold kimono dress with her hair in a long, high ponytail.

"Good! You're here, we can finally begin," said Miranda.

"Sorry I'm late," replied Valen.

"It's fine. They can wait. Are you ready?" asked Miranda.

Valen nodded. Miranda waved her hands in the air. Several panels on the wall flipped over to reveal rectangular gold-framed mirrors behind them. The shadowy figures appeared in each of the mirrors.

"Now that we're all here, I'll keep this meeting short as I'm sure we all have other things to attend to," stated Miranda.

They all nodded in agreement.

"I'm sure you're all aware by now of our … latest setback. We lost not only the former Blademaster, who was under our control, but we also now have to deal with another one. And we lost our black knight commander, Gideon," said an irritated Miranda.

"Pity, I've always liked Gideon," a shadowy figure replied.

"Gideon was an arrogant fool! He became so fixated on wielding that sword, he let it cloud his judgment. He strayed from our plans and suffered for it," snapped Miranda.

"What's become of Gideon, then?" asked one of the figures.

"Apparently this new Blademaster, a mere child, mind you, found Aleron's box and managed to use it on him," revealed Miranda.

"This is the same child who managed to survive the Minotaur that Gideon sent after him. I'm becoming more and more impressed," admitted one of the figures.

"Be that as it may. He could prove to be more of an issue than first anticipated," replied Miranda.

"And what will become of the black knights?" asked another one of the figures. "They don't know much. We don't have to worry about them spilling any info if caught and interrogated. Any info that was obtained from the raid at the Silverrun mines was old information, anyway. It won't do them much good anyway. We keep those idiots in the dark for a reason. They'll just go back into hiding until we call from them again. It's not like they have any other options," revealed Miranda.

"Pity for Gideon, but this still could be advantageous for us. Convince the child to give the box to the council for safekeeping and take it from there. We could use that kind of power on our side if it is as powerful as the old legends say," suggested another figure.

"We tried that. He wouldn't give it up and was tight-lipped about what he did with it," replied Miranda.

"So, what do we do now?!" growled another figure.

"Nothing's changed, we stick to the plan. In fact, our fortunes may have changed for the better now that the Blademaster is a child. He'll be all the more easy to manip-ulate," announced Miranda.

"Good. I don't know about any of you all but I'm get-ting a bit antsy. I am not one for all this sneaking around," said another one of the figures.

"Patience! That moron Gideon lacked it, and look where that got him. We only get one shot at this. So far, the council doesn't suspect anything. I've seen to that. Leon, thankfully, doesn't remember anything from Gideon's time inhabiting his body, and they're so desperate to sweep this whole thing under the rug as an isolated incident since they have no one to pin it on," replied Miranda.

"Aye, the lass be right, we've come too far to blow it now," agreed one of the figures.

"Just continue with your tasks, like before. You'll be contacted if anything changes, understand?" asked Miranda.

The figures all signified that they understood Miranda's orders and then disappeared from the mirrors. Miranda turned to Valen, who was standing behind her.

"You're sure about all of this?" asked Valen.

"I've never been more sure about anything in my life. Soon, we'll be a family again," exclaimed Miranda. She smiled at Valen.

The sunlight was strong as a gentle breeze blew through the restaurant's outdoor garden, softly swaying the nearby flowers as Alice sat at a table on the restaurant's patio with her stepmother and younger sister, Sophia. Sophia was a seven year old girl with long brown hair, fair skin, and green eyes. Like her mother, Sophia didn't have an accent.

The three of them were dressed in beautiful formal summer dresses with nice large hats, as were all the females around them. The men wore fancy formal summer dress suits. Everyone was happily chatting amongst themselves.

"It's so nice of you to have finally joined us on one of these trips, Alice. Viola loved coming out with us," said Mrs. Liddell.

"Yeah!" added an excited Sophia. Alice smiled. Since returning home she decided to be much more open and kinder to her stepmother. Their relationship had improved greatly.

"Thanks for inviting me. I'm just sorry I didn't come along sooner," Alice replied.

Mrs. Liddell smiled. "You're here now. That's what's important."

A waiter walked over and placed three teacups on the saucers already in front of them. He then filled each cup up with hot water before going to check on the nearby tables. Sophia attempted to drink from her teacup, but it was too hot.

"Careful, Sophia. You don't want to burn yourself," warned Mrs. Liddell.

Sophia slumped down in her chair. "I'm hungry," she complained.

Mrs. Liddell stopped stirring her tea. "Those finger sandwiches should be here by now. I'll go check to see what's going on." She got up from the table and went inside.

Sophia once again attempted to drink from her teacup, but the tea was still too hot.

"No, Sophia. Like this," instructed Alice. She stirred her hot tea a few times before bringing a spoonful up to her mouth. She blew on it, softly, for a few moments before drinking it.

Sophia attempted to mimic her older sister, but blew too hard. She blew all the tea off her spoon.

"Softly, blow like this," repeated Alice. She blew again on the tea in her spoon, hovering just above her teacup. As she blew, a sudden blast of freezing cold air came from Alice's mouth. It hit the spoon and encased it in a solid chunk of ice.

Alice sat in shocked silence. She put the spoon down next to her teacup, whose top was also now encased in ice.

"Cool! How do I do that?!" Sophia excitedly asked. Alice remained in a stunned silence.

Mrs. Liddell walked over to the table. "It'll be just a few more minutes," she began, before noticing Alice's frozen teacup and spoon. "Alice—did you—?" Mrs. Liddell asked. Alice slowly nodded, with a large smile growing on her face.

Matthew was sitting in his bedroom on his computer, still in his school uniform. It had been several months since his adventure. He was working on an essay for English class. He had to write a report about *Romeo and Juliet*. They were reading the play in class. Matthew found it completely uninteresting.

On his computer desk sat the lucky rock Leon had given him. So far it had seemed to work for Matthew. He got a B on a math test that he didn't study for. Math was always his worst subject. As he typed away on his keyboard, the rock seemed to move.

Matthew looked at the rock. It was still. He stared at it for several moments but it didn't move an inch. He went back to typing his essay. Suddenly, the rock moved again. He stopped typing and stared at the rock again. He continued to stare at the rock for a full minute but it still didn't move.

"I must be going crazy," he thought to himself. He continued working on his essay. This time, the rock fell over, causing him to jump up from his desk.

Matthew examined the rock up close. The rock began to roll back and forth. First slowly, and then more forcefully. After a few minutes of this, some parts of the rock began to crumble away until it broke in half.

Out from one half of the rock crawled a small, lizard-like creature. It was a foot long, from head to tail, with jet black scales, big electric blue eyes, and long thin wings.

It was a baby dragon. The young creature let out a small high-pitched screech.

"Mom! Mom! Mom!" Matthew shouted as he ran from his room in excitement.

"What? What is it!?" Elizabeth replied from the other room.

"The rock that Dad gave me, there was something in it. You gotta come see this!" He tugged at his mother's arm.

"Okay, okay," she replied.

The creature looked around, observing its new surroundings, before letting out another high-pitched screech.

This time, tiny blue sparks of electricity came from its mouth.